The Mysterious Romance of Murder

The Mysterious Romance of Murder

Crime, Detection, and the Spirit of Noir

David Lehman

Cornell University Press

Ithaca and London

Untitled prose poem ["The blonde took her teeth out of my hand . . ."] from *Nothing in the Dark* by Fred Muratori is reprinted by permission of the author. Copyright © 2021 by Fred Muratori.

"Noir" by Angela Ball. Copyright © 2021 by Angela Ball. Used by permission of the author.

"At the Ritz" and "The Book's Speech" from *Then, Suddenly* by Lynn Emanuel, published by the University of Pittsburgh Press. Copyright © 1999 by Lynn Emanuel. Used by permission.

"The Mysterious Romance of Murder" is a substantially revised version of an essay of the same title first published in the *Boston Review* (February 1, 2000).

"Poetry Noir" includes material revised from the essay "Shades among Shadows," previously published in *The Writer's Chronicle*, 2000.

"Here's to Crime!" is a substantially revised version of an essay of the same title first published in *Tin House Magazine*, 2005, and reprinted in *Food & Booze: A Tin House Literary Feast*, edited by Michelle Wildgen (Tin House Books, 2006).

"Among My Souvenirs" is a substantially revised version of an essay of the same title first published in *Boulevard*, Spring 2010.

"Dashiell Hammett's Priceless Patter" was first published in *The American Scholar*, 2015.

"Paperclip" (Raymond Chandler) was first published in the *New York Times Book Review*, May 20, 2001. Reprinted by permission.

"*Black Friday*" (David Goodis) and "Orange Noir" (Charles Willeford) have been revised substantially since they were first published in *Tin House Magazine*, 2005.

"Hitchcock's America" is a revised version of an essay first published in *American Heritage*, April/May 2007.

"Strangers and Mirrors," "An Exchange of Bullets in Belfast," "Blind Accidents," "Epitaph for a Genre," "Shadow of Evil," "A Reluctant Spy's Conversion," "Gangsters in Love," and "Rogues' Gallery" were first published in the "Talking Pictures" column on *The American Scholar* website between 2019 and 2021.

First published 2022 by Cornell University Press
Printed in the United States of America

Library of Congress Cataloging-in-Publication Data

Names: Lehman, David, 1948– author.
Title: The mysterious romance of murder : crime, detection, and the
   spirit of noir / David Lehman.
Description: Ithaca [New York] : Cornell University Press, 2022. |
   Includes bibliographical references and index.
Identifiers: LCCN 2021048703 (print) | LCCN 2021048704 (ebook) |
   ISBN 9781501763625 (hardcover) | ISBN 9781501763632 (epub) |
   ISBN 9781501763649 (pdf)
Subjects: LCSH: Detective and mystery stories—History and criticism. |
   Detective and mystery films—History and criticism. | Murder in
   literature. | Murder in motion pictures.
Classification: LCC PN3448.D4 L425 2022 (print) | LCC PN3448.D4 (ebook) |
   DDC 809.3/872—dc23/eng/20211208
LC record available at https://lccn.loc.gov/2021048703
LC ebook record available at https://lccn.loc.gov/2021048704

Rowe was a murderer—as other men are poets.
—Graham Greene, *The Ministry of Fear*

Contents

Part III. Auteurs

Part IV. Dreams That Money Can Buy

The Mysterious Romance of Murder

Introduction

THE MYSTERIOUS ROMANCE OF MURDER

In the fratricide in the fourth chapter of Genesis, the murder mystery has its starting point. Man and woman have fallen. Eden exists as a mental construct or a dead metaphor. Expelled from paradise, Cain kills Abel and is banished from human society, though he is protected from harm by his stigmata. An omniscient God plays the role of detective, and the culprit speaks the line about his brother's keeper before getting off the stage forever, a marked man.

The alternative point of departure derives from Greek tragedy, Sophocles's Oedipus trilogy, in which the crimes are parricide and incest, and the culprit is also the detective, whose relentless drive toward the truth will eventuate in the lifting of the plague that has afflicted the polity—at the expense of his eyesight, his reputation, and the life of his mother and wife. Guilt, and the liberation from guilt, whether by expiation, confession, or justice, is inevitably one thing the mystery genre is about. Knowledge, and the possibility of acquiring it, distinguishing truth from fiction, is another. In detective novels, the initiating act of terminal violence—which characteristically takes place offstage—doubles as a beguiling riddle. Only two people knew what happened. One of them, being dead, can't tell you; the other one won't. The progress from ignorance to truth, mystery to enlightenment, parallels that from order disturbed to order restored. Identifying the murderer, the detective cleans up a case of violent disorder. We begin with a corpse and a smell as of corruption, the smell of guilt pervading all. We end with the unmasking of the culprit, whose expulsion will absolve all the rest. To this extent at least, the entire genre is optimistic, affirmative.

Murder, Graham Greene wrote in a film review in 1938, "is a religious subject; the interest of a detective story is the pursuit of exact truth, and if we are at times impatient with the fingerprints, the time-tables and the butler's evasions, it is because the writer, like some early theologians, is getting bogged down in academic detail."[1] In its emphasis on "exact truth," an exactness possible only in a world of fingerprints, timetables, blood types, and DNA, the genre presents itself as an antidote to modern fiction, in which the theme of uncertainty is pronounced. The protagonist of Henry James's story "The Figure in the Carpet" (1896), for example, fancies himself an expert on the work of Hugh Vereker, the novelist he most admires—only to be told by Vereker that all the critics, the interlocutor included, have "missed my little point," "my secret," "the thing for the critic to find," "like a complex figure in a Persian carpet." The "figure in the carpet" has become shorthand for the secret message that defies detection in a work of art or life experience. Ambiguity is all. In Joseph Conrad's *Heart of Darkness* (1899), for a second example, the climactic revelation is the

---

1. Greene was reviewing the 1937 French film *L'alibi*, directed by Pierre Chenal and starring Erich von Stroheim. *A Slight Case of Murder* is the movie's English title. Greene's review appeared in *The Spectator*, June 17, 1938. See *Graham Greene on Film: Collected Film Criticism, 1935–1939* (New York: Simon & Schuster, 1972), 192.

exposure of a lie that has the effect of compromising our whole edifice of understanding. In stark contrast, the detective story proceeds from disclosure to closure; from the discovery of the body in the first chapter to the identification of the murderer in the last; from secrets and signs amassed and analyzed to the final grouping of the suspects, like the return of the cast at the end of a well-made play, with the villain or villains marked for banishment and, during curtain calls, absolution conferred on the poor players strutting and fretting their hour upon the stage. Murder becomes a "religious subject" if you believe in a last judgment.

Gertrude Stein, who called the detective story "the only really modern novel form," has an analysis that has always fascinated me. (You can piece it together from passages in *Everybody's Autobiography* and in her 1936 lecture "What Are Master-Pieces, and Why Are There So Few of Them?") Stein explained that the detective story "gets rid of human nature by having the man dead to begin with the hero is dead to begin with and so you have so to speak got rid of the event before the book begins." In a detective story, she also observed, "the only person of any importance is dead" and so "there can be no beginning middle and end" in the conventional sense. Stein helps to account for why time in a detective novel flows not in a straight line but in two directions concurrently: there is the time of the action culminating in the violent event that occurs just before the book begins, and there is the narrative time of the detective's reconstruction of the events leading to that moment. Stein's arguably more important insight is that the discovery of the corpse represents the termination of an action at the same time that it initiates a new action, and since this is so, it makes sense to regard the detective as a new hero who emerges at the precise moment when his predecessor, the traditional hero of fiction, meets his violent end—just as Nancy Allen replaces Angie

Dickinson as the heroine in the elevator scene in Brian De Palma's *Dressed to Kill* (1980). The scene of the crime is the locus of the transition from a flawed hero (the victim) to one who is better equipped for survival (the detective, even as improbable a duo as Nancy Allen and the teenaged Keith Gordon).

The figure of the detective as a distinctively modern hero suggests that truth in modern industrial society is concealed, distorted, fabricated—or, as happens in Edgar Allan Poe's "The Purloined Letter" (1844), effectively concealed by being left out in the open, unnoticed by those who neglect surfaces in favor of depths. The detective proceeds on the assumption that the truth can be learned and is empirically verifiable. Brainwork is the key. Fierce mental energy is needed to decipher coded messages, to expose lies and resolve contradictions, to pull off false noses and masks, to interrogate witnesses (some of whom are mendacious, others merely self-serving or frightened), to interpret textual evidence, and to reconstruct an entire sequence of events from scattered hints.

"Always an Orangutan"

Every so often somebody reprises Edmund Wilson's famous put-down of detective novels, "Who Cares Who Killed Roger Ackroyd?" (1945). Wilson regarded the genre as terminally subliterary, either an addiction or a harmless vice on a par with crossword puzzles. But the truth is that for every Edmund Wilson who has resisted the genre, there are dozens of intellectuals who have embraced it wholeheartedly. The enduring highbrow appeal of the detective novel is one of the literary marvels of the last century. How to account for the genre's popularity? And what does it tell us about ourselves? More than half a century after he asked it, Edmund Wilson's question continues to beguile us. All we have lost is his scorn.

W. H. Auden, whose 1948 essay "The Guilty Vicarage" remains one of the best things ever written about thrillers, wrote that the murder mystery "is the dialectic of innocence and guilt." An Agatha Christie mystery (as opposed to the celebration of criminal mischief and mayhem in, say, Quentin Tarantino's *Pulp Fiction*) announces that the angel in humankind is superior to the animal, the ego can establish its mastery of the id, though the impulse to rebel against authority is great. And yet the mystery's ground zero is Hobbes's view of the moral universe: the conviction that in the state of nature, man is not a noble savage but a natural-born killer. In Poe's "The Murders in the Rue Morgue" (1841), the world's first official detective story, the culprit is a pet ape, like a Darwinian nightmare ahead of the fact. (Poe's story antedated Darwin's *Origin of Species* by eighteen years.) In the act of shaving, with razor in hand as he has seen his master do it, the orangutan is interrupted and runs away in a panic. He kills two women because they happen to reside in the place where his rage and fear blindly take him. The entire genre is testimony to this image of the ape beneath the skin. The man in the tuxedo with the concealed dagger in his jacket pocket is a murderous monkey in a monkey suit, and the female of the species is as deadly as an asp.

In his poem "Mysteries" (1994), Terence Winch narrates that he has been reading "The Murders in the Rue Morgue." The orangutan solution strikes him as "pretty ridiculous." But he finds himself thinking about Poe and talking about the story, and when at dinner he tells his friends Doug and Susan about it, "Doug / suggested that he and I collaborate / on a series of detective stories in which / the murderer is *always* an orangutan."

The lesson of the poem, beyond its humor, is indefinite. Is it that what appears ridiculous may become something quite different if taken to an extreme? Or is it that some ideas for fiction are best left in a conceptual state? Both, perhaps. Doug's idea of a "series of detective stories in which / the murderer is *always* an orangutan" is so pithily stated that it makes the composition of the stories themselves superfluous.

In its easygoing way Winch's narrative hints at the uncanny strangeness of the mystery genre's inaugural story, in which the "ridiculous" murderer is nothing less than Darwinian man in an arrested evolutionary state, or perhaps Hobbesian man in the state of nature. The primal murderer, Poe is suggesting, is the unshackled id: a creature of brute desire and limited intelligence, but not devoid of finer aspiration, including the desire to be human. Look how manlike he is. He is capable of feeling guilty, of fearing punishment. He is aware of his resemblance to human beings and proves, indeed, that the homicidal impulse can originate in a clumsy effort at civilization. Note that the orangutan consults a mirror not only for narcissistic but also for mimetic purposes; it is surely significant that the brute begins his murder spree when he is discovered in the act of aping the sailor who owns him. But note, too, that the notion of the double, always strong in Poe, is taken to a logical extreme in the story, in which the detective, Dupin, and his unnamed sidekick make one double, and the murdered mother and her daughter make a second. It is tempting to say that the murderer is also a double, the product and emblem of a divided consciousness, half human and half brute. So when Dupin says of the sailor that though he did not himself commit the murders he was "implicated" in them all the same, it is a remark that vibrates with meaning.

Poe's Dupin stories represent an antithetical force balancing the impulse governing such of his tales as "The Black Cat," "The Fall of

the House of Usher," and "The Tell-Tale Heart," which involve gratuitous acts of cruelty and the nightmare of being buried alive. In
a century riddled with self-destructive doubles—Victor Franken-
stein, Dr. Jekyll, Dorian Gray—you could argue that Dupin is able
to contain his double in both senses of "contain," if we identify
Dupin's own double as the antagonist he foils in "The Purloined
Letter," Minister D——, with whom he shares a first initial and
much else. Allegorically, Dupin represents the unified ego mediat-
ing between the warring impulses of the ungovernable id and the
wrathful superego.

Watching a movie like *The Talented Mr. Ripley* (1999) or its 1960
French predecessor, *Purple Noon*, with Alain Delon (both adapted
from Patricia Highsmith's 1955 novel), allows us to indulge the
murderous id with impunity. The same is true of certain stories
by Roald Dahl. But these are exceptions. Starting from Wilkie Collins's *The Moonstone* (1868)—which T. S. Eliot called "the first,
the longest, and the best of modern English detective novels," and
which inspired Dickens to begin his unfinished last novel, *The
Mystery of Edwin Drood* (1870)—the vast majority of mystery
novels reassure us that human depravity can be controlled and, in
the end, defeated by the forces of justice if not always by what Poe
called "ratiocination."

The primary conventions of the classic whodunit—from locked
rooms to dullard cops, wrongly accused bystanders, precious documents hidden in plain sight, and eccentric sleuths accompanied
by loyal friends who will tell the tale—originate with Poe. Sherlock
Holmes, the most famous of the Great Detectives, was made in
the image of Poe's Dupin. A fundamental assumption common
to both is that the more outré the incident the better, because, as
Holmes puts it, "the very point which appears to complicate a case
is, when duly considered and scientifically handled, the one which

is most likely to elucidate it." The difference is that Dupin and Poe's unnamed narrator are not all that interesting as characters, while Holmes and his narrator, Dr. Watson, come so vividly to life that visitors to London still trek to 221B Baker Street, where, according to Conan Doyle, the pair resided from 1881 to 1904. (Tourists hoping for a real-life glimpse of these purely fictional characters must satisfy themselves with the Sherlock Holmes Museum.) When Holmes's creator tried to kill him off, the outcry was such that Doyle had little choice but to bring Holmes back—a case of an author at the mercy of his own character.

The definitive dialogue between Holmes and Watson distributes two words between them:

"Excellent," I cried.
"Elementary," said he.

But Watson's narrative duties go beyond admiration and wonderment. He is always willing to lend a hand and to bear true witness. In *The Hound of the Baskervilles* (1902), he sees an unknown figure on the moor, "black as an ebony statue," and exclaims that the man "might have been the very spirit of that terrible place." Watson does not know that it is Holmes's silhouette that he sees. Nevertheless, the description of the great detective, aloof, "as if he were brooding over that enormous wilderness of peat and granite which lay before him," rings true. In a gothic universe of desolate wilds, Holmes is the hero who does not succumb to curses and superstitions. There is something of the uncanny about him.

Like Poe's Dupin, Holmes is a mind reader, able accurately to chronicle the train of thoughts in his silent friend's mind. One glance is all it takes for Holmes to observe that a certain visitor "has at some time done manual labor, that he takes snuff, that he is a Freemason, that he has been in China, and that he has done a considerable amount of writing lately." Beyond these "obvious facts," Holmes says he "can deduce nothing else," a masterly example of what has come to be called the humble brag.

Holmes is a genius whose contempt for the police matches his own exalted sense of superiority. (About the police officer in "The Red-Headed League" [1891], he remarks, "He is not a bad fellow, though an absolute imbecile in his profession.") Where Holmes is singular, his sidekick Watson is definitively ordinary except in his fierce loyalty to his partner. As the fleshed-out version of Poe's unnamed narrator, Dr. Watson is the most famous instance of the universal wingman— the genial fellow who tells the story, lends a hand, brings his old army pistol at Holmes's request, and is always six chess moves behind his companion. He may be pleasantly obtuse (Christie's Captain Hastings, who narrates the adventures of Hercule Poirot) or dashing as he makes his rounds in service to an oversized armchair detective back home (Archie Goodwin in Rex Stout's Nero Wolfe series). The narrator represents the fallible reader, along for the ride, ready to express our astonishment as the case gets solved. As the wonderfully named E. M. Wrong put it in 1926, "The detective's friend acts in the dual capacity of very average reader and of Greek chorus; he comments freely on what he does not understand."[2]

Unlike Watson, who has an eye for an attractive woman, Holmes is a confirmed bachelor with a bundle of oddities and eccentricities. Expert at the art of disguise, he turns up here as a harmless clergyman, there as an asthmatic old mariner. He has written "a little monograph on the ashes of 140 different varieties of pipe, cigar, and cigarette tobacco." He is a very capable fellow, and quite self-assured. "Burglary has always been an alternative profession

2. E. M. Wrong, "Crime and Detection" (1926), in *The Art of the Mystery Story*, ed. Howard Haycraft (New York: Grosset & Dunlap, 1946), 22.

had I cared to adopt it, and I have little doubt that I should have come to the front," he confides in "The Adventure of the Retired Colourman," the last story in *The Case Book of Sherlock Holmes.*

Subject to long periods of lethargy from which he is desperate to escape, Holmes takes cocaine, plays the fiddle, and fires his patriotic pistol to shoot the initials "VR" (for "Victoria Regina") into the wall of his sitting room. Solving mysteries is an expedient way to overcome the ennui to which he is prone. Little else can absorb his insatiable curiosity or divert him from his gloom. His worldview is definitively pessimistic: "We reach. We grasp. And what is left in our hands at the end? A shadow. Or worse than a shadow—misery." With his fits of melancholia, Holmes has some of the traits of the Romantic rebel as defined in the poetry of Charles Baudelaire. "My life," Holmes reflects, "is spent in one long effort to escape from the commonplaces of existence. These little problems help me to do so." In effect, Holmes is a mentally superior murder addict who rejects the hopelessly prosaic world in favor of perverse pleasures, flowers of evil. It is one of the paradoxes of the genre that Holmes, the most unconventional and extraordinary character, in some ways a bohemian, in all ways a nonconformist, is the one who restores the moral and social order.

In the Fall of a Beam

In the American hard-boiled tradition, the hero is singular in a different sense. A loner by temperament, fiercely independent though possibly down-at-the-heels, caustic in speech, wounded but game, the city-dwelling private eye restores order but only after disrupting a contrived and artificial order in which venality is hidden from view. He is, as Raymond Chandler said of himself, a "ferocious romantic," and he works alone. The death of Miles Archer, Sam Spade's partner, at the beginning of *The Maltese Falcon* (1930) establishes a precondition for the whole hard-boiled genre. "Have the Spade & Archer taken off the door and Samuel Spade put on," Sam tells his secretary in his brisk, unsentimental way. The sleuth's partner, potentially a Watson, a Boswell, or a Sancho Panza, is dead and more or less forgotten from the start. He has become that least loved, most dispensable individual: the victim, who exists entirely in the past tense. No, the hard-boiled detective can be accompanied by no one. He is a martyr to Emersonian self-reliance, a tough guy attracted to women who are bad for him: assorted femmes fatales in whom the Freudian connection between Eros and Thanatos is made explicit.

The setting of Dashiell Hammett's *Red Harvest* (1929)—Personville, pronounced "Poisonville"—suggests the allegorical locale that attracted Hammett and his followers: a place where the private eye can function as a kind of catalyst for violent change. With his sturdy self-reliance, the hard-boiled sleuth in his gray fedora resembles the lone, no-nonsense lawman played by Gary Cooper in Westerns. He is proof that violence is needed to contain violence and that one just man will prevail over the corrupt mob and timorous crowd. An insubordinate cuss, the sleuth knows that insubordination becomes an admirable trait in an age when the torturer's first line of defense is that he was merely following orders. His alliances are temporary and grounded in deep suspicion; he can count on no one, least of all the client who's footing the bill. Many hard-boiled dicks used to be cops but left because their attitude toward authority was like Steve McQueen's in *Bullitt* or Clint Eastwood's in *Dirty Harry, Magnum Force,* and *The Enforcer.* Though there is a chase and a shootout still to come, *Bullitt* reaches its moral climax in the one word that Frank Bullitt, the cop played by McQueen, barks when his antagonist, a venal senator, says, "We must all compromise." McQueen's one-word response rhymes with his character's name: "Bullshit."

In the morally ambiguous world of *The Maltese Falcon,* Hammett's best book, Spade is described as a "blond Satan." He is (the other characters constantly exclaim) a wild and unpredictable man, and his motives are never quite clear. The priceless jewel-encrusted falcon—which turns out to be a fake—is the unholy grail that obsesses the book's entertaining cast, and Spade is not entirely immune from the lure of the hunt.

The story of Flitcraft, a Tacoma man who disappeared one day after a falling beam narrowly missed him in the street, helps explain Spade's "existential" disposition. Flitcraft (says Spade, telling the story) left his wife and family, his job, and severed all his ties, because "the life he knew was a clean orderly sane responsible affair. Now a falling beam had shown him that life was fundamentally none of these things." The awareness that he could be wiped out in an instant caused him to flee the life he had been living, a life that had been "sensibly ordered" and was therefore "out of step" with a universe of blind chance. Tracked down by the detective, Flitcraft turns out to be living in Spokane with a second wife more like the first than they are different. "I don't think he even knew he had settled back naturally into the same groove he had jumped out of in Tacoma," says Spade. "But that's the part of it I always liked. He adjusted himself to beams falling, and then no more of them fell, and he adjusted himself to them not falling."

Where Spade differs from Flitcraft is that he will not settle down, will not deny the epiphany of the falling beam. Life is not a reasonable affair, and he will not act reasonably. Randomness is all; there is no special providence in the fall of a beam. The Flitcraft parable presents the key to the detective's character and attitude, but it is also a parable about murder mysteries in general, which begin with "a clean orderly sane responsible" situation that gets violently disrupted by the equivalent of "a falling beam." And just as Flitcraft returns to "the same groove he had jumped out of," the conventional detective novel returns to its initial state of rest. Why does Spade tell the Flitcraft story to Miss Wonderly, alias Brigid O'Shaughnessy? Perhaps to make the point that he, unlike Flitcraft, prefers the world of chaos and anarchy to an artificial retreat. In Raymond Chandler's *The Long Goodbye* (1953), Philip Marlowe articulates this position. He rejects a sober, safe small-town life, with "an eight-room house, two cars in the garage, chicken every Sunday and the *Reader's Digest* on the living room table, the wife with a cast-iron permanent and me with a brain like a sack of Portland cement. You take it, friend. I'll take the big sordid dirty crooked city."

In the books Marlowe smokes a pipe, plays chess (or tries to solve chess puzzles), refuses the advances of lusty clients or associates, gets slugged and spat at regularly by the police. Unlike the character as marvelously portrayed in the movies by Humphrey Bogart and Dick Powell, he leads a chaste life. A bottle of scotch will have to do. He has a cop friend, Bernie Ohls, who, with an unlit cigar in his mouth, says, "I quit smoking. Got me coughing too much." Bernie asks why Marlowe persists in pursuing nasty cases of enormous complexity in which everyone involved is doing his or her best to get him to drop the matter. It can't be for the money, there's so little of it in his line of work. The answer: "I'm a romantic, Bernie. I hear voices crying in the night and I go see what's the matter. You don't make a dime that way."

W. H. Auden argued that Chandler's detective stories are "serious studies of a criminal milieu, the Great Wrong Place," and should be read "not as escape literature, but as works of art." At its least complicated, Chandler's moral vision is based on a species of class resentment. "To hell with the rich," Philip Marlowe says in *The Big Sleep* (1939). "They made me sick." The book begins in the Sternwood mansion and ends in the oil sump where the

Sternwood money comes from and where, now, Rusty Regan sleeps the big sleep. The plot thus illustrates Balzac's remark that if you follow any fortune to its source, you will uncover a crime. But the texture of Chandler's novels is thickened immeasurably by their allegorical dimension. Philip Marlowe's very name suggests the pull of romance: the playwright Christopher Marlowe of the "mighty line," or possibly the sailor and adventurer named Marlow who penetrates the infernal center of Conrad's *Heart of Darkness*.[3] In Philip Marlowe's Los Angeles, the casinos and clubs that beckon are like the bowers of bliss—all ersatz glitter—that test the epic hero embarked on a Renaissance quest romance. The place is beyond redemption, and the hard-drinking hero is somewhat quixotic in his mission. Chandler compares him to a knight-errant in the opening pages of *The Big Sleep*, and the last name of the woman his client hires him to find in *Farewell, My Lovely* (1940) is "Grayle." Clever cracks keep Marlowe from looking ridiculous as he targets a windmill: "I felt like an amputated leg."

Dame Agatha and Co.

What humor there is in hard-boiled novels and films noirs is provided by wisecracking dialogue and acute insights, such as this observation from Helen Nielsen's *Sing Me a Murder* (1961):

3. It cannot be a coincidence that Christopher Marlowe, the Elizabethan dramatist, a colorful duel-fighting fellow, has lent his last name, with or without a final *e*, not only to characters in Conrad and Chandler but also to figures of some importance in E. C. Bentley's *Trent's Last Case*, Eric Ambler's *Cause for Alarm*, Dennis Potter's *The Singing Detective*, and two movies based on novels by Cornell Woolrich: Roy William Neill's *Black Angel*, in which the victim is a singer named Mavis Marlowe, and Robert Siodmak's film adaptation of *Phantom Lady*, which Woolrich wrote under the name William Irish.

"When a man mentally undresses a woman, it's merely sex, but when a woman mentally dresses a man he's in dire danger of matrimony." The screenwriter and executive producer Dick Wolf displays a mastery of poker-faced wit in, for example, the episode of *Law & Order* that aired on October 30, 1990. Detective Greevey (George Dzundza) questions a bodega proprietor about the hike in the price of a ham sandwich. "I didn't know ptomaine had gone up that much," Greevey says, to which the vendor replies, "We don't use any of that stuff. It's all homemade."

In the classic whodunit, the situation itself may have strong comic possibilities. T. S. Eliot pointed out (in his introduction to the English-language translation of Paul Valéry's *The Art of Poetry*) that the detective novel is the only genre, other than certain kinds of stage comedy, in which "the *unexpected* is a contribution to, and even a necessary element of, our enjoyment." The elaborate artifice built around a challenging puzzle can have the charm of a riddle, as in Ellery Queen's *The Chinese Orange Mystery* (1934). That murder can coexist with the comic imagination is demonstrated in *Kind Hearts and Coronets* (1949), in which Alec Guinness plays multiple murder victims, and *No Way to Treat a Lady* (1967), in which five women are strangled by a histrionic, limerick-reciting Rod Steiger disguised as a priest, a plumber, a beat cop, a gay dandy in a blue blazer, and a middle-aged woman, with accents and costumes to match. There is an element of romantic comedy in such films as *The Thin Man* (1934), with urbane William Powell and Myrna Loy as Dashiell Hammett's Nick and Nora Charles, and Stanley Donen's *Charade* (1963), with Cary Grant and Audrey Hepburn playful in Paris, in which surprise is the better part of suspense and the villain is unmasked at the very end.

Tom Stoppard's 1968 play *The Real Inspector Hound*—a travesty of murder mystery dramas on the order of *The Bat* by Mary

Roberts Rinehart—explores the meeting place of detective story and farce. But it is also a reminder of the enabling irony of the detective genre: that it transmutes the cruelty and brutality of human nature into a species of entertainment, presenting homicide not as an ethical violation or tort but as an aesthetic spectacle, a parlor game with rules. It is a civilized way to pass a social evening.

In the detective novel, wrote Auden, "the corpse must shock not only because it is a corpse but also because, even for a corpse, it is shockingly out of place, as when a dog makes a mess on a drawing room carpet." The analogy suggests a world of country house weekends, Mediterranean cruises, tropical island resorts, an archaeological dig, even a plane ride from Le Bourget to Croydon: the terrain of Agatha Christie. The proper way to read a puzzle by Christie is as a version of pastoral. She offers up an idyllic setting in which everyone knows everyone else and no one seems to work except the servants. In this garden there are serpents; in fact, just about everybody has a false front. Nevertheless, it is a closed and orderly community temporarily disturbed by violent death and ultimately restored to the Way It Was after a brief brain-teasing diversion.

There has never existed a more cunning artificer of homicide than Dame Agatha. Nor has anyone made shrewder use of the least-likely-suspect ploy or the basic incongruity summed up well by Anthony Lane as "maleficence emerging in the most genteel of contexts, like strychnine in the tea."[4] Christie's triumph was to have fulfilled Thomas De Quincey's irony-charged vision of murder as an aesthetic experience. "Enough has been given to morality; now

---

4. Anthony Lane, "Murder Most Fun," *The New Yorker*, December 2, 2019, 76.

comes the turn of Taste and the Fine Arts," De Quincey declared in "On Murder Considered as One of the Fine Arts" (1827). "A sad thing it [the murder] was, no doubt, very sad; but *we* can't mend it. Therefore let us make the best of a bad matter; and, as it is impossible to hammer anything out of it for moral purposes, let us treat it aesthetically, and see if it will turn to account in that way." G. K. Chesterton developed the idea. "A crime is like any other work of art," Chesterton's detective Father Brown says in "The Queer Feet" (1910). "Don't look surprised; crimes are by no means the only works of art that come from an infernal workshop."

"The game is afoot," Holmes says when he hurries Watson into action as "The Adventure of the Abbey Grange" begins. Murder, like sex, can be considered not merely as an art, but also as a game, a competition, a battle, an act of passion, or—in the phrase of a gentleman in Bruce Hamilton's very British *Too Much of Water* (1958)—"the best of all blood sports." A suspect in Christie's *Hickory Dickory Death* (1955) presents "the controversial challenge that crime was a form of creative art—and that the misfits of society were really the police who only entered that profession because of their secret sadism." Christie does not endorse this notion, but it was she who put the aesthetic theory of murder into practice most successfully in *Murder on the Orient Express* (1934), *The ABC Murders* (1936), *Death on the Nile* (1937), and *And Then There Were None* (1939). In her hands, murder is rather like a work of art: a creative challenge, theatrical, requiring careful planning and the ability to improvise before a live audience.

Christie is nothing if not clever. In *Lord Edgware Dies* (1933; also published as *Thirteen at Dinner*), the solution to the mystery hinges on the double meaning of a phrase overheard in a luncheon conversation: does the "judgment of Paris" refer to classical myth (Hector's brother choosing among three goddesses) or to French fashion designers and critics? Why, in *The Clocks* (1963), is the unidentified dead man found in a blind woman's sitting room with four extraneous clocks, each reading 4:13, a little more than an hour in advance of the right time? Scattering red herrings where they will do the most good, Christie brought the convention of the least likely suspect to its apotheosis, pinning the murder in one of her books on the narrator—and on all the assembled suspects in another.

There are games within games. In *Cards on the Table* (1936), four detectives sit at one table, four suspects at another, playing bridge after a dinner thrown by their mysterious host, who makes a crack in bad taste about murder as an art form. He pays for it; is stabbed to death while the games are going on. Somehow the stabbing goes unnoticed. Each of the four suspects has a violent death in his or her past. I have read the book twice, seen it both onstage and in a television dramatization, and—I say this in tribute to Christie's brilliance as a puzzle maker—could probably read it again without any annoying recollection of who the killer is revealed to be.

If the murderer is an artist, an artificer, and a game player, the detective is the great critic—or what Oscar Wilde dubbed "the critic as artist." And in the person of Hercule Poirot, the fussy little Belgian with the egg-shaped head, Christie created an immortally eccentric detective who owes his triumphs to the "little gray cells of the brain." Poirot succeeds not in spite of being a caricature but because of this condition. As a bundle of quirks, he is highly theatrical, made to order for a skillful actor. He has been memorably impersonated on-screen or on television by Albert Finney, Peter Ustinov, David Suchet, and Kenneth Branagh. In September 1975, when *Curtain*, Christie's last Poirot, was published, the *New York Times* reported the fictive detective's death on its front page, a rare distinction.

Christie's prose has been dismissed as serviceable at best, but this is unjust. She writes so directly and with so little artistic pretension that the ease of reading makes her riddles all the more maddening—and the easier to adapt from the page to the stage, radio, film, and television. In a simple sentence she can convey something essential about the class-conscious English murder mystery. In *The Clocks*, a minor character wonders to herself, "How was she to get the potatoes on for the Irish stew if detective inspectors came along at this awkward hour?"

If you're reading Agatha Christie to get a picture of English provincial life, you're reading her for the wrong reason. But an incidental pleasure of her books is how quickly and astringently she depicts persons from different classes and separates the ones she respects from the scoundrels. Of a typist with "a mild worried face like a sheep," we're told on page one of *A Pocket Full of Rye* (1953) that her job was to boil the water for tea but that she "was never quite sure when a kettle was boiling. It was one of the many worries that afflicted her in life." That is nearly all that needs to be said about her in this puzzler fashioned after a nursery rhyme. Christie's sense of proper order is summed up in her approval of a minor character, the governess in *Murder in Retrospect* (1942), who had "the enormous mental and moral advantage of a strict Victorian upbringing, denied to us in these days—she had done her duty in that station of life to which it had pleased God to call her, and that assurance encased her in an armor impregnable to the slings and darts of envy, discontent, and regret."

The mood of postwar Britain, an air of grumpiness and resentment, may be inferred from such of Christie's novels as *Mrs. McGinty's Dead* (1952) and *Funerals Are Fatal* (1953; also titled *After the Funeral*). Complaints are common about shortages, the rationing that lasted for years following the end of World War

II, and the newly created National Health Service. Skeptical note is taken of the spread of government bureaucracy. All you need to say is you're from "UNARCO," the acronym of a nonexistent government agency, and you're in. Xenophobia remains pervasive. Mind you, "foreign" in Christie has always meant dangerous and untrustworthy. "Who's to know what reason foreigners have for murdering each other, and if you ask me, I think it's a dirty trick to have done it in a British aeroplane," the wife of an airline steward says in Christie's *Death in the Clouds* (1935). On second thought, "there's Bolshies at the back of it."

Poirot had one strategy for dealing with the general suspicion of "foreigners" during World War II. "It was no moment for trying to be English," he reasons in *Murder in Retrospect*. "No, one must be a foreigner—frankly a foreigner—and be magnanimously forgiven for the fact." By 1952, seven years after V-E Day, he is not above dispensing Gallic wisdom, explaining to the British inspector that "a *secret de Polichinelle* is a secret that everyone can know. For this reason the people who do not know it never hear about it—for if everyone thinks you know a thing, nobody tells you."

A fop from the continent with a taste for aperitifs, a surfeit of *amour propre*, and a willingness to play the mountebank, Poirot fits right into tradition. No doubt because of Poe and Conan Doyle, the detective in the classic murder mystery is an outsider, and not always because he is a dandy (Poe's Dupin); a fleshed-out late Victorian version of the same, wearing a deerstalker and smoking a bent pipe (Holmes); a bespectacled man of the cloth with a rolled umbrella and a penchant for paradoxes (Chesterton's Father Brown); or a patrician oenophile with a monocle and a manservant (Lord Peter Wimsey). He may be an obese cultivator of orchids (Nero Wolfe). She may be a feminist literature professor at Columbia who drinks, smokes, and is married but "neither uses his name nor wears his ring" (Kate Fansler in Amanda Cross's novels).

The most famous female detective is Christie's Jane Marple, the smartest old lady in the village, rising always to the occasion, whether it be the discovery of a body in the library or what Mrs. McGillicuddy saw out the window of the 4:54 from Paddington: a man strangling a woman in the window of the train going the opposite way. Among the actresses who have brought Miss Marple to life are Margaret Rutherford, Angela Lansbury, and Joan Hickson. To Rutherford, star of *Murder, She Said* and three other Miss Marple movies, Christie dedicated her 1962 novel *The Mirror Crack'd from Side to Side*. That novel was the basis of the 1980 movie *The Mirror Cracked*, with Lansbury as Jane Marple heading a cast that included Elizabeth Taylor, Kim Novak, and Geraldine Chaplin. In retrospect that movie looks like a trial run for the popular 1980s television series *Murder, She Wrote*, in which Lansbury plays Jessica Fletcher, author of detective novels, a Maine widow and inveterate traveler, who is living proof that a single woman of a certain age is not to be trifled with. The third in my list of favorites, Joan Hickson, played Jane Marple in the BBC series that ran between 1984 and 1992. Many years earlier, Christie saw the young actress in a 1946 theater adaptation of *Appointment with Death* and wrote to her, "I hope one day you will play my dear Miss Marple."

Miss Marple has definite views. "Human nature is much the same everywhere," she believes, and therefore her little village, St. Mary Mead, can serve as a universal model. In *A Pocket Full of Rye*, she notes with disapproval that "a group of quite reasonably intelligent women showed incredible ignorance of correct procedure" during a medical emergency. But Jane Marple can be quite generous with the well-meaning police detective who does his best even if he is not her intellectual equal. In the same book, a pair of similes defines Miss Marple's relation to Inspector Neele, whose intelligence she respects, and to whom she reveals the solution to a chain of murders, "rather in the manner of someone explaining the simple facts of arithmetic to a small child." When she has provided her theory, the inspector wonders how he will prove it. "You'll prove it," Miss Marple says, nodding at him "encouragingly as an aunt might have encouraged a bright nephew who was going in for a scholarship exam."

Under the Sign of W. H. Auden

As an English professor at a major metropolitan university resembling Columbia, Kate Fansler—the heroine of the novels Columbia professor Carolyn Heilbrun wrote under the pseudonym Amanda Cross—is literary, learned, a tireless defender of victimized women and opponent of sexism in the English department. Within the first fifty pages of *Poetic Justice* (1970), we encounter a performance by the Living Theatre ("the entertainment principally consisted of the members of the cast removing their clothes and urging, gently of course, that the audience do likewise"), unwashed radicals, the generation gap, and a list of then-typical New York disasters that makes one feel almost nostalgic ("strikes, garbage uncollected, snow unremoved").

With the campus uprisings of 1968 fresh in everyone's mind, Amanda Cross captures the astonishment of the moment. She is appalled "that a bunch of half-baked, foul-mouthed Maoist students could bring a great university to a standstill, could be followed in their illegal acts by nearly a thousand moderate, thoughtful students, but above all could reveal that the University had never really been administered at all." Kate can tell a mean literary anecdote. "You're accusing me, in your ever polite way, of being like the dreaming lady in an anecdote of Kenneth Burke's. She dreamed a brute of a man had entered her bedroom and was staring at her from the foot of her bed. 'Oh, what are you going to do to me?' she asked, trembling. 'I don't know, lady,' the brute answered; 'it's your dream.'"

Each chapter of *Poetic Justice* begins with a well-chosen epigraph from Auden. Perhaps the author took her cue from Nicholas Blake, whose detective, Nigel Strangeways, bears the name of a Manchester prison. Each chapter of Blake's *The Corpse in the Snowman* (1941) begins with an epigraph from Shakespeare, Dryden, Marlowe, and others of their ilk, and "the problem of evil" rates a mention. In *A Question of Proof* (1935), Nigel's first chronicled adventure, we learn that at Oxford he answered all his examination questions with limericks. In *End of Chapter* (1957), he analyzes characters by the appearance of their rooms. One is a "museum of false starts." Another is a "mausoleum of dead ends." Lines of poetry from T. S. Eliot, Emily Dickinson, Thomas Hardy, and John Donne accompany Nigel's investigation like a soundtrack.

In *A Question of Proof*, Strangeways is said to have "alienated the [Oxford] dons, [who] have no taste for modern poetry." If he is a houseguest, beware. "He can't sleep unless he has an enormous weight on his bed. If you don't give him blankets enough for three, you'll find that he has torn the carpet up or the curtains down." Shades of Wystan Auden. But then Nicholas Blake is the pseudonym of C. Day Lewis, a celebrated poet in the Auden circle and a translator of *The Aeneid*, who went on to become England's poet laureate.[5] In *Thou Shell of Death* (1936), possibly Blake's best book, the

---

5. "I must confess to a weakness for Mr. Day Lewis's Nigel Strangeways, because some of his habits were taken from mine," Auden wrote, qualifying his observation that often the most cunning artificers of crime puzzles "invent the most intolerable detective heroes."

victim is said to have been based on T. E. Lawrence. Fergus O'Brien is rich, dashing, heroic, a ladies' man, and the motives for killing him are many; there is a will, a blackmail scheme that goes awry, a jilted lover, an unlucky rival. A quotation from *The Revenger's Tragedy* helps Nigel Strangeways arrive at the right solution—and establish the possibility of a posthumous murderer. The book contains my three favorite sentences in the Blake oeuvre. In one of them, Hercules is described as the Bulldog Drummond of Greek myth; in a second, we encounter "the utter caliginous inspissated fog" in Nigel's mind; in a third, a man whose car keeps stalling gets out, pulls up the bonnet, and tinkers with the insides in a process that "was, like the Roman Catholic Church, a triumphant blend of faith and ritual."

The Whisper in the Gloom (1954) is not one of Blake's best, but it does illustrate a fundamental fact about the classic detective story. The solution is almost necessarily prosaic, but the problem may be wonderfully eerie: a dying man slips a piece of paper to a boy he doesn't know, with the boy's name and age written on it.

Auden's spirit presides over *The Horizontal Man* (1946) by Helen Eustis, who borrows the poet's epigraph that instructs us to honor "the vertical man" while ruefully admitting that we attach more value to "the horizontal one." Eustis, an alumna of Smith College, sets her story there, disguised as "Hollymount College"—perhaps to distinguish it from nearby Mount Holyoke College. The victim is a young poet, and if you knew who was who in the literary world in 1946, you might recognize a few of the characters. Back then, the revelation of the killer's identity shocked readers, presaging the abnormal psychology informing one of Hitchcock's signature works.

Of a dormitory house mother (Miss Sanders), who remains the confidante of a former student, now a faculty member (Freda), Eustis tells us that "Miss Sanders found herself relegated (or elevated) to a position in Freda's life like that of a superannuated nanny in a noble

English household, who, having dandled the young lady in the family in her infancy, now bends a deferential ear to her debutante confidences." The simile, beautifully elongated, evokes the default context of the classic detective story: the patrician family estate, replete with retainers. Freda herself, in conversation, does an admirable job of summarizing the double pleasure of murder mysteries as "the pleasure of vicarious violence, and the pleasure at the detection and punishment of the crime of another. In the first we can enjoy the emotional outlet without undertaking the penalty, and in the second we can shiver deliciously with the knowledge that we cannot be found out, since our share in the business was secret, and of the mind."

Skullduggery

The spy novel is the detective story's close cousin. It is significant that Charles Latimer, the hero of *A Coffin for Dimitrios* (1939), arguably Eric Ambler's greatest prewar novel, is an acclaimed writer of old-school detective stories who now, as he crosses European borders on the trail of a singular criminal, comes into contact with the real thing as opposed to the "tidy book-murder" in his fiction. Like the detective, the spy is a figure you can do a lot with. He or she may be wholly innocent of spycraft, a civilian on holiday, or a professional working for an intelligence service. The innocent, like Charles Latimer and other Ambler heroes, gains an education. The professional renews a cycle of betrayals and disloyalty oaths.

In "The Guilty Vicarage," Auden wrote that the interest in the spy stories "is the ethical and eristic conflict between good and evil, between Us and Them." So long as there is no doubt about the meaning and validity of these pronouns, the formula makes sense. Somerset Maugham's World War I agent Ashenden is a veteran traveler who goes from one episode of skullduggery to another in a different venue, foreign and exotic. *Ashenden* (1928) goes a long way toward demystifying what Rudyard Kipling in *Kim* called "the Great Game," but there is no moral ambiguity in the spy's identity as a British agent, loyal to his country. In World War II movies from *Casablanca* to *The Guns of Navarone*, the choice between Us and Them could not have been easier. The Nazis were ideal foes— and still are. But the Cold War complicated things. So much of the fighting took place in secret, in the mind and the imagination, in threats and in gambits, that inevitably a cloud of unknowing descended upon the game being played, be it poker, a board game, charades, "Capture the Flag"—or, finally, a game without rules.

Three premises:

1. In a war between nuclear powers that dare not use weapons, except via surrogates or in metaphor—where who "blinked" first is
   the victor's boast—the gathering of information is more necessary than ever.[6] While technology has provided new equipment, it
   has also created new opportunities for miscreants.

2. The double agent is, by definition, not only duplicitous but also
   capable of leading several lives—to the point where the usual
   distinctions between truth and fiction get blurred even in the
   agent's own mind. The task must be a nearly impossible one if,
   as Auden writes in *The Prolific and the Devourer*, "it is folly to
   imagine that one can live two lives, a public and a private one.
   No man can serve two masters."

3. Who better to epitomize treachery and treason than a trusted
   confederate, the honorable Brutus in *Julius Caesar*, Kim Philby
   in MI6?

6. If the United States could be said to have won the Cuban Missile Crisis,
it is because, in turning his ships back from the Caribbean, Nikita Khrushchev
"blinked" first. "We're eyeball to eyeball," Secretary of State Dean Rusk is supposed to have said to national security adviser McGeorge Bundy, "and I think the
other fellow just blinked."

There was always the risk that ideology could trump patriotism. And what happens to loyalty as an ideal, if not a prerequisite, when a high-placed citizen of one nation embraces the governing ideology of that nation's enemy? Out comes the Judas figure.

John le Carré's *Tinker, Tailor, Soldier, Spy* (1974) retells aspects of the Cold War espionage story with the greatest resonance not just in Britain but in all the West, that of the Cambridge-educated Guy Burgess, Donald Maclean, and Kim Philby, who worked at the highest levels of British intelligence and defected to the Soviet Union—the first two in 1951, Philby twelve years later—but only after years of revealing state secrets to the Russians. *There was an enemy within.* And, the reader infers, our own government was in no hurry to inform us that said enemy came from the ranks of the privileged few, who went to the best schools, belonged to the best clubs, and drank cocktails with the most amusing people. Philby, the most enigmatic in the group, and his cronies were as if singled out from boyhood for positions of leadership and responsibility. They took up the cause of Communism as practiced in the Soviet Union when they were Cambridge students in the 1930s, and they were dead serious about it, joining British intelligence to serve their masters in the KGB.

It took until 1979 for the British to reveal that a fourth agent who spied for the KGB was no less a personage than Sir Anthony Blunt, the distinguished art historian, author of an acclaimed study of Nicolas Poussin, and supervisor of Queen Elizabeth's royal collection. After he was denounced and stripped of his knighthood, Blunt said he had made "the biggest mistake of [his] life" out of his "enthusiasm for any anti-fascist activity." This sounds hollow; whiskey was a better recourse for Blunt than such a lame effort at self-exculpation. He knew better, after all; in 1951, when the KGB ordered him to go to Moscow, he refused, having come to the realization that he would sooner run any risk in England than be forced to live in Russia, the nation he had served to the detriment of his own. Yet not until he was publicly unmasked in 1979 did he say anything about what he had done. The wonder is that the British government agreed for so long to grant him immunity and to shield him from public exposure. After being outed, Blunt quoted E. M. Forster's famous statement that if given the choice, he would hope to have the guts to betray his country rather than his friends, and perhaps that was the death knell for a wicked doctrine that was presented rather more romantically in le Carré's *The Spy Who Came in from the Cold*, both book (1963) and film (1965).

As for Philby, this happy-go-lucky fellow who drank too much but was charming, how did he manage to escape detection for so long? Burgess and Maclean defected in 1951, Philby not until 1963. How did Philby do it? How did he hoodwink his colleagues, who were, let us remember, alleged experts at this sort of thing? One old boy, recollecting his days as an operative, chuckled as he opined that one should never, in matters of intelligence, rule out the possibility of incompetence. This notion stands behind one of the greatest of all spy novels, Graham Greene's *Our Man in Havana* (1958). The book is founded on the idea that "intelligence" in the espionage sense—secret knowledge—is as likely to be a fabrication, a rumor, or a fear as a fact; "intelligence" is where credibility and gullibility shake hands and go together to the nearest bar. A satire on espionage as an enterprise, *Our Man in Havana* presents a Cuba monitored by imaginary spies controlled by James Wormold, a vacuum cleaner salesman who can use the easy money from intelligence headquarters in London. The designs for the cleaners he sells, reproduced out of scale, can be seen to look like military installations. These Wormold feeds to the home office, where they arouse grave concern, if not the nuclear anxiety that marked the Cuban Missile Crisis in October 1962, foreshadowed here.

For all the ambiguity and irony that sneaks into books by Greene and le Carré, the Us versus Them formula remains durable. Laurence Olivier plays the evil Nazi dentist in one movie (*Marathon Man*, 1976) and the dogged Nazi hunter in pursuit of Dr. Mengele in a second (*The Boys from Brazil*, 1978). Both films have their attractions, but I cannot leave unpraised Gregory Peck's performance as the villain in *The Boys from Brazil* or the road rage car race with which *Marathon Man* begins, pitting two old men, a Jew in one car and a German in the other, and not just any German but the brother of an Auschwitz torturer. Mutually assured destruction for the two men is one consequence; the plot of the movie is the other.

A quartet of standouts from the 2010s have in common a basis in historical fact: Kathryn Bigelow's *Zero Dark Thirty* (2012) about the pursuit and execution of Osama bin Laden; Steven Spielberg's *Bridge of Spies* (2015), in which, in the early 1960s, the Soviet spy Rudolf Abel (played by Mark Rylance) is exchanged for the downed US spy plane pilot Francis Gary Powers; Ben Lewin's underrated film *The Catcher Was a Spy* (2018), about Moe Berg, the Princeton-educated Major League Baseball player who had an amazing facility for languages and was recruited by Allied intelligence to carry out a critical mission in Nazi Germany; and *The Spy* (2019), the Israeli television series based on the exploits of Eli Cohen, the Mossad agent who infiltrated the highest ranks of a hostile Syrian government in the 1960s. In the last named, Sacha Baron Cohen portrays the hero with the double identity, the young Israeli husband and father whose persona as a charming Syrian plutocrat vaults him into the inner circle of the radical Ba'athists who seized power in Damascus in 1963.

If the defining condition of the age is paranoia, the spy genus is home to two subspecies illustrating the point. Call the first of these the fear of mind control, or thought control, programmatically achieved by hypnosis. There are two noteworthy films about sleeper agents developed by nefarious forces in China or Russia. In John Frankenheimer's *The Manchurian Candidate* (1962), the queen of diamonds in a deck of cards is the trigger. When the decorated war hero sees the card, he goes into a trance and obeys the first command he hears. Thus triggered, Staff Sergeant Raymond Shaw overhears the bartender at Jilly's tell a story with "jump in the lake" in the dialogue, and the next thing we know, Raymond has followed orders into Central Park lake. In Don Siegel's *Telefon* (1977), a line from the last stanza of Robert Frost's "Stopping by Woods on a Snowy Evening" triggers a long-dormant Russian saboteur. A peaceable car mechanic, a regular beer-drinking guy, gets a phone call, hears the line, goes into a trance, drives his truck full of explosives into a US Army base, and you, the viewer, think that, contrary to what Auden wrote in his elegy for Yeats, maybe poetry can make something happen.

An equally compelling subgenre, that of the conspiracy narrative, emerged not long after the assassination of John F. Kennedy on November 22, 1963. The events of that day remain engulfed in doubt; the official version is unconvincing. The theories are many, and the gain for fiction and cinema is considerable, though at a cost; epistemological uncertainty has displaced objective truth in our secular philosophy. Charles McCarry's *The Tears of Autumn* (1974) speculates in fiction, Oliver Stone's *JFK* (1991) in film, and I would call attention to the assassination of Hyman Roth in *The Godfather, Part II* (1974), which echoes the televised shooting of Lee Harvey Oswald and substantiates Michael Corleone's assertion that if history teaches us anything, it's that you can kill anyone.

An arresting new development in the espionage genre is *Fauda* (begun in 2015; in its third season in 2020), the Israeli television series about an elite counterintelligence unit and its dealings with

Hamas and the Palestinian Authority, themselves at odds. The title, an Arabic word that translates roughly as "chaos," is an apt term for skullduggery in the Holy Land and specifically for the complex and emotionally challenging situations that confront the various agents, their antagonists, and their loved ones. "Fauda" is also, David Remnick reports in *The New Yorker*, "the Mayday code word used by the Israeli special forces when a mission goes belly up."[7]

Watch *Fauda* immediately after a well-made Hollywood thriller, and the first thing that hits you is the feel of the authentic that *Fauda* has. I'm a big fan of *Clear and Present Danger* (1994), in which Harrison Ford performs heroics in combat with a South American drug cartel. But its charm is that of fantasy. The characters run true to type. The handsome high-minded hero happens to be a marine and CIA higher-up but could easily be a campus heartthrob. His pretty wife Cathy is more formally known as Dr. Caroline Ryan, an ophthalmic surgeon. Cathy's lunch friend is having an affair with a suave operator who snaps her neck when he needs to cover his tracks. The dishonorable politician mouths words not because he believes them but because it is expedient to do so. The dedicated army officer is betrayed by his own government. The self-satisfied cocaine kingpin smokes cigars in his grand hacienda.

In *Fauda*, the agents look like agents, not actors; attractive, to be sure, but not so much as to beggar belief; and they have complicated personal lives. The crises are believable and all too literally explosive. While most of the focus is on the Israelis, the Palestinians are not caricatures, nor are they uniformly unsympathetic, and the tragedy is how little anyone can do to prevent the violence and death. There is the hopeful

7. David Remnick, "How Do You Make a TV Show Set in the West Bank?," *The New Yorker*, September 4, 2017, https://www.newyorker.com/magazine/2017/09/04/how-do-you-make-a-tv-show-set-in-the-west-bank.

portrayal of an officer of the Palestinian Authority who dreams of the prosperity that would follow a peace agreement with the Israelis. Unfortunately, his own son betrays him, collaborating with, of all people, a renegade terrorist who operates in the name of ISIS.

What the genre demands by way of suspense and surprise occurs with the inevitability of current events. Innovative terrorist tactics produce unintended effects. There is a romance between a Palestinian doctor and an Israeli agent that goes well beyond the *Romeo and Juliet* formula, for each has strong reason to suspect the worst of the other. The opportunities for deceit and deception are many, and the characters with whom you identify are far from invincible. The politically orthodox will predictably find fault with *Fauda*, because it favors the Israelis, because it makes the commandos look heroic, or because of the series' allegedly relentless machismo. Such and similar objections would also shame us for enjoying any number of great movies; it is almost always lamentable to subordinate aesthetics to politics. In any case, the drama is so engrossing that avowed anti-Zionists confess to binge-watching it.[8]

The Avenging Chance

Three other subgenres—each of which could be subdivided further—should not be overlooked in any survey of the murder mystery: the police procedural, the inverted detective story, and the locked-room murder, a metonym for the "impossible" crime that defies reason and empirical evidence and invites us into the realm of the uncanny.

8. See Yasmeen Serhan, "Watching Israeli TV's *Fauda* as a Palestinian," *The Atlantic*, June 8, 2018. By contrast, an outraged opinion piece by a self-described "Palestinian living in the occupied territories" appeared in the Israeli newspaper *Ha'Aretz*: George Zeidan, "'Fauda' Isn't Just Ignorant, Dishonest and Sadly Absurd. It's Anti-Palestinian Incitement," *Ha'Aretz*, April 24, 2020.

Ed McBain—the pen name of Evan Hunter—is the undisputed master of the police procedural, in which, as in real life, crimes are solved, or not, by the authorities. I would argue that the cops of McBain's 87th Precinct are the model for the heroes of nearly all the New York–based cop shows on television, from *Law & Order* to *Blue Bloods*. McBain came to the same conclusion and had one of his characters, the obese Ollie Weeks, announce it in his 1984 novel *Lightning*. If not for the prohibitive expense ("prolly cost me a fortune"), Ollie says he would sue the producers of *Hill Street Blues*, the Emmy Award–winning TV show that ran from 1981 to 1987, for modeling the show's Charlie Weeks after him. The offensive character has Ollie's last name and his distinctive set of prejudices. "That kind of shit can give a *real* cop a bad name," Ollie tells a fellow officer.

What's more, the name of the lead in *Hill Street Blues*, Furillo, is similar in vowel formation, pronunciation, and ethnic origin to that of Carella, McBain's peerless hero. As Ollie puts it, "How many wop names are there in this world that got three vowels and four condiments in them, and *two* of those condiments happen to be the same in both names?" The brilliant barbarism "condiments" for "consonants" must have given McBain some satisfaction, but the legal system did not. McBain considered filing suit but refrained from doing so when told that such litigation would cost him at least a half million dollars. Asked whether the producers of *Hill Street Blues* had consulted with him, McBain said, "No, of course they didn't," explaining to a *Guardian* reporter in 1990 that "if you come in to steal my jewels, you don't say 'May I come in tonight through the window please?'"[9] Previously there had been

9. See Paul Abbott, "Did *Hill Street Blues* Rip Off Ed McBain's 87th Precinct Series?," *CrimeReads*, October 15, 2019, https://crimereads.com/did-hill-street-blues-rip-off-ed-mcbains-87th-precinct-series/.

other, more kosher efforts at adapting McBain's cops to screens both large (*Cop Hater* in 1957 and *The Pusher* in 1960) and small (thirty episodes of *87th Precinct* in 1961 and 1962). Akira Kurosawa based his must-see 1963 movie *High and Low* on McBain's *King's Ransom.*

When it comes to seemingly impossible crimes, the police procedural's motto is "There must be a flaw somewhere," and this is usually a reliable assumption, certainly in McBain's books, if only because of the workings of chance—although there are notable stories in which the American sheriff or the British superintendent of police gets it completely wrong: Flannery O'Connor's "The Comforts of Home" (1965) for one, and Arnold Bennett's "Murder!" (1927) for a second. In "Lamb to the Slaughter," Roald Dahl's most famous short story (1953), the police devour the murder weapon, a leg of lamb which had been frozen when used as such. E. W. Hornung, creator of *Raffles*, summed up the relation of diligent cop to great detective: "Though he might be more humble, there's no police like Holmes."

In the inverted tale, the detective enters the scene belatedly, or even as something of an afterthought, as we observe everything from the point of view of the criminal, often an ingenious individual, sometimes an extremely lucky one, who gets away with a fiendish plot, a murder or even a series of murders, until one day it catches up with him or her, sometimes by the merest quirk of fate. R. Austin Freeman invented the genre in *The Singing Bone* (1912), although you can trace the seeds back to Dostoyevsky's *Crime and Punishment* (1866). Julian Symons's *The Man Who Killed Himself* (1967) is an excellent variant of the inverted type. The novel, in which justice and poetic justice coincide, details the two lives of a man who is henpecked in one of them and behaves like a bounder in the other.

The popular 1970s TV series *Columbo*, with Peter Falk in the title role, is a monument to the inverted formula. Columbo, the dogged LAPD lieutenant wearing his raggedy raincoat, driving his battered old car, always gets the better of the overconfident villain with the ironclad alibi that gets broken because of one chance detail. If, say, a murderer's alibi depends on his having a drink with a friend at precisely nine p.m., he may doctor the friend's glass and consign him to two hours of oblivion during which he can leave, do his foul deed, return, turn the friend's watch back to nine o'clock, and wake him up. What the murderer hasn't counted on is that Columbo, for all his self-deprecating antics, is as perceptive as he is persistent. He has learned that the friend was obsessive about time and always set his expensive watch ten minutes ahead. Alibis depending on watches never hold up.

Roy Vickers, in the inverted stories he wrote in the 1940s and 1950s, created a Scotland Yard bureau, the "Department of Dead Ends," devoted to the detritus of closed cases, oddments that will have an afterlife either because criminals repeat themselves or because a stray incongruous piece of new evidence makes an old, very cold case soluble. In *The Department of Dead Ends* stories (which first appeared in 1938), the detectives revisit long-shut cases only, as the author says in "Marion, Come Back," "at a tangent—when a ripple from one crime intersect[s] the ripple from another." The ripple may come in the form of a signet ring, for example, or a toy, a volume of Ella Wheeler Wilcox's poems, or an antique snuffbox. In one of the stories a man has figured out a way to murder his successive wives in public. He will cease getting away with it after eliminating the third wife, because of the interference of what Anthony Berkeley calls "The Avenging Chance," a brilliant story that the author later expanded into *The Poisoned Chocolates Case* (1929).

To an extent, both Frederick Forsyth's novel *The Day of the Jackal* (1971) and Fred Zinnemann's 1973 movie of it conform to the inverted type of storytelling. The focus of the novel—which is at once a political thriller, a police procedural, and a spy story—is always on the professional assassin hired to kill the president of France. About the Jackal, we know little except that he is blond, British, and remarkably good at what he does. Even the cop on his tail, though always a street or two behind, has "a grudging respect for the silent, unpredictable man with the gun who seemed to have everything planned to the last detail, including the contingency planning." Though we know that he does not succeed, the author manages to sustain the suspense, because the Jackal is so capable of improvising, so imaginative, and so gifted in both the martial arts and the use of firearms that we almost instinctively take the dashing assassin's side—a guilty pleasure from which the foreordained conclusion absolves us.

The book testifies to the cult of professionalism, and the novelist, a journalist by training, is true to his trade and creed. Most mystery writers are content to name guns, not to tell you how they work. Forsyth shows you the pistol up close, being assembled. With meticulous detail he describes how an expert gunsmith goes about fabricating what he calls "one of my masterpieces, a beautiful specimen": a made-to-order long-range rifle that can be disassembled to avoid detection and can fire mercury-tipped bullets banned by the Geneva Convention because such a bullet can "go off like a small grenade when it hit[s] the human body." Besides giving us the lowdown on forging a passport or explaining how a silencer works, Forsyth takes the trouble to remind us, too, that while a man may be tortured in secret for the information he may have, the world outside goes on as normal: "Along the banks of the Seine the couples strolled as always on summer nights, hand in hand, slowly as if drinking in the wine of dusk and love and youth that will never, however hard they try, be quite the same again."

Perhaps in homage to "The Murders in the Rue Morgue," many mysteries concern murders committed in a room that seemingly permitted neither entry nor exit. I have elsewhere called John Dickson Carr "the Houdini of whodunits," who has, I would add, a lock on the locked-room murder. In *The Three Coffins* (1935), he incorporates a lecture on the subject with the thoroughness of Edward G. Robinson running down types of suicide in *Double Indemnity* (1944). The uncanny is Carr's realm. "It is not impossible," Dr. Gideon Fell, Carr's detective, says in *The Problem of the Wire Cage* (1939) when a corpse turns up on a muddy clay tennis court and the only footprints near it are those of the one person who couldn't have committed the murder. "It is only incredible."

You're in Carr country if you're a penniless patrician cadging a meal at a hotel and, when quizzed for your room number, you say room 707 at random, and it turns out that there's a corpse in that room, and the corpse is that of your cousin's wife, whose husband was murdered in the identical way (strangulation) at a country estate a fortnight past. That's how the table is set for us in *To Wake the Dead* (1938). The man arrested for the first murder is in jail and could not possibly have committed the second. Was it the work of a copycat? No way. Gideon Fell explains: "These two murders are the work of one person: anything else, my boy, would be artistically wrong, and I have an unpleasant feeling that someone behind the scenes is managing matters with great artistry."

High-Class Murder

To writers whose work does not properly belong to the mystery or espionage genre, the conventions of same have proved irresistible. Vladimir Nabokov enjoyed manipulating them for his own pre-postmodernist purposes. In *The Real Life of Sebastian Knight* (1941), the first of his novels written in English, Nabokov offers the plot summary of a purely conceptual novel titled *The Prismatic Bezel*, which is not only "a rollicking parody of a detective tale" but also a "wicked imitation of many other things," such as "the fashionable trick of grouping a medley of people in a limited space (a hotel, an island, a street)." Up to a point the plot seems made to order for Agatha Christie. It turns out that all the lodgers in a boardinghouse are related in some manner. "The novelist occupying the front bedroom is really the husband of the young lady in the third floor back. The fishy art-student is no less than this lady's brother," and so on until "the numbers on the doors are quietly wiped out and the boarding-house motif is painlessly and smoothly replaced by that of a country house." New clues surface, a bumbling detective appears, the room with the corpse is discovered to be empty, and after "a moment of ridiculous suspense," the sleuth removes his beard, wig, and glasses, and the dead man returns to life. "You see," says Mr. Abeson with a self-deprecating smile, "one dislikes being murdered."

Of the modern writers attracted to detective fiction, none has tested the limits of detection more fruitfully than the Argentine master Jorge Luis Borges. In the detective story Borges found an apt vehicle for his master image of the labyrinth. In "The Garden of Forking Paths" (1941), the characters engage in a learned discussion of labyrinths until with shocking abruptness a seemingly gratuitous murder is committed. The murder is solved in the last sentences of the story in a totally surprising way that makes it a small parable about modern warfare, in which death and destruction are meted out arbitrarily and yet in accordance with a design. The sequence of events in Borges's "The South" (1953) can be read on at least three levels: literal narrative, dream, and allegory. The story reaches the level of the uncanny to which detective novelists aspire and very rarely approach.

In "Death and the Compass" (1942), perhaps his most celebrated detective story, Borges subverts a convention established by Agatha Christie in *The ABC Murders*. The homicidal idea that the murderer in Christie's novel exploits is that the appearance of a series of crimes tends to deflect attention from any one of them; thus, crimes A and B might have been committed for the sole purpose of making C seem part of a series. In chasing down a serial killer, the police would overlook the particular motives accounting for the one murder in which the criminal or criminals had a real interest—just as the police in "The Purloined Letter" overlook what is or should be obvious. The riddle stumps the cops but not, of course, Hercule Poirot.

But where Poirot succeeds, the intellectual hero of "Death and the Compass," a mentally superior detective named Erik Lönnrot, outsmarts himself. The clues seem to point to a criminal design in the shape of an equilateral triangle: the design would be complete when the third in a series of three murders takes place. That's what the cops think. Only Lönnrot apprehends that the design of the plot is actually a rhomb. Correctly interpreting the clues and the signs, he realizes that a fourth murder must occur. He can even determine the date, the time, and the place. But what he doesn't realize, as he hurries to avert the calamity, is that he must die to complete the murderous design: this murder is his. He has solved it with his life. Detection and death are one.

Rather than reassure the reader, a Borgesian fable like "Death and the Compass" or "The South" sends one shivering into the dank night of an ancient Manichean heresy, a world in which the forces of evil have an equal shot at defeating the forces of good for the simple reason that rationalism, and indeed high intellectual ability, can be put to malevolent use.

Umberto Eco's international bestseller *The Name of the Rose* (1983) pays elaborate, if ironic, homage to Borges. The most compelling character in this medieval murder mystery is the blind librarian Jorge of Burgos. And just why Eco made his culprit the spitting image of Jorge Luis Borges, a blind librarian, may be the most interesting mystery lingering in the air after the novel ends.

Graham Greene observed that "a high-class murder is the simple artistic ideal of most film directors." It's worth lingering over this remark. The detective novel in all of its many manifestations depends on a strong narrative line. It offers story, plot. I would add that with its sturdy conventions the murder mystery has affinities with poetic form. In *Cue for Murder* (1942), Helen McCloy observes that "the construction of a plausible hypothesis" within the narrow limits of a crime puzzle is "a mental exercise as strict, and therefore as stimulating, as the composition of a sonnet." As the sonnet to the whodunit, the sestina or pantoum suits film noir. The poet Lynn Emanuel writes that "watching film noir is like being in the presence of a miraculous sestina in which the lush presence of repetition is felt subliminally"—to the effect that "form (repetition) is content in these films."[10] Finally, murder mysteries and thrillers are modern in exactly the sense that "modern" means "of the twentieth century": they are already a bit dated, glamorous and

---

10. Michael Gilbert, the outstanding British crime novelist, agrees that "the detective story is the sonnet. It is precise, neat, satisfyingly symmetrical, constrained, but sustained, by the nicety of its form." In contrast, in Gilbert's view, "the thriller is the ode. It has no formal rules at all. It has no precise framework. It has no top and, heaven knows, no bottom." Gilbert's essay "The Moment of Violence," in which this statement appears, is quoted in Martin Edwards's introduction to a 2019 paperback edition of Gilbert's *Death Has Deep Roots* (1951).

seedy at once, fit vehicles of nostalgia as well as of the more violent and passionate desire that culminates in murder.

THE BOOK TO which these pages are introductory is divided into five parts in line with a strategy that I call "centripetal," while my editor favors "kaleidoscopic." Without allegiance to any single critical theory, I favor multiple perspectives in approaching crime, detection, and noir, a field of modern literature and cinema that I enthusiastically recommend. Part one is devoted primarily to the spirit of noir and what I have called the hard-boiled romance. In part two, three great noir props take center stage: drinks, smokes, and songs. Part three consists of looks at some favorite authors and directors, including Maugham and Ambler, Hammett and Chandler, Rex Stout, Ed McBain, David Goodis, Charles Willeford, Ida Lupino, and Alfred Hitchcock. Part four focuses closely on films from the crime and espionage canon, such as *Double Indemnity*, *Odd Man Out*, *The Stranger*, *The Lady from Shanghai*, *The Asphalt Jungle*, *The Killing*, *Cape Fear*, *The Counterfeit Traitor*, and *Once Upon a Time in America*. Part five is reserved for a flight of fancy in the belief that the end is assured even if the means are as speculative as an astrology reading.

Two of the readers over my shoulder, who whisper in my ear as they observe what I write, are W. H. Auden and Graham Greene. They put in regular appearances in this book, for which I will always be grateful.

I

KILLER STYLE

1

Cracking Wise

A double bill of *The Maltese Falcon* (John Huston, 1941) and *The Big Sleep* (Howard Hawks, 1946) makes for a perfect initiation into the romance of the hard-boiled 1940s shamus as well as to noir as a cinematic style, though purists might object that neither movie technically qualifies as a noir, for neither film is a eulogy to human failure. On the contrary, the hero in both films emerges intact, if the worse for wear. But the black-and-white style of the films, the look of the actors, the hooch in the pocket flask, the patrician in the wheelchair confined to his greenhouse, the wild daughter, the guns, the shadows, the cigarettes, the background music—all work together to create a template for noir.

In *The Maltese Falcon*, Mary Astor is the vixen who plays the helpless-female card, uses her body to best advantage, and pulls the trigger on Sam Spade's partner. In *The Big Sleep*, Lauren Bacall in peek-a-boo haircut, beret, and houndstooth check shows off her legs and her comic talent, and sings "And Her Tears Flowed Like Wine" ("She's a real sad tomato, she's a busted valentine"). Peter Lorre (Joel Cairo) and Sydney Greenstreet (Kasper Gutman, the "Fat Man") lend their considerable talents to *The Maltese Falcon*, in which the gunsel, played by Elisha Cook Jr., takes it on the chin. Fate doesn't treat poor Elisha much better in *The Big Sleep*, in which, however, his character shows rare nobility and courage. In both movies, Humphrey Bogart plays essentially the same fellow with wide-brimmed fedora, trench coat, and perpetual cigarette, though his name is Sam Spade in *The Maltese Falcon* and Philip Marlowe in *The Big Sleep*.

Not blessed with the looks of a Cary Grant or Gregory Peck, Bogart had been good as a hoodlum or bootlegger, a Cagney sidekick in flicks of the thirties, or an unlucky truck driver playing second fiddle to George Raft in Raoul Walsh's *They Drive by Night* (1940). With his matchless ability to leer, wince, flash a fiendish grin, and blow his top, Bogart excelled as a paranoid or psychopath, whether cast as a homicidal painter married to Barbara Stanwyck (*The Two Mrs. Carrolls*, 1947) or a prospector in Mexico (*The Treasure of the Sierra Madre*, 1948). In Nicholas Ray's noir classic *In a Lonely Place* (1950), Bogey plays an embittered Hollywood screenwriter, who may love Gloria Grahame but, when transported by rage, may direct a friend to tighten his wrists around a surrogate woman's neck in a choke hold. In *The Caine Mutiny* (1954), Bogart is Captain Queeg of the US Navy during World War II, who obsesses over strawberries and plays with marbles while metaphorically losing his own. But it was as a brokenhearted café owner in *Casablanca* and a private eye in *The Maltese Falcon* that Bogart attained leading-man status. And it is Bogart as the detective hero, stripped of his illusions, equipped with a derisive wit, and handy with a gun, that defines his place in cinema history. A cynic with a sentimental streak, he is virile, quick on his feet, comfortable in his body, never at a loss for a wisecrack; and though he makes you wonder, in the end he can be counted on to do the right thing.

Not until he was forty-one did Bogart become a leading man. In Walsh's *High Sierra* (1941), for which John Huston wrote the screenplay, Bogart plays Roy Earle, nicknamed "Mad Dog," an ex-con on the lam after a heist goes wrong. Roy dies on a mountain-top, but not before winning the love of Marie (Ida Lupino). Even Bosley Crowther, the film critic for the *New York Times*, with his astonishingly low batting average, had good words for Lupino and Bogart: she was "impressive as the adoring moll," and he displayed "a perfection of hard-boiled vitality." Then, these concessions aside, Crowther was his usual self, adding, "As gangster pictures go—if they do—it's a perfect epilogue." The right word would have been *prologue*, as what followed was a whole new genre of crime and noir movies. *The Maltese Falcon* was the next picture Bogart made.[1]

Huston's *Maltese Falcon* was true to Dashiell Hammett's novel; Hawks's *Big Sleep* was a fantasia on Raymond Chandler's. Having at its center a priceless artifact that turns out to be a fake, *The Maltese Falcon* has some of the qualities of a parable. The film is as tightly plotted as the book; Huston had the good sense to reproduce Hammett's dialogue. The plot of *The Big Sleep* is, contrarily, even more incoherent and hard to decipher than the novel on which it is based. (At one point the screenwriters, who included William Faulkner, wrote Chandler to find out who killed a certain character. Chandler cabled back, "I don't know.") The principal actors go in and out of character, but it doesn't matter, because the dialogue is unmatched for sexy banter. When Bogart hails a cab, the taxi driver turns out to be a pert young woman, to whom he says, handing her a tip, "Here you are, sugar, buy yourself a cigar." She hands him her card. "If you can use me again sometime, call this number."

"Day or night?"

"Night's better. I work during the day."

---

1. Bosley Crowther, "'High Sierra,' at the Strand, Considers the Tragic and Dramatic Plight of the Last Gangster," *New York Times*, January 25, 1941.

The Maltese Falcon ends with Mary Astor imprisoned behind the bars of an elevator going down. The snap in Bogart's dialogue with her is not merely decorative. "If they hang you, I'll always remember you," he tells his costar, somewhat to her disbelief, because she has always had her way with men. If *The Maltese Falcon* is not a genuine noir, it is because Bogart resists Mary Astor. She can be resisted because she is not Marlene Dietrich or Barbara Stanwyck. And besides, Bogart won't play the sap for anybody.

Asked by a cop what all the fuss was about, Bogart, holding the sculpted bird, gives Shakespeare the last word: "the stuff dreams are made of."

"Thin as an Honest Alibi"

It was one of Hammett's achievements to have fashioned a murder mystery that would satisfy the requirements of the form in a fresh idiom, an urban setting, and without the moral complacency of the country mansion sort of novel against which the hard-boiled crime writer was rebelling. The cold-bloodedness in Hammett makes for a nice corrective to the lure of gentility and ivory tower self-satisfaction that you may find in an intricately plotted murder mystery written by an Oxford don under a pseudonym. Of his boss, the overweight operative in one of Hammett's stories says, "We used to boast that he could spit icicles in July, and we called him Pontius Pilate among ourselves, because he smiled politely when he sent us out to be crucified on suicidal jobs." The writing has speed and immediacy: "For the next six hours I was busier than a flea on a fat woman." Two operatives tail a criminal duo: "If they split, I'll shadow the skull-cracker, you keep the goose."

Hammett was Chandler's acknowledged master, but as a sheer stylist the student surpassed the mentor. Chandler's similes and sarcastic hyperboles ("a stare that would have frozen a fresh-baked potato") are full of attitude in the contemporary New York sense. They describe two things: the thing they're supposed to describe and Marlowe's reaction to it. A girl in *Farewell, My Lovely* gives him "one of those looks which are supposed to make your spine feel like a run in a stocking." The wealthy area known as "Idle Valley" makes Marlowe feel "like a pearl onion on a banana split" in *The Long Goodbye*, and the television commercials he watches "would have sickened a goat raised on barbed wire and broken beer bottles." Such wisecracks are classic figures with the prettiness removed, defense mechanisms raised to an aesthetic ideal. Yet Marlowe can also be insistently literal, as when he encounters a piece of modern sculpture. Its owner "negligently" identifies it as "Asta Fial's *Spirit of Dawn*." Marlowe replies, "I thought it was Klopstein's *Two Warts on a Fanny*."

The wisecrack may be the modern American equivalent of the French aphorism, and some of your best examples will have come from Chandler. With his cracks, similes, and muted hyperboles, Chandler established a rhetorical style. Consider, from the story "Trouble Is My Business" (1939): "She was sitting behind a black glass desk that looked like Napoleon's tomb and she was smoking a cigarette in a black holder that was not quite as long as a rolled umbrella." Sometimes the effect is deliberately incongruous, but more often what these similes communicate is a world-weary snarl accented by a certain amount of resentment, misanthropy, and misogyny. "Faces like stale beer," "thin as an honest alibi," "unperturbed as a bank president refusing a loan"; a woman's laugh likened to "a hen having hiccups," a man's smile "as faint as a fat lady at a fireman's ball." In *The Lady in the Lake* (1943), an elevator "had an elderly perfume in it, like three widows drinking tea." In *Playback* (1958), Marlowe describes himself as "old, tired, and full of no coffee."

In *The Real Cool Killers* (1959), Chester Himes adapts the hard-boiled simile to the Harlem of detectives Coffin Ed Johnson and Grave Digger Jones. Street thugs "were jabbering and gesticulating like a cage of frenzied monkeys." When a white woman with a "high-pitched proper-speaking voice" reports a crime, it is with "the smug sanctimonious of a saved sister." On the avenue, "red-eyed prowl cars were scattered thickly like monster ants about an anthill."[2]

"As Romantic as a Pair of Handcuffs"

From the movies, I would offer this very abbreviated supplemental list of wisecracks and other rhetorical flourishes:

- *Colorful similes.* "He was as helpless as a sleeping rattlesnake," Orson Welles says of his employer in *The Lady from Shanghai* (1947). Sometimes the analogy conveys more than the speaker may have intended, as when, in *The Big Heat* (Fritz Lang, 1953), Gloria Grahame tells Glenn Ford, "You're about as romantic as a pair of handcuffs."
- *Local slang.* "Cow on a slab," the waitress shouts to the short-order cook when a customer orders a steak sandwich at a diner in *Try and Get Me* (Cy Endfield, 1950).
- *Gallows humor, pointed puns.* As a verb "split" means "divide," but as a noun it denotes the parceling out of ill-gotten gains. Thus, in André de Toth's *Crime Wave* (1954), the trigger-happy mob boss (Ted de Corsia) says, "Wait till you see the split we get," and the

---

2. The style endures. Reviewing *Knives Out* (2019), a mystery movie that "bears a sheen of smugness," Anthony Lane writes that the sleuth in the movie "smokes cigars as long as fountain pens" and that the survivors of the deceased "are about as lovable as the flu." Anthony Lane, "Pastiche and Politics in 'Knives Out,'" *The New Yorker*, December 2, 2019, 76–77.

reluctant robber (Gene Nelson) replies that if things go wrong, "we'll split the gas chamber."

- *General bitchiness:* In *White Heat* (Raoul Walsh, 1949), Virginia Mayo complains, "Cody, my radio ain't working again," and Cody (James Cagney) snaps back, "What do you want for it, unemployment insurance?"
- *Insults and a thumb in your eye:* Vera (Ann Savage), the fatal female in *Detour* (Edgar G. Ulmer, 1945), tells off Al (Tom Neal), the male accomplice she has only just met: "Shut up. You're making noises like a husband." Vera wants them to sell the car that belonged to the deceased fellow foolish enough to pick up hitchhikers. Al wonders whether she would expect a "small percentage" of the profits. Vera: "Well, now that you insist, how can I refuse? A hundred percent will do." Al: "Fine. I'm relieved. I thought for a moment you were gonna take it all." Vera: "I don't wanna be a hog."

2

Paradise of the Damned

EIGHTEEN NOTES ON NOIR

1. *The Dark Mirror*

"What is noir?" In *Somewhere in the Night*, his 1997 study of the genre, the poet Nicholas Christopher phrases his answers as questions to indicate their inadequacy. "A state of mind, an aesthetic school, a philosophy, an ethos, a sensibility, an attitude, a symbolic system? Something undefinable—a kind of raw poetry, like the snatch of a ghost sonata one hears at the outskirts of the necropolis? Or is it, first and foremost, a *style*?"

Noir shares in all these things, and the resort to metaphor is the result. Christopher opts for "the dark mirror" reflecting the underside of American urban life, a place as full of vice and fallen angels as the Paris evoked a century earlier by Charles Baudelaire in his poems and prose poems. I like Christopher's metaphor, because the mirror is the locus of the uncanny, where the double's twin halves meet and sometimes recoil from the encounter, and I'm fond of Robert Siodmak's 1946 movie *The Dark Mirror*, in which Olivia de Havilland plays twin sisters, one virtuous, the other vicious, a popular Hollywood trope.

Fumbling for a definition, I'll second Christopher's list, double down on *style*, and add an epigraph from Baudelaire's *Intimate*

Journals. After rejecting what others say is the greatest pleasure in "Love"—to give, to receive, to enjoy "the pleasure of pride" or the "voluptuousness of humility"—Baudelaire asserts that "the sole and supreme pleasure in Love lies in the absolute knowledge of doing *evil*. And man and woman know, from birth, that in Evil is to be found all voluptuousness."

In exactly this sense, movies informed by the spirit of noir are love stories featuring a man and a woman who are damned from birth, exiled from Eden, and drawn together by an erotic and transgressive impulse so strong that it overrides all scruple and moral restraint. The Argentine cop in *Gilda* (1946), who has watched Gilda (Rita Hayworth) and Johnny (Glenn Ford) constantly quarrel, says, "You two kids love each other very terribly, don't you?"

"I hate her," Johnny replies.

"That's what I mean," the cop says.

2. Déjà vu All Over Again

"Some things that happen for the first time / seem to be happening again": Lorenz Hart's definition of déjà vu (from his lyric for "Where or When") applies with a vengeance to noir. Accidents seem predetermined; events occur as if repetitions of themselves. Exhibitionists in gaudy undergarments perform for laid-up photographers across the airshaft. The surgeon with a cigarette dangling from his lips gives the escaped con a new face, and says "There's no such thing as courage. There is only fear." The gumshoe has taken a beating. "You're a tough guy," he tells himself. "You've been sapped twice, choked, beaten silly with a gun, shot in the arm until you're crazy as a couple of waltzing mice. Now let's see you try something really tough like putting your trousers on."

"From thirty feet away she looked like a lot of class," Philip Marlowe says, sizing up a frail, in *The High Window*. "From ten feet away she looked like something made up to be seen from thirty feet away." The damsel-in-distress sobs to the police: "I've told you all I know." Husband Zachary Scott of the pencil mustache and contemptuous sneer knits his brows but can't help looking bitchy: "There's nothing for you to be ashamed of." Both are lying. Eve Arden officiates at a party for the suspects, witnesses, and extras. "It's a shame to waste two perfectly good mouths on you," she remarks when a pair of gossiping girlfriends get on her nerves. But the true noir note is sounded by the red-haired temptress in a South American nightclub: "If I had been a ranch, they'd have called me Bar None."

When there's a knock on the door, the chances are that a man with a gun will enter the room and shoot first, ask questions later. *What do you want me to do, count to three like they do in the movies?* The veteran prizefighter refuses to throw the bout and gets beaten in the alley. The pampered invalid has a panic attack, picks up the phone, and dials the emergency number she has been given. A voice answers, "City morgue." The dead return to life. A businessman survives the attempt on his life by his wife and her lover, but everyone thinks he is dead, and he doesn't correct the impression.

"Lieutenant Diamond, you have a very expensive name."

Sooner or later we're at a club or fancy restaurant. The young couple believes in love at first sight. "It saves a lot of time." We leave New York, go to Los Angeles, Reno, Chicago, Mexico, the state penitentiary, a lost highway, a truck stop, and a fleabag hotel, but for some reason we keep returning to San Francisco. There is also a suitcase stuffed with twenty-dollar bills, a crooked cop, a flask of whiskey, a missing key, and a pair of lethal scissors on the desk. The cast includes a sensitive Korean War veteran (James

Edwards), a loyal flat-mate (Ann Sothern), and a sinister litigant (Robert Emhardt). There's a stick-up in the parking lot, a confusing plot, a lot of rain, and a lot of cigarettes.

It was an easy genre to like. The French were crazy about it.

3. "Moonlight Serenade"

Fog, rained-on streets, cigarettes in dark rooms, an unmade bed. A curtain is drawn ("the man in the hat standing at the streetlamp had been following her since morning"). Two shot glasses flank a half-empty flask on the table. The key turns. The door opens slightly. A shot rings out. There is the sound of footsteps hurrying down stairs and then, in the fleabag hotel room where the dead man lies, a gauze curtain rustles lazily in the half-open window. Across the street you can see a "CHOP SUEY" sign in faded red neon. On the record player the same record plays over and over: it is "Moonlight Serenade" by the Glenn Miller band, and later, when the hero in the movie, who is suffering from amnesia or battle fatigue, dances with his sweetheart at a nightclub, the band is playing "Moonlight Serenade" and that is the moment when he senses that something is amiss.

Noir is where pessimism meets desperation, and darkness is as visible as in Byron's vision of stars that "wander darkling in the eternal space, / Rayless, and pathless, and the icy earth / Swung blind and blackening in the moonless air."[1] Free will is a mug's game. "Whichever way you turn, fate sticks out a foot to trip you," Al (Tom Neal) says in *Detour*, and though it is difficult to credit his version of events, this statement is true enough.

---

1. Lord Byron, "Darkness," lines 3–5.

Noir is the paradise of the damned. It is where foolproof plans meet their graveyard fates. The plans are always foolproof. An ex-con and three buddies plan to rob the safe of a jewelry store on the rue de Rivoli in Paris, and they do it, in thirty minutes of film time without music or talk. They even make off with the loot, but. . . . Surely this is a sentence that should end with "but."

Noir is one last heist, one roll of the dice. Risk is requisite. "Got to take chances," Johnny (Paul Henreid) tells his co-conspirators in *The Hollow Triumph* (1948). "That's the overhead in our racket."

4. One Roll of the Dice

Is gambling the central vice around which the others—smoking, drinking, whoring, thieving, playing with guns—are the satellites? You might wonder. Gambling movies are a genre unto themselves. In Jacques Demy's *Bay of Angels* (1963), Jackie—a platinum-haired Jeanne Moreau, glamorous in a white Pierre Cardin suit—goes from one roulette table to another in Nice and Monte Carlo. She smokes furiously. Lucky Strike is her brand. Jackie is a compulsive gambler, and unapologetic about it. "The happiness gambling gives me can't be compared to any other," she says. It's what she likes to do on a date, and it's how she manages her romance with Jean (Claude Mann), the young Parisian bank teller who has left job and family behind now that the gambling bug has bitten him. "What I love about gambling is this idiotic life of luxury and poverty," Jackie says. "And also the mystery—the mystery of numbers and chance." The first time she walked into a casino, she says, she felt as if she had entered a church.

In caper movies, the crooks play cards, poker usually, to kill the time while waiting for the big score. They cheat, fight, accuse one another of cheating. They have rules, if only in order to break them. Rule number one: never trust a dame. Rule number two: see rule number one. Life with a dame is a gamble, and the odds are fifty-fifty at best. Yet you walk right into the trap. A young hood will talk too much to impress the girl he's in bed with, not realizing that she will share the information with her next partner, a pimp who has turned informer to save his own skin. Or a henpecked croupier's wife will make an anonymous phone call spilling the beans about the planned casino robbery. Both these things happen in Jean-Pierre Melville's *Bob le flambeur* (1956), a noir with a sharply ironic edge.

Bob (Roger Duchesne), Melville's eponymous *flambeur* (or "high roller"), gambles as incessantly as he smokes. Famous in the underworld of Montmartre and the streets around place Pigalle, where life and vice begin as night descends, Bob has done prison time, but he once saved a cop's life; he has scruples; and he has earned a lot of favors. But he is in thrall to Fortuna, the Roman goddess. He plays the horses, rolls the dice, bets on cards, flips a coin before making a trivial decision. He even keeps a one-armed bandit in his apartment, and plays it. Planning to rob the casino at Deauville, a seaside resort town in Normandy, Bob assembles the necessary cohort. The night comes. The heist is scheduled for five in the morning. The gang waits nervously. Bob, discarding his usual raincoat and snap-brim in favor of a tuxedo, is supposed to walk around the casino, watching out for any untoward last-minute development. He is, however, so addicted a gambler that he can't help going to the tables. He plays roulette and baccarat and loses all track of time as he embarks on a wildly improbable winning streak, accumulating a small fortune, attracting a crowd of admirers. "Lady luck, his old mistress, made him forget why he was there," the narrator comments. Because of the informer's phone call, the police ambush the robbers in front of the casino at five o'clock. Gunfire erupts. Bob's protégé is killed. Bob himself is arrested but has a glint in his eye when the casino's delivery men deposit his winnings into the trunk of the police car that will take him to jail. In an American noir, he wouldn't get to keep the dough.

The all-or-nothing gamble is to noir what the pursuit of marriage is to Jane Austen's heroines. The heist is the loser's last shot at redemption. "One roll of the dice and then we're through forever," Ed Begley enthusiastically says, recruiting a partner in crime, Robert Ryan, in *Odds Against Tomorrow* (1959), which some consider the last genuine noir. (Films from following years would be characterized as neo-noir.)[2] When Ryan, a specialist in portraying bigots, learns that Harry Belafonte will be the third man on the team, he throws Begley's words back at him. "One roll of the dice, doesn't matter what color they are, so's they come up seven," he says. You know then that Begley's bet will turn up snake eyes. You had an inkling when Begley paid off Belafonte's debt to a loan shark, which Belafonte incurred because his horses never win. "I got rid of a headache," Belafonte says. "Now I have cancer." *Odds Against Tomorrow* ends with an explosion and the indistinguishable corpses of enemies in life, one black, one white, united in death. The camera pulls back. The road signs say "Stop" and "Dead End."

2. There is little sense arguing about labels or end dates. *Bay of Angels* has been called a "post-noir gambling picture." The neo-noir category is handy for movies shot in color, such as *Chinatown, The Getaway, Black Widow, The French Connection, The Usual Suspects,* and *Jagged Edge.* Some neo-noirs declare themselves to exist in strict relation to the noir tradition, as *Body Heat* is essentially a remake of *Double Indemnity.* Whether *The Manchurian Candidate*—that is, John Frankenheimer's black-and-white film from 1962 rather than its 2004 remake—qualifies as a noir or a neo-noir may quicken academic disputation, but the salient point is that the movie is a masterpiece.

5. "An Existential Allegory"

Noir is the product of the 1940s, the late forties especially. Men wear belted trench coats and wide-brimmed fedoras on a tilt. (Dana Andrews wins the award for best fedora.) A dark double-breasted suit with peaked lapels and a pocket square is a favored look. Women wear great hats, some with veils, and long black gloves. A winning outfit might feature a black velvet cocktail dress, dangling earrings, and a bejeweled choker with a pendant, but there are many alternatives, and a girl doesn't like to be seen twice in the same dress by a man she likes. (A course in forties noir should be mandatory for every student of fashion design.) Everyone smokes. Bourbon is another equalizer: everyone drinks. Favorite hangouts include casinos, racetracks, roadhouses, and cafés in which somebody bangs out a Hoagy Carmichael tune while a leggy blonde wearing black seam stockings sits on the piano, crossing her legs, and sings. The style is compatible with Edward Hopper's pictures of alleys, hotel rooms, and all-night diners on the one hand, and Franz Kline's black-and-white abstract paintings of the 1950s on the other.

The French seized upon the poetic possibilities of this rough-hewn American style just as, a century earlier, they'd grasped Poe's importance before his compatriots did. Noir became the existentialists' preferred form of imported fiction. As James Naremore writes in *More Than Night*, his 1998 study of the genre, French critics celebrated noir "as if it were an existential allegory of the white male condition." Nicholas Ray's movies (*In a Lonely Place*, *They Live by Night*) were interpreted as dark parables of "moral solitude." In the late 1950s, Jean-Luc Godard directed *Breathless* with Jean-Paul Belmondo and Jean Seberg, François Truffaut made *Shoot the Piano Player* based on a David Goodis novel, and all at once a French art cinema based on the Hollywood thriller was born. Meanwhile, Albert Camus declared that James M. Cain's noir novel *The Postman Always Rings Twice* had inspired him to write *The Stranger*. "You were a fool not to be born a Frenchman," the British author Rebecca West told Cain. "The highbrows would have put you in with Gide and Mauriac if you had taken this simple precaution."

Both Samuel Fuller's *Pickup on South Street* (1953) and Robert Bresson's *Pickpocket* (1959) are about guys who ride the subway to lift the wallets of unsuspecting riders, but in the former, an American movie, the guy does it for money, whereas in the French film, it is to test out a theory. There, in a nutshell, are two rival national conceptions of what noir is about.

6. Failure

Noir is the flip side of the American sunny-side-of-the-street dream of success. Noir is what you get if you take Chandler's "Great Wrong Place" and substitute a more fallible detective for Marlowe. As Harry Jordan, the narrator of Charles Willeford's *Pick-Up* (1955), says in all caps and italics, "*FAILURE*" is the meaning of noir in a single word: "Somehow, I wasn't surprised. Harry Jordan was a failure in everything he tried. Even suicide."

In the noir novel, temptation can't be resisted, mental fatigue makes failure inevitable, and well-educated family men can become bums overnight, suddenly, for no reason you can give. Villains play mind games. Consider the work of the underrated Fredric Brown. *Murder Can Be Fun* (1949), a variant on the theme that life copies art, is about a murder-mystery radio serial, whose episodes, written but not yet produced, depict ingenious ways of committing homicide. In the first episode, which the scriptwriter keeps in a desk drawer and has not shown anyone, the killer has donned the disguise of a Santa Claus costume and beard—and that is exactly what a murderer does. The news item turns the bedeviled writer into a detective.

The title of *Knock Three One Two* (1959), an even better voyage to the zero of the night, refers to a code between a husband and his wife, who should not, with a serial killer rapist on the loose, undo the chain lock and open the door unless she hears three knocks, a pause, then one knock, a pause, then two. The chief character, Ray Fleck, is a reckless gambler, an unfaithful husband, and a schemer whose plans get more desperate and illogical with each drink he takes. He needs to make five hundred bucks to cover his gambling debts. Ruth, his wife, whose patience is wearing thin, works at a restaurant owned by a man with a crush on her. Ray buys his newspapers from a benevolent half-wit with a guilt complex. Ray also visits Dolly, a woman of easy virtue, whose main squeeze is Mack Irby. Then there's a friendly cop—and the killer. All these characters, and the plot twists that Ray Fleck sets in motion when his debt becomes due, converge in two climactic chapters that justify the author's reputation as a master of the surprise ending.

The difference between noir and murder mystery can be summed up by situation. In the murder mystery, the corpse of a steelworker is found, with a bullet hole in his chest, in a room locked from the inside with windows shut and latched and no sign of forced entry. The cops would write it off as suicide except for the fact there's no gun in the room. The crime looks impossible but will be solved—eventually—after two other persons are found in the same condition, a beautiful ballet dancer in her twenties and a retired judge.

In the noir, a drifter with no visible means of support hitchhikes to a small town where, with his skill as a car mechanic, he gets a job at a filling station and body shop, and all goes well. He even has a honey of a girlfriend, as pure as the water in a country brook, until his former business partner shows up and threatens him unless he returns to Los Angeles, his real life, and his beautiful, ruthless ex-mistress. Return he does. Only the sweet girlfriend survives.

7. The *Chingona*

More often than not, *cherchez la femme* is the rule. Indispensable to the script is the femme fatale thereof—beautiful, ruthless, deadlier than the male she attracts and exploits, and less apt than he to confuse lust with love. In any relationship with her, the forces of Thanatos are constantly threatening to create a crisis that the forces of Eros must confront. She is Barbara Stanwyck in *Double Indemnity*, Rita Hayworth in *The Lady from Shanghai*, Jane Greer in *Out of the Past*, Lana Turner in *The Postman Always Rings Twice*, Gene Tierney in *Leave Her to Heaven*, Lizabeth Scott in *Pitfall*, Marilyn Monroe in *Niagara*, Joan Bennett in *Scarlet Street*, Jean Simmons in *Angel Face*. She is, to use the Mexican term for a badass woman, a *chingona*—someone who, when her fatally wounded husband stumbles in, tells him to take a taxi to the hospital (Marie Windsor in *The Killing*). She is sometimes entangled with a rich man, a husband or a lover, often sinister; he may be a racketeer (Kirk Douglas in *Out of the Past*) or a histrionic defense attorney hobbling on crutches (Everett Sloane in *The Lady from Shanghai*). She tends to be attractive, pragmatic, greedy, and faithless. As Sterling Hayden tells Marie Windsor in *The Killing*, "You've got a great big dollar sign there where most women have a heart."

It makes sense that many noir fans are women, as the women in the movies are active agents in the plot, and not mere background figures, mothers, sisters, or objects of romantic desire. In addition to her other charms, the femme fatale wields an extraordinary amount of power.

Lizabeth Scott of the arched eyebrows and flip hairstyle, who looks great in a strapless dress with sequin embellishment, is sometimes put down as merely a lesser Lauren Bacall. Well, I don't know. Isn't that a little like saying that Duke Snider was a lesser Mickey Mantle? Or that Hector was a lesser Achilles? Bacall is tops; my friend Suzanne Lummis would award the "femme fatale" laurels to Bacall and her "low, sly, silky voice" telling Bogart, in *To Have and Have Not* (1944): "You know you don't have to act with me, Steve. You don't have to *say* anything, you don't have to *do* anything. Or, maybe just whistle. You know how to whistle, don't you, Steve?"

I, too, prefer Bacall but believe that Scott is badly underrated. Not every movie she's in is a winner, but one worth seeing multiple times is *Too Late for Tears* (1949), in which she begins in innocence and ends in malevolence, using and discarding Arthur Kennedy and Dan Duryea along the way. The plot, an illustration of the adage that avarice is the root of all evil, begins when a bag of money lands in the back seat of the convertible that Scott's husband (Kennedy) is driving with his wife seated beside him. When they get home and open the bag, they quarrel about what to do with the dough. He wants to turn it in; she wants to keep it. From that moment on, Scott's capacity for criminality and intrigue grows. She is more devious than we had a right to expect. For a murderess, Scott has an icily beautifully front.

8. The Root of All Evil

The implicit assumption in film noir is that evil exists, whether as an entity in itself or as a perverted form of love: love for the wrong thing, the love of money, itself valued far beyond its intrinsic worth or purchasing power.

The New Testament's warning *radix malorum est cupiditas* (greed is the root of evil) meets its match in Virgil's *omnia vincit amor* (love conquers all). If the two Latin aphorisms can coexist, it is because, as "conquers" implies, there may be a battle, even a war, between "love" and all else, and will anyone argue that the side of Eros is always the side of righteousness? Moreover, Cupid, the Roman god of the erotic life, exists in the very word for avarice, *cupiditas*. With his bow and arrow in hand poised to link lovers, Cupid is the counterpart of the Greek Eros, son of the goddess of beauty—Aphrodite in Greek, Venus in Latin—whose lineage embodies the perhaps self-evident idea (self-evident certainly to the manufacturers of makeup) that passionate desire and intense attraction follow from the sight of a pleasing appearance. But where Eros leads directly to the erotic as a subset of the aesthetic, the linguistic linkage of Cupid and cupidity suggests a trail that may take us from love and longing to concupiscence (Saint Augustine's term for "sinful lust") on the one side and cupidity (the covetousness prohibited by the Ten Commandments) on the other. In Caravaggio's great painting *Amor Vincit Omnia*, a mischievous naked eagle-winged Cupid tramples happily over musical and mathematical instruments, pen and manuscript paper—the *omnia* of civilization.

In Latin, another name for Cupid is Amor.

9. Shades among Shadows

The darkness in film noir is not a function of the lighting alone. The movies suggest that we, ordinary law-abiding civilized human beings, are attracted, tempted, and even seduced by the types of vice depicted on the screen. We envy the recklessness of gamblers and con men and thieves, their appetite for risk and their aversion to life as a cog in a machine, a working stiff on an assembly line or in a heartless bureaucracy. If we understand the bank robber's rationale ("because that's where the money is"), it's because we understand the singular importance that we have invested in money as the universal unit of exchange.[3]

At the same time, these movies imply a world of shades among shadows, and no absolutes. They associate sexual passion with mortality, and some of them insist that the electric impulse linking man and woman is so powerful as to override all other imperatives. For its sake men and women would commit larceny, even homicide, though of course the money has something to do with it too.

In noir, sex is a prize but also a consummate killer. We love forbidden fruit and we transgress with the ease of our first parents. The intensity of desire creates a motive for murder, whether acted on or not, and makes guilt and paranoia inevitable. The tensions between man and woman animate noir, are palpable, feel real. "Can't live with them, can't live without them": the fundamental things apply as time goes by. Yet love has a surprisingly short shelf life, and once the bloom is off the orgasm, anything can happen.

In brief, a man or woman may kill for many reasons beyond the pursuit of cash and jewelry, the desire to facilitate an inheritance, eliminate a rival, or surmount an obstacle to the acquisition of wealth. The killer may act out of rage, revenge, jealousy; on a wicked impulse; during a struggle; in self-defense; because it is a

---

3. With all the literature devoted to it, money remains an intellectual problem—a subject for endless discussion, like the problem of evil. Norman O. Brown has advanced the view that money is "nothing other than deodorized, dehydrated shit that has been made to shine," but this can hardly be the last word on the subject.

professional job he or she is performing; or even out of ideological hatred or religious fervor. And yet, and always, the money has something to do with it too.

10. The Villain as Hero

In a burgeoning literature of antiheroes, there is also the phenomenon of the villain who steals not our hearts or souls but our rapt and prolonged attention during which we root shamelessly for the bad guy who robs, kidnaps, kills, gets caught, escapes, talks his way out of one crisis after another, is always one step ahead of the cops, and is, until the final shootout, as impossibly lucky as the guy who draws a fourth ace at the poker table when the other players are "all in."

We can, in other words, align ourselves with a thoroughly despicable if charismatic character, such as the French gangster Jacques Mesrine as played by Vincent Cassel in Jean-François Richet's riveting two-part 2008 movie *Mesrine: Killer Instinct* and *Mesrine: Public Enemy Number One.* By any standard, Mesrine is a villain, a most resourceful one, who frightens even hardened cops. He is a bully, a scoundrel, a repeat offender as a kidnapper and killer. A con artist quick with a glib but somehow credible lie, he has remarkable sangfroid. A French nationalist, he committed atrocities in the Algerian War in 1959; now, in the 1970s, it may suit him to join forces, or pretend to join forces, with militant left-wing outfits. A shameless publicity hound, he is good at manipulating the media, proclaiming himself a revolutionary when he is really just a thug. A man without a conscience, he ends a marital dispute by sticking his gun into the mouth of his terrified wife to teach her that his gangster "friends," two of whom are watching, will always mean more to him than his spouse and children. Yet for all that he should arouse our moral disgust and censure, Mesrine fascinates the viewer, all 246 minutes of his story.

To be sure, the success of the movie depends on the movie-maker's great skill at manipulating us. Given the performance of Vincent Cassel, we are quite ready to believe him to be the type of *Übermensch* that Nietzsche had in mind. Given the charm, bravery, and good looks of the adoring women who sleep with him, we believe he must be awfully good in bed. The gripping narrative is, furthermore, a tall tale told by a liar. *Mesrine: Killer Instinct*, part one of the movie, in which he performs heroics in a prison break, was based on Mesrine's own self-serving account of his life in crime, *L'instinct de mort.*

But none of this is enough to explain why the viewer watches not in revulsion but as if mesmerized by the arrogance, the inventiveness, the wickedness of this homicidal hoodlum, who is, on some level, the projection of what we must secretly, guiltily, half-consciously imagine ourselves to be or to desire.

11. "Baby, I Don't Care"

In the noir scenario, the detective is eliminated, vanquished, or reduced in stature, significance, or virtue. Witness the fate of Jeff Bailey (Robert Mitchum) in Jacques Tourneur's *Out of the Past* (1947). When we first meet Bailey, he runs a gas station in a hick town in California. A man out of his past turns up—a man named Joe, about whom we're later told that he "couldn't find a prayer in the Bible." But he has no difficulty finding Bailey; the garage sign with Bailey's name on it catches his eye. ("Small world." "Or big sign.") You can't escape the past, and when it catches up with you, it explodes the identity you would construct for yourself. Not Bailey but Markham is his real name, Mitchum tells the sweet, wholesome girlfriend he has managed to acquire in the rural village. He was a professional detective in New York three years ago, "maybe more," when he got a call from a high-powered gambler . . . and we go into a flashback, like a dream within a dream.

This is a movie in which characters constantly seek, often find, and always lose. Big operator Whit Sterling (Kirk Douglas) hires Jeff to find the woman who shot at him, Whit, four times and absconded with $40,000 of his ill-gotten gains. Jeff goes to Acapulco in search of the lady in question, Kathie Moffat (Jane Greer). Acapulco in *Out of the Past* is the quintessential romantic place of escape: beach houses, palm trees casting shadows in early evening, gambling joints where the point is to bet big, as if life itself were a reckless wager. Jeff finds Kathie there, but instead of accomplishing his mission, he falls in love with her, and then keeps falling. Kathie denies taking the $40,000. Jeff: "Baby, I don't care."

"I never saw her in daylight," Mitchum informs us by voice-over. "How big a chump can you be? I was beginning to find out." When Whit and his henchman unexpectedly turn up, Jeff and Kathie flee to San Francisco. For a time they keep a low profile. They begin to venture out, going to the usual gambling places and racetracks, and that is when Fisher (Steve Brodie), Jeff's ex-partner from his New York days, turns up. "Pay me off and I'll be quiet," Fisher says. Kathie shoots him. "You didn't have to kill him," Jeff says. Oh, yes, she did, she hisses. "You would have just beaten him up and thrown him out." Fisher is dead, and Jeff knows himself to be implicated irrevocably in his death.

What Jeff Bailey does is exactly what Sam Spade refuses to do in *The Maltese Falcon*. Bogart playing Spade recognizes he has a duty to his dead partner and acts accordingly. He resists Brigid O'Shaughnessy (Mary Astor) because she has already lied to him when he put his trust in her and he refuses to make the same mistake twice; he turns her in to the police. When Jeff in *Out of the Past* throws in his lot with Kathie, he terminates his identity as a detective no less surely than the army deserter Don José terminates his identity as a soldier in *Carmen*. Inevitably, Kathie betrays Jeff. The flashback concludes with the revelation that she has the missing $40,000 in her bank account after all.

Jeff informs his girlfriend that he never saw Kathie again. She ran out on him. But when we return from the flashback's past tense to the unfolding present, Jeff has his second go-round with Kathie, and the wholesome country girlfriend doesn't stand a chance. In the interim Kathie has regained Whit's confidence (Jeff isn't the only man under her spell) and has promptly pinned Fisher's death on Jeff. She is a cheat, a murderer, and a liar, and Jeff knows all this. Yet when, in the shadows, with the light illuminating their faces, Kathie says, "I've never stopped loving you," Jeff forgets everything else. Not that he's naïve. He knows what is going to happen. Yet he will let her betray him again. Sam Spade's phrase fits the case perfectly: Jeff has "played the sap" for Kathie. Or in Mitchum's own word, the "chump."

This is the crucial spin that noir put on the detective novel: the transformation of the detective from the man of reason to the chump, a victim not so much of lust as of a force of sexual attraction so deep, so dark, and so irresistible that there's no reason not to call it love. "Jeff, we've been wrong a lot, and unlucky a long time," Kathie tells Jeff in *Out of the Past*. "I think we deserve a break."

"We deserve each other," Jeff growls. And so they do. The melodrama they enact is the noir equivalent of certain immortal lyrics from the Rodgers and Hart song "I Wish I Were in Love Again": "the double-crossing of a pair of heels," "the self-deception that believes the lie," "the classic battle of a him and her."

12. From Triangle to Chevron

The typical noir plot involves conspiracies and betrayals. Two or three collaborate until self-interest pulls them asunder. Spousal homicide is an evergreen. A man and a woman conspire to eliminate her husband and enrich themselves in the process, but she betrays him or he betrays her and both end up in the morgue. Elaborate plots, ingenious or crude, are hatched to eliminate the obstacle to erotic pleasure—pleasure that is the greater because it is transgressive. Greed augments passion until it displaces it. The use of violent means to remove one side of the romantic triangle and thus convert it into a V shape occurs as a sort of criminal orgasm: what Baudelaire called *criminelle jouissance*. After climax, all is downhill.

While there is sometimes a competent investigator on hand, more truly representative of the noir is the detective who succumbs to the lure of a woman impersonating his client's wife (Hitchcock's *Vertigo*), the detective who falls in love with the victim of the homicide he is investigating (Otto Preminger's *Laura*), or possibly the dying fellow trying to figure out who murdered him (Rudolph Maté's *D.O.A.*). In the last named, a notary public named Frank Bigelow (Edmund O'Brien) swallows a slow-acting poison, a "luminous toxin" that will kill him before the week is out. The movie has a celebrated opening sequence: Bigelow walking down the police department's hallway to report his own death by murder. A doctor has explained to Bigelow that there is no cure for the luminous toxin and that he has approximately one week to live before the poison will kill him. Just time enough to find out who did it—and make sure they get what's coming to them—before checking out for good. Bigelow gets to speak the two-word interrogative sentence that informs film noir: "Why me?"

13. "Why Me?"

"Why me?" is asked by bewildered fellows whose lives have been turned upside down—as the biblical Job's was, we read, because of a capricious wager between God and the devil. "Why me?" is uttered a lot in noirs, and not always in terminally dire circumstances. "Why me?" Anne Bancroft asks Aldo Ray in Jacques Tourneur's *Nightfall* (1956). "I used to ask myself the same question," he says, lighting her cigarette at the bar—the initiating gesture of a romance or a fling. She'll have another martini. He's drinking vodka. He's wanted for murder. She says, "You're the most wanted man I know."

But sometimes the circumstances that have you cornered and saying "Why me?" are indeed terminally dire. The threat to life and limb, or to sanity, may be an accident, the result of trespassing in another person's scheme or dream, as when Bigelow in *D.O.A.* (1949) drinks a poisoned cocktail at a hotel bar in San Francisco, where he's gone for a few days just to get away from his life, his job, and his girlfriend in Los Angeles.

Or the upheaval may be staged-managed, directed by a malevolent auteur, as happens to Scottie (James Stewart) in *Vertigo* (1958) when Gavin Elster hires him to pursue his wife. "Why me?" Scottie directs the question to Judy (Kim Novak) as they climb the tower's stairs for the second time, but it is really a rhetorical question, asked of the cosmos, implying that we are in the dark about what is happening to us and why, and it raises grander questions, too, about existence and identity. "Why me?" is the central question of paranoia, itself one of the more aesthetic of psychotic conditions, because the world of data, noises, and signals has a special existence for the paranoid; everything is about him or her. The noir equivalent of French existential anguish in the face of the absurd is "Why me?"

When Delmore Schwartz quipped that "even paranoids have enemies," he summed up the mood of noir. It is not only the neurotic who has at one time or another felt singled out by destiny for an incomprehensible fate.

14. Gun Crazy

The walking stick with concealed blade wielded by George Macready in *Gilda* may be the most blatant phallic symbol in all of film. Aside from this special case, the universal phallus in noir is a gun—a Colt 1903 pocket hammerless, for example, or a Smith & Wesson I-frame. "Such a lot of guns around town and so few brains," Marlowe says to a pistol-wielding palooka in *The Big Sleep*. "You're the second guy I've met within hours who seems to think a gat in the hand means a world by the tail."

Gun Crazy (Joseph H. Lewis, 1950) is an ode to the pistol, the revolver, and the automatic. The movie is something of a costume show. When we meet Laurie (Peggy Cummins), she is a sharpshooter wearing a carnival sideshow cowboy suit. Bart (John Dall) is also a sharpshooter, and after he and Laurie link up and embark on a spree of robberies, and they are on the lam, he disguises himself at one point by trading in his duds for a naval officer's uniform and cap. They also disguise themselves as a respectable, prematurely middle-aged couple in dowdy eyeglasses.

Both are crazy about guns. One reason Bart is attracted to Laurie is that she is so comfortable handling a pistol. It is significant that he is a pacifist before she casts her spell over him. She is the "bad" one, the one who pulls the trigger when they rob a meatpacking company's payroll office, but then again here, as in *Bonnie and Clyde*, it is the power of the fatal female not only to corrupt her partner but also to bring out the manly beast in him.

The partnership between hero and heroine is a bond which they can't dissolve, try as they might. They "go together the way guns and ammunition go together," as Bart tells Laurie. They are in it till death do them part. When they plan to split up and go their separate ways in two cars going in opposite directions, they cannot go through with it. They know the path they have chosen will lead to a fatal end, but while they can, they go to an amusement park and enjoy the rides like a couple of giddy teenagers. They can't help themselves. Their very desperation adds to the sexual energy between them.

15. Identity Crisis

Identity is not something you can take for granted in the dicey universe of noir. Sometimes the guy driving the car drops dead of a heart attack and you, who hitched the ride, take his wallet, his money, and his name, rolling the dead man's body behind a bush (*Detour*, 1945). A beleaguered doctor may fake his suicide if a patient who resembles him has a heart attack in the doctor's office after hours, though the disposal of the body is always a tricky affair (*Nora Prentiss*, 1947). An innocent man's alibi depends entirely on a witness with a distinctive hat but without a name (*Phantom Lady*, 1944). Passports can be forged, and names changed for a whole host of reasons. By marriage, for example. Velma Valento, the showgirl Marlowe (Dick Powell) was hired to find in *Murder, My Sweet* (1944), has become Mrs. Helen Grayle (Clare Trevor), a wealthy man's wife.[4] You didn't think Miss Wonderly was Brigid O'Shaughnessy's real name in *The Maltese Falcon*, did you?

4. *Murder, My Sweet* is one of two movies adapted from Chandler's *Farewell, My Lovely*. In the 1975 movie with Chandler's title, Robert Mitchum played Marlowe.

The theme of the double, which dates back to Poe, implies that you can split an identity in roughly the same way that a common stock can split its shares except that the binaries are not morally neutral. If there are twins, one is going to be vicious, but who can tell them apart? A hoodlum and a psychiatrist would be dead ringers if not for the scar that disfigures the latter's face. After eliminating his double, the killer carves a scar on his own cheek—on the wrong cheek, as it happens. Does he get away with the impersonation? Maybe, but not with the dead man's gambling debts, in *The Hollow Triumph*, a title with a strong noir resonance.

Let's say you're a journalist in a remote corner of Africa, frustrated because you are there to report on a despotic government, not to challenge it. When the only other English-speaking fellow around, someone who looks vaguely like you, dies of a heart attack, you can take his place, and make yourself the deceased one, if you have a knife and glue to alter the passports. What will happen? Viewers of Michelangelo Antonioni's *The Passenger* (1975), with Jack Nicholson, are still wondering.

16. "God Bless Him"

In college I went to see *Gone With the Wind* at a big theater near Times Square. On Clark Gable's first appearance, at the base of a spiral staircase, the middle-aged woman sitting next to me exclaimed, "God bless him!"

Certain actors should not play the damaged noir hero. Clark Gable, the "King of Hollywood," tops my list. Just as Gregory Peck is always righteous, Gary Cooper ever the strong, silent type, and the older Spencer Tracy a figure of gravitas, Clark Gable is a winner. He radiates confidence, and confidence is a self-fulfilling prophecy, the antithesis of noir. In *It Happened One Night* (1934), Gable is the hard-nosed newsman who, much to his surprise, falls in love with Claudette Colbert, a runaway heiress, and despite misunderstandings, she feels the same way and leaves her groom at the altar to prove it dramatically. The role won Gable the Oscar for best male lead, and for the rest of the 1930s, Gable defined masculinity whether he was paired with Jean Harlow, Joan Crawford, Myrna Loy, Vivien Leigh, or Carole Lombard, who married him. He led the mutiny on the *Bounty*, standing up to the tyrannical Charles Laughton. He was Scarlett O'Hara's true love, a dashing soldier of fortune who exits the scene defiantly and with pride intact; you'd hardly know all that he has lost during the course of the movie. He is all bravado: "Frankly, my dear, I don't give a damn."

World War II did nothing to tarnish Gable's image. As an aerial gunman Gable flew five combat missions in Europe in 1943. He won medals and was promoted to the rank of major. Returning to Hollywood, the war hero starred in *The Hucksters*, which is what Madison Avenue ad men were called before the *Mad Men* era. The casting is perfect, because like an ordinary salesman on steroids, the huckster sells confidence, and that is what Gable has in spades.

Any Number Can Play (1949) has all the trappings of a noir, but in the end it is a Clark Gable movie. Gable owns a moneymaking casino but has a lousy relationship with his bratty high school–age son (Darryl Hickman). He also has a newly diagnosed heart condition. His wife (Alexis Smith) loves him. So does Mary Astor, but he is a one-gal guy. The wise move would be to clear out, quit the gambling racket, and affirm family ties. And so he does, though not before he coolly wins a major showdown at the dice table and foils a robbery by a couple of cheap gunmen. Why not start from scratch? Just give away the joint. But how best to do it? Gable offers a preposterous wager to the guys who have worked loyally for him: their $5,000 against the entire casino, furnishings and all, which is easily worth ten times that amount. High card wins. The guys draw a ten. You win, Gable says, and only on the street, with loving wife and adoring son at his side, does the now middle-aged hero reveal that he really drew a jack and won the bet. That's Clark Gable.

17. The Element of Style

Why noir now? What accounts for its growing fan base?

To the extent that noir evokes a certain amount of nostalgia for the stylistic signatures of the recent past, here are some leads:

1. John F. Kennedy went hatless, and the fedora was old hat.
2. The surgeon general declared that cigarettes are bad for you, which killed cigarette commercials and, eventually, despite much resistance, smoking.
3. The Vietnam War was decisive in dividing the good guys from the bad, the hip from the square. People older than thirty were obsolete. Came the Beatles, dope, etc., and the bad haircuts of the 1970s. Eventually, let's skip some years, and this is something no one forecast, parents began to emulate their children, and today, on the Las Vegas strip, you may encounter proles in oversized unisex Yankee jerseys rather than suits and ties for the men, slim tailored suits or cocktail dresses and chic hats for the women, in a casino presided over by the tuxedo-clad racketeer of a forties movie.
4. Rock 'n' roll, which displaced jazz as the nation's characteristic sound, is incompatible with the spirit of noir. The sound of noir is a jazz-inflected soundtrack punctuated by classic American popular songs as performed by vocalists, pianists, or a band.
5. Dialogue is crucial to noir. The triumph of technology was a triumph of color and special effects at the expense of dialogue and the more literary qualities of a movie. Black-and-white cinematography, one of the defining aspects of noir, allows for the

subtleties of chiaroscuro. The characteristic noir mood does not feel natural in Technicolor.

In sum, we have discarded hats, cigarettes, an ideal of sartorial elegance, the popular music of a bygone era, and the value placed on conversation, wit, and the American wisecrack.

Noir characters may make foolish choices, but they always look like grown-ups and never seem to question that they are adults—they do not need a neologism ("adulting") to describe the difficulty of the endeavor. Notwithstanding their weaknesses, they are more articulate than most of us, and more literate. The clothes they wear, the cigarettes they smoke, the cocktails they drink, and the music in the background are elements not just of style but of meaning.

18. "That Old Black Magic"

Why me? Why would a poet get hooked by noir? Could it be that the poet's identity in our society has more in common than meets the eye with that of a hard-boiled gumshoe, a noir loser, an accidental spy, a wrongly accused suspect? The detective can't be in it for the money, since there's so little of it, and important people may look at you the way an entomologist looks at a beetle. Someone is forever warning the sleuth off the case. This is the poet's predicament, too. And the poet has a natural sympathy with the victim of circumstantial evidence, the underdog, the dame who has a right to sing the blues, the person who gets plucked out of his or her native setting and thrust into a macabre plot.

The poet is a sucker for style as a form of flirtation. I can never get over the idea that the women in noir are as stylish as they are dangerous, the gangsters drive great-looking cars, and many of the background songs ("Tangerine," "How Little We Know," "Laura,"

"Too Marvelous for Words," "That Old Black Magic") have lyrics by Johnny Mercer.

I write this sentence on September 1, 2019, exactly eighty years since the day when Germany invaded Poland, World War II began, and W. H. Auden wrote "September 1, 1939." The fifth stanza of that poem, the one about the bar where "The lights must never go out, / The music must always play," conveys something essential about the spirit of noir. The bar, that noir fixture, can be understood metaphorically as a fort—or as home.

Poetry Noir

The patron saint of poetry noir is Kenneth Fearing. Celebrated by mystery mavens for his novels *The Big Clock* (1946) and *Dagger of the Mind* (1941), Fearing is not nearly as widely acknowledged for his staccato-paced "bop" poems with jagged edges and explosive comic book exclamations ("wham," "pow"). His Depression-era poems are bitter, colloquial, urban, noisy, and polyvocal. The titles of the poems themselves tell a tale: "Flophouse"; "If Money"; "Manhattan"; "Jackpot"; "Payday in the Morgue." "How Do I Feel?" begins, "Get this straight, Joe, and don't get me wrong." Fearing is sometimes tagged as a "proletarian poet," which may be the kiss of death. It is in any case misleading; Fearing's radical skepticism extended to the politics of the left. The buoyantly satirical "Cultural Notes" ends with a belligerent speaker at a meeting: "Shut your trap, you. The question is, what about Karl Marx?" When Fearing was asked whether he was a member of the Communist Party, he said, "not yet."

The diction and tone of such poems as "Dirge" and "X Minus X" were startlingly new in 1935. "Dirge," an elegy for the "executive type," the "fellow with a will who won't take no," may be compared with Auden's "The Unknown Citizen" as a profile of the organization man, who lives in a city, works for a company, and is governed by metrics, statistics, and the bottom line, under the gaze of a gigantic clock. Fearing has a penchant for "wow" words: "And wow he died as wow he lived, / going whop to the office and blooie home to sleep." The last words of "Dirge" are "bong, Mr., bong, Mr., bong, Mr., bong." The language is supercharged though not necessarily with meaning: "awk, big dipper; bop, summer rain."

The typical young urban couple is profiled in "X Minus X," in which we are told that "his life" is the stock market ticker and "her dream" is a magazine, their friend is the radio, their enemy the rent collector, their adviser the salesman, their destiny the boulevard, and their paradise the dance hall. There will not be a happy ending to this story.

Upon graduating from high school in Oak Park, Illinois, Fearing was voted "wittiest boy and class pessimist." In a 1951 article, *Newsweek* reported that as a young man in New York City, Fearing had been walking along, composing a traditional sonnet on a classical theme, when an elevated train roared by overhead, and all at once he changed his verse style, ditching meter and rhyme in an effort to capture the noise and pressure of big city life. Apocryphal or not, the story, with suitable modifications, could furnish the opening gambit of a dime novel.

The hard-drinking, twice-married Fearing made enough money from *The Big Clock*, book and movie, that he could begin his daily drinking in the morning. He drank, suffered from blackouts, and died alone, a month shy of his fifty-ninth birthday. Sounds like the hero of a noir, doesn't it?

IN RECENT DECADES, noir as a style, an attitude, and a bundle of useful conventions has entered American poetry in an emphatic way. Here in its entirety is an untitled prose poem from a sequence titled *Nothing in the Dark* by Fred Muratori:

> *The blonde took her teeth out of my hand and spat my own blood at me.* In isolation, an almost incomprehensible sentence, courtesy of Chandler, but a story in itself. And what about the eerie grace of *The woman stood up noiselessly behind him and drifted back, inch by inch, into the dark back corner of the room.* Not perfect, almost if not certainly ruined by the repetition of *back*, but in life I have often witnessed such imperceptible edging, sometimes by women, often by men. Guilt is no different retreated from than withstood. That's a Philip Larkin line in its bones. He was just a surname away from Marlowe, and would probably have been quite good at this game: nondescript, unmarried, few friends, his hand quick to the gundrawer at the suggestion that routines he had spent a lifetime perfecting were about to be disrupted by a livid husband, or a beautifully enraged widow.

Noir here begins as a style and becomes a way of confronting experience. The elision between the two Philips, the fictional detective Marlowe and the mortal English poet Larkin, is enacted in the syntax itself, which moves from Raymond Chandler's style of observation to the flat statement that "guilt is no different retreated from than withstood," an echo of Larkin's great poem "Aubade," where death is "no different whined at than withstood." If novels are mirrors, the mystery novel is the mirror in which Philip Larkin might look and behold Philip Marlowe, "just a surname away."

In her poem "Noir," Angela Ball turns to a different literary affinity, appropriating the last line of Whitman's "Song of Myself" as the unlikely launching pad for a noir excursion:

> I stop somewhere waiting for you, my aficionado of Noir:
> An honest man is lured into vice, a squeeze on the down-low,
>   murderous insurance.

The night disc-jockey introduces a number: his wife and her beau
   enter an embrace.
A towering miscreant crashes in flames—too late for the good
   man manqué.
I wait for you under the dark marquee whose lights have circled
   each atom of our past. Please catch up.

In a sense this is a love poem to "my aficionado / of Noir," luckier
than the "good man manqué" in the movie that the couple will
see if he shows up—if, that is, he has not been lured into vice or
claimed by death. "I wanted to invoke the particular kind of darkness that I see as part of the film genre: the knowledge that at any
time anyone may be caught up in the machinations of a force,
both natural and perverse, that turns life toward decay and death,"
Ball explains. "I hope to reconnoiter with 'you'—a dead love—by
means of this force. The poem begins with Walt Whitman's line as
a magic charm, hoping to invoke the great lover of death and enlist
him in my cause."[1]

For Lauren Hilger in *Lady Be Good* (2016), the poet's primary
cinematic model is Ivy Smith, "Miss Turnstiles" in *On the Town*,
but there are other invitations to romance in music (Beethoven's
Seventh, Gershwin, Arlen, Fats Waller) and the movies. There's
Lauren Bacall in *To Have and Have Not*: "I have to join the gang at
the piano. / They need me to sing right away." For the woman in
Double Indemnity, "having a husband"—and here the poet inserts
a block of empty space before completing the sentence—"is a
problem." In the movie, Walter Neff expresses wonder that "murder can sometimes smell like honeysuckle." In Hilger's poem, this
is reduced to essentials in a sentence fragment: "Honeysuckle also
called hysteria."

---

1. Angela Ball, letter to the author, July 3, 2020.

Lynn Emanuel fuses the noir and the postmodernist impulses in her book *Then, Suddenly*. Consider this passage from "At the Ritz":

All up and down the avenue, blondes—lacquered
in intelligence, sarcasm, babeness, and money—
gossiped into the ears of investment bankers
so impeccably groomed you could see them
checking their Windsor knots in the chrome
toes of their wing tip shoes.

Blondes, sarcasm, "babeness," money: essence of noir. The poem describes the beginning of an affair ("He was so handsome that when he walked in / the room just rearranged its axis from south / to north"; "Against her mink a gardenia erupts in a Vesuvius / of white") and ends with quiet, sinister streets that look "grainy" as an old black-and-white movie: "the pale, small stares of the hotel / lobby, a taxi hauls a smudge of exhaust into place, / and a town staggers to its feet as he follows her like a prisoner / into the sentence of the story." Elsewhere, in "The Book's Speech," Emanuel writes that a certain dress—the one that recurs in the book—"is not a dress really, it is heartache-waiting-to-happen in / the train station of the small town where the rainy evening / is a window, black and shiny, where the passengers are / planted like flowers in the rubber pots of their galoshes." From the train station in the rain, that marvelously evocative bleak landscape, to the Chandleresque simile that clinches the deal, Emanuel paints it noir.

As does Kevin Young, whose *Black Maria* (2005) consists of eighty poems in the form of a conceptual five-reel movie; conventions are lampooned and renewed, tropes and clichés recur with a twist ("here comes the bribe"), and the resources of poetry and the language of cinema merge. The passage that begins "She wore red like a razor—cut quite a figure" ends "Between us, this sweating, a grandfather clock's steady tick, soundtrack of saxophones sighing." Young's poem follows this "voice-over" narration: "Boy meets girl. Girl meets The City. Nights she sings for her supper under the stage name Delilah Redbone; days she avoids the super, and the casting couch. Boy and girl rendezvous: his place, her place, a no-tell motel, who can tell. Aliases and ambushes. Throughout, a hint of crime, or at least a world in which everyone's a suspect. Is she too good (or bad) to be believed? Can anyone be believed? Stay tuned."

How to account for the particular attraction that noir holds for contemporary poets? Having tangled with this question myself, I asked a few poet friends to comment. Suzanne Lummis argues that the poem noir can "conjure a kind of dark laughter in the face of the inevitable."[2] James Cummins, author of *The Whole Truth* (1986), a book of sestinas featuring Perry Mason and company, maintains that noir is a comic genre. "The first great irony in noir is that it isn't tragedy; it's only melodrama, at best," Cummins says. On the larger question of what attracts poets to noir, Cummins refers to the lovers in *Double Indemnity*: "Walter's in love with his own genius, not Phyllis; and Phyllis doesn't love anybody. Sounds like poets to me."[3]

Lynn Emanuel likens noir style to the "lush" workings of the sestina form:

> What I love about film noir is its repetitions; the manner in which
> a delimited number of images and plot elements are circulated
> and recirculated through a film and through the genre as a whole.

2. Suzanne Lummis, letter to the author, August 27, 2019.
3. James Cummins, letter to the author, June 23, 2020.

Watching film noir is like being in the presence of a miraculous sestina in which the lush presence of repetition is felt subliminally. I love the way form (repetition) is content in these films. I love film noir because it is the most stylish and stylized of American film forms; these films feel "poetic" in their valorizing of style. I admire their insistence that style is more important than mere event— unlike Westerns which celebrate event. Finally, the genre is so compact. Watching these films, I often feel I am watching an oeuvre by a single author. Again, I think, because the films are so formally restricted, there is a strong family resemblance among them. Watching film noir is close to the experience of reading chapters in a long book. Even when the film is over, you are invited to feel that the story continues in its elegant, paranoiac, American way.[4]

The late Diann Blakely, whose book of poems *Farewell, My Lovelies* (2000) announced the noir shading in her work, associated noir with nostalgic desire. She described herself as a "perversely proud member of the junk culture decade otherwise known as the '70s," who "came to be a noir fan after becoming, in my teens, an ardent and lifelong fan of what are now called the neo-noirs." When I asked her to explain the depth of her interest, Blakely offered a series of associations: the theme music *of The Untouchables* on TV, Truman Capote's *In Cold Blood*, "Bull Connor and his legion of soon-to-be-unemployed-steel-worker supporters," "the logical outcome of belief in original sin *and* urbanization." "Or was it because the bitter and troubled and violent city [Birmingham, Alabama, where she grew up] was so beautiful at night, the molten steel pouring in white flashes through blackness and the distant streetlights, when seen from the suburban hills, glowing more interestingly than the stars?"[5]

4. Lynn Emanuel, letter to the author, August 15, 1998.
5. Diann Blakely, letters to the author, November 7, 1997, and July 25, 1998.

For L. S. Asekoff, too, a curious nostalgia (for the "trailer courts and bungalows of James Cain's post-war 40s America") has something to do with his appropriation of noir elements for his verse. Asekoff's poem "Film Noir" begins with the universal noir landscape, which is dominated by "the Inferno / Bar & Grill." In noir there is, in Asekoff's words, a "nostalgia here for cars with running boards, America on the move, the first neon nights, the black/white irrealities of a world-that-never-was, except in the movies of my/our childhood."[6]

Nostalgia, yes, but also anxiety, as fate deposits us in the dreamscape Nicholas Christopher evokes in *Desperate Characters* (1988). "It's not a good place to be alone," but aloneness is your fate, and it is hurtling you past a desolate landscape consisting of abandoned cars, rusty railway tracks, padlocked courthouses, stores with cobwebbed mannequins, and a police station where under a single lightbulb you can see the silhouettes of two cops playing darts.

6. L. S. Asekoff, letter to the author, October 12, 1998.

4

Five Noir Poems

*"Perfidia," the earliest of these poems, was written in 1989 at
the Pittsburgh airport during a layover between a flight from
Los Angeles and one to New York. Many viewings of* Laura,
*Otto Preminger's 1944 movie, gave rise to my poem of that
title, a pantoum. "Witness to a Murder" is the title of a 1954
movie. In "The Formula," I wanted the title to stand for the
MacGuffin in many novels of intrigue (the papers, the secret
document, the purloined letter, "the process") and for the plot
template itself, with its predictable episodes and lines. "Just a
Couple of Mugs," the prose poem, was written for this book in
summer 2019.*

Perfidia

You don't know who these people are, or what
They'll do to you if you're caught, but you can't
Back out now: it seems you agreed to carry
A briefcase into Germany, and here you are,
Glass in hand, as instructed. You rise to dance
With the woman with the garnet earrings, who is,
Of course, the agent you're supposed to seduce
And betray within the hour. Who would have known
You'd fall in love with her? Elsewhere the day

Is as gray as a newsreel, full of stripes and dots
Of rain, a blurred windshield picture of Pittsburgh,
But on the screen where your real life is happening
It is always 1938, you are always dancing
With the same blonde woman with the bloodshot eyes
Who slips the forged passport into your pocket
And says she knows you've been sent to betray her,
Or else it is seventy degrees and holding
In California, where you see yourself emerge unscathed
From the car crash that wiped out your memory,
Your past, as you walk into a gambler's hangout
On Sunset Boulevard, in a suit one size too large
And the piano player plays "Perfidia" in your honor,
And the redhead at the bar lets you buy her a drink.

Laura

Then the doorbell rang.
Time for one more cigarette.
It wasn't Laura's body on the kitchen floor.
He is not in love with a corpse.

Time for one more cigarette.
The venomous drama critic insinuates
He is in love with a corpse.
It's a typical male-female mix-up.

The venomous drama critic knows
He is sane.
It's a typical male-female mix-up.
He thinks she is dead and she thinks he is rude.

Is he sane?
Each wonders what the other is doing in her living room.
He thinks she is a ghost and she thinks he is rude
When the picture on the wall becomes a flesh-and-blood woman.

Each wonders what the other is doing in her living room.
It hasn't stopped raining.
The picture on the wall becomes a flesh-and-blood woman:
Gene Tierney in *Laura*.

It hasn't stopped raining.
"Dames are always pulling a switch on you,"
Dana Andrews says in *Laura*.
There was something he was forgetting.

"Dames are always pulling a switch on you."
It wasn't Laura's body on the kitchen floor.
There was something he was forgetting.
Then the doorbell rang.

Witness to a Murder
—Barbara Stanwyck (1954)

She saw a murder.
She bought all the papers.
She pocketed the murdered woman's earrings.
She called the police.
She smoked a cigarette.
She told her story and was not believed.
She deduced that the door had been tampered with.
She answered the doctor's unreasonable questions reasonably.
She heard the woman say one thing: "Show Mr. Peabody into the
    library, please."
She didn't back down.
She insisted she saw the ex-Nazi, author of *Age of Violence*, kill the girl,
    "Joyce Stewart."
She didn't write the threatening letters that were typed on her
    machine.
She didn't get ticketed, just scolded, for speeding on a scary
    mountainous road.

She took the elevator down.
She ran in the street.
She hurried up the black-and-white steps pursued by shadows.

The Formula

"Some people would pay a lot of money for that information."
It wasn't said with menace, but that was the effect.
In her purse she had the tiniest camera
anyone in the control room had ever seen.
Like many widows her age she had transferred
her suspicion from the Germans to the Russians.
Berlin remained the center of the struggle,
which it had been since 1945 and maybe even earlier.
Of little use to her now was the pistol she kept in her underwear drawer.
Love had left her life except in its abstract and spiritual forms,
yet in her loins desire waxed and waned with the moon.
She had a matter-of-fact attitude toward sex.
It had been months since her last confession.

The formula was encrypted in a postcard of the Stephansdom
she had given her niece to mail to London
from the postbox at Friedmanngasse 52
three weeks and four cities ago, but
the man in the black trench coat couldn't know that.
"I shall have to ask you to come with me,"
he said, and she tried to place the accent.
Latvia? The Ukraine? They were arguing about something
inside, but the voices subsided when they led her into the room.
"Relax. If I wanted you dead, you'd have been—"
He left the sentence unfinished. "Oh yes," he said,
"I've had my eyes on you. Your perfume is nice,
very nice, but you may not get to wear it
where you're going." At his signal the others left the room.
"Unless—" There was a bottle of whiskey
and two shot glasses. Outside the fog rolled in
and dour men in motor caps rowed their small craft

in the canal to the base of the dungeon
while two black cars idled down the road.

Just a Couple of Mugs

1.

The man wears a pinstripe suit with peak lapels and pleats in his pants, the woman a collarless jacket and black leather gloves, with a single flower behind her left ear or a yellow bonnet with a dark brown band. The question is what they should do with the stolen money.

2.

Dana Andrews and Linda Darnell hate each other in a hotel room with sink in San Francisco. They have just had a fight or gone to bed; maybe both. "I'm waiting for something to happen," he says. Then: "Nothing's going to happen." He takes off, goes to the Blue Gardenia, and catches the bartender's eye. "What'll it be?" "I'll have a double scotch." (Pause). "Make that a single scotch." (Pause). "I'll settle for a beer." Those are the best lines he gets.

In the Blue Gardenia, Nat Cole sings and Anne Baxter drinks too many Polynesian Pearl Divers. In a side street, Jean Hagen recites a poem by Robert Burns and gets hit in the eye by her ex-fiancé. She can sing, too. "You're hired." "I get forty dollars a week plus bail money."

3.

The challenger shows his hand: three kings. In the ensuing melee, a pendant with three diamonds goes missing.

In the shabby hotel room, the down-on-his-luck guy with the loosened tie says, "I can change." Ha. She knows the only way a man can change is if he is a football player in his street clothes heading to the locker room where he will don his uniform and helmet before practice.

In a side street, a pawnbroker makes an offer for the pistol that is aimed right at him. "Be careful with that thing," he says.

"Do I look like a murderer?" the man with the pistol says.

And the pawnbroker answers, "Do I look like a pawnbroker?"
The plan was foolproof. No one was supposed to get hurt.

4.

Ann Sheridan gets stuck on a roller coaster while the assassin
goes after her husband, and Dan Duryea claims he killed the old
man not for the jade but because he had been hypnotized and was
in a trance. Ida Lupino mesmerizes the courtroom with a tirade
concluding, "History to the defeated may say Alas but cannot help
or pardon."

In the car, the radio switches from "Tangerine" to the second
movement of Schubert's "Unfinished." In the elevator, the man says
"shut up" and kisses the woman hard. At police headquarters, the
commissioner says, "There are times when I regret being a policeman." Nobody knows what happened to the money. The ex-lovers
unite in a beach café in Peru. Raymond Burr plays the heavy.

5.

The chief admonished the insubordinate son of a bitch before
rewarding him with a promotion. And then he went back to work,
as though nothing had happened.

II

THE ELEMENTS OF CRIME

*I*n part one I wrote about wisecracks ("Cracking Wise") and made mention of the styles of dress, the hats, and the guns of noir. Here is a leisurely look at three other elements of crime: drinks, smokes, and saloon songs.

5

Here's to Crime!

*Breeze looked at me very steadily. Then he sighed. Then he picked the
glass up and tasted it and sighed again and shook his head sideways
with a half smile, the way a man does when you give him a drink
and he needs it very badly and it is just right and the first swallow is
like a peek into a cleaner, sunnier, brighter world.*

The writer is Raymond Chandler, the book *The High Window*
(1942), and the narrator Philip Marlowe, the shamus who has
just sociably mixed a drink for a cop. Not a very exotic drink, but
an ordinary highball (ginger ale, ice cubes, and a shot of rye whiskey): a drink once ubiquitous, now hopelessly passé. Yet it brings
out the lyric poet in Chandler, who studied his Hemingway and
knew that a succession of terse clauses connected by the common-
est of conjunctions can produce sublime effects.

The hard-boiled detective novel came into being during the rau-
cous last years of Prohibition, and the genre is soaked in whiskey,
sinfulness, and the dark—as if time stopped during a New Year's
Eve of the soul at four a.m., when the celebration has subsided and
someone has to go around mopping up the mess. The detective in
Chandler, Hammett, and their successors is a loner who may not
have a secretary, but he reliably has a bottle of whiskey in the desk

drawer and a hip flask in his pocket, and he reaches for one or the other when bad news hits. In an early chapter of *The Maltese Falcon* (1930), Hammett's Sam Spade gets a middle-of-the-night phone call informing him of his partner's violent death. During the next fifty minutes, Spade smokes exactly five cigarettes and downs three wineglasses full of Bacardi.

Spade's drinking and smoking mark him as a more ambiguous hero than any official guardian of the law. Yes, in the end he does the right thing, but you can never be sure of this unpredictable fellow with an unfiltered Camel dangling from his lower lip and a glass of rum in his hand.

For all the booze in Hammett, Chandler is really the king of the cocktails. Philip Marlowe without a drink is very nearly as unthinkable as Bogart without fedora, belted trench coat, and unfiltered cigarette. Some of Marlowe's drinking is compulsive, yet it brings him a certain sardonic pleasure. A chapter of *The Lady in the Lake* (1943) begins with Marlowe regaining consciousness after a blow to the head: "I smelled of gin. Not just casually, as if I had taken four or five drinks of a winter morning to get out of bed on, but as if the Pacific Ocean was pure gin and I had nose-dived off the boat deck." A chapter later he regains his thirst: "I went back to the whiskey decanter and did what I could about being too sober."

The cocktail occurs in the narrative stream of Chandler's prose the way a *waka* might punctuate the narrative of Lady Murasaki's *Tale of Genji*. Though Marlowe doesn't mind drinking alone, he also revels in the cocktail hour as a social ritual, regardless of the venue. No accident that in *Farewell, My Lovely* (1940), Marlowe's tone-setting first meeting with his client—the oversized, loudly dressed Moose Malloy (who is "about as inconspicuous as a tarantula on a slice of angel food")—takes place in a cheerless bar where the two men drink whiskey sours.

Chandler was very particular about his drinks and liked switching favorites from book to book. In *The Lady in the Lake*, a "wizened waiter with evil eyes and a face like a gnawed bone" serves Marlowe a Bacardi cocktail; we'd probably call it a daiquiri (juice of one lime, two shots of rum, sugar). By the time of *Playback* (1958), Chandler's last book, Marlowe has switched to ordering double Gibsons, a very serious drink, consisting of gin and vermouth as in a martini but with a cocktail onion substituted for the olive or lemon twist.

Chandler liked gimlets so much he included a recipe in *The Long Goodbye* (1953). In the book Marlowe and his pal Terry Lennox make a habit of meeting at Victor's and drinking gimlets. "What they call a gimlet is just some lime or lemon juice and gin with a dash of sugar and bitters," Terry Lennox says scornfully. "A real gimlet is half gin and half Rose's Lime Juice and nothing else. It beats martinis hollow." (I am afraid that this formula results in a drink far too sweet for the taste of any martini man or Gibson girl—it's more a cordial than a cocktail.) Yet even the flawed gimlets at Victor's do the trick: "I like to watch the man mix the first one of the evening and put it down on a crisp mat and put the little folded napkin beside it. I like to taste it slowly. The first quiet drink of the evening in a quiet bar."[1]

From the point of view of managing transitions, the cocktail is a great prop in Chandler's hands. The offer of a drink can lubricate

1. Having come down hard on Chandler's gimlet recipe, I feel I owe the reader a compensatory delight. Consider the Negroni. Some recipes call for one third gin, one third sweet vermouth, and one third Campari. Instead of the red vermouth I suggest Byrrh; instead of the Campari, substitute Cynar. Shake. Add the juice of half a lime, plenty of ice cubes, shake vigorously, and top it off with club soda. As for the gimlet, the best I can do is pour a shot and a half of ice-cold gin in a rocks glass, mix in a teaspoon of Rose's Lime Juice Cordial, stir, and serve with two ice cubes.

a reluctant witness ("a guy that buys me a drink is a pal"), pacify a cop, or romance a frail. Drinking cocktails is how Marlowe gets from one chapter to another, or from a flashy nightclub to the back office where a tough guy in a pinstriped suit and two-tone wing-tips tries to buy him or threaten him off the case.

Think of all the bridge sentences in which a cocktail figures in Chandler's novels. You can convey the atmosphere of the narrative if not the narrative itself from a loose assortment of them: "I carried the drink over to a small table against the wall and sat down there and lit a cigarette." "It made my head feel worse but it made the rest of me feel better." "He finished his drink at a gulp and stood up." "I liked him better drunk." "Then you let me cuddle you." "Then you cracked me on the head with a whiskey bottle." "This is harder than it looks." "He lifted the empty glass and brought it down hard on the edge of the table." "I finished my drink and went after him." "His whiskey sour hadn't seemed to improve his temper." "I needed a drink badly and the bars were closed."

The cocktail shared by two persons of either sex is both a social ritual and an expression of intimacy in Hammett and Chandler. The first sign of betrayal is a doctored drink, as when the Fat Man slips Sam Spade a Mickey in *The Maltese Falcon*. The most popular toast in detective fiction generally is "Here's to crime," or "Success to crime," though Chandler gets off a beauty in *The Big Sleep* (1939), his first novel, in the scene in which the thug gets ready to administer a fatal dose of poison to a luckless but honorable small-time crook: "Moths in your ermine, as the ladies say." The character of old General Sternwood, Marlowe's client in *The Big Sleep*, is delineated in dialogue centering precisely on what the two men are, or are not, drinking. Sitting in a greenhouse, wrapped in a heavy bathrobe, the general is now belatedly paying the price for a dissipated life. No longer allowed to drink, he nostalgically recalls that he used to take his brandy with champagne, "the champagne as cold as Valley Forge and about a third of a glass of brandy beneath it." Marlowe enjoys his drink ("brandy and soda") and his cigarette, and the general enjoys watching. "A nice state of affairs when a man has to indulge his vices by proxy," the old man says "dryly," a most apt adverb. If the scotch and sodas in Hammett's *The Thin Man* signal sophistication, the cocktails in Chandler seem to stand for virility.

Though the drinking is much more measured in the classic detective novel as practiced by Agatha Christie and Dorothy Sayers, both authors use alcoholic references to help establish the character of their detective heroes. Sayers has a story, "The Bibulous Business of a Matter of Taste," in which two characters claiming to be Lord Peter Wimsey are asked to prove it in a wine-tasting competition. The real Wimsey, a connoisseur of fine French wines, can unerringly tell a Chevalier-Montrachet 1911 from a Montrachet-Aîné of the same year. In Christie's Hercule Poirot novels, the great detective's love of aperitifs, like his waxed mustache, his French name, and his hobby of growing artichokes, distinguishes him from the rest of the cast. We're never allowed to forget that Poirot is an eccentric as well as a foreigner. With a hopeful air, he seems always to be offering the Scotland Yard inspector a variety of cordials—crème de menthe, Benedictine, crème de cacao—and is forever disappointed when the beefy British policeman chooses British beer.

Fans have commented on the haute cuisine in Rex Stout's detective novels. Fewer have noticed the sometimes strategic use to which the novelist puts beverages. Stout's sleuth is Nero Wolfe, a man of pure mind and seemingly dysfunctional body. He is huge, perhaps the fattest detective in a genre full of fat detectives, and he rarely vacates his armchair except to tend his prize orchids. He has a surly disposition, and would prefer to read books than take on a case. And though he is a gourmet, with a world-class chef on the premises ("squabs with sausage and sauerkraut, in the dining room of the old brownstone house on West Thirty-fifth Street"), he likes to guzzle beer. The narrator is Archie Goodwin, Wolfe's chief subordinate, who is dashing and charming if always one mental step behind Wolfe, as befits a narrator in the Sherlock Holmes–Dr. Watson tradition. A running gag is that he-man Archie drinks milk while his egghead boss goes for the hops, a German brew called Remmers. "I'm going to cut down to five quarts a day," he says in *Fer-de-Lance* (1935). "Twelve bottles. A bottle doesn't hold a pint."

Archie may favor milk, but he knows how to behave when it's cocktail time, and so does Wolfe's client Mrs. Bruner in *The Doorbell Rang* (1965). Archie has taken the attractive woman to lunch at a fancy midtown restaurant. His opinion of her goes up when she orders, and enjoys, "a double dry martini with onion"—he had pegged her for Dubonnet or sherry, and no onion. He has a martini himself, he tells us, to "keep her company."

It could be said that cocktails figure in detective fiction the way they figure in urban life. But there is another explanation for the significance of the cocktail in thrillers. Georges Simenon, the creator of Jules Maigret, the introspective French inspector with the penchant for his pipe and an aperitif or two in a café, came to the United States to live for a time after World War II. He stopped drinking wine with his meals and now drank cocktails before them: "Manhattan after Manhattan, then dry martini after dry martini." He had always enjoyed drinking but never before felt like an alcoholic. "From one end of the country to the other there exists a freemasonry of alcoholics," he remarked.

Is it possible that the hard-boiled detective novel, the noir movie, and even the comic thriller derive some of their energy from the national American fellowship of alcoholism?

W. Somerset Maugham, an Englishman residing in Cap d'Antibes, offers proof that the appeal of the dry martini extends across the Atlantic Ocean. Ashenden, Maugham's spy, declines the offer of a glass of sherry. "To drink a glass of sherry when you can get a dry Martini is like taking a stagecoach when you can travel by the Orient Express," he says.

You can view Hitchcock's *North by Northwest* as a progress from alcoholism to redemption. The hero played by Cary Grant is, when the film begins, an advertising man with a nagging mother and a drinking problem. The movie hops from one locale to another, and a way to keep track is through the drinks he either has or orders: martinis with business associates at the Plaza, the bottle of bourbon force-fed him by the bad guys at the Long Island estate, a Gibson on the train with Eva Marie Saint, scotch in her hotel room, and more bourbon after the fake shooting at Mount Rushmore. This sequence of drinks is seemingly indiscriminate and would be indigestible, which is part of the point, but it's noteworthy that he doesn't drink the bourbon he asks for after the fake shooting—it's a ruse to get rid of an unwanted visitor. In the course of his adventures, Cary Grant has graduated from his dependencies, and in the end has Eva Marie Saint in his arms to show for it. But then he is Cary Grant. More common in the literature and cinema of crime and detection is the unreformed alcoholic who celebrates the state of intoxication with the verve of Baudelaire, whose most famous prose poem is titled "Enivrezvous": "Get Drunk."

When, in *The Thin Man*, Nora asks Nick, "Why don't you stay sober today?" he answers for everyone in the hard-boiled tradition: "We didn't come to New York to stay sober."

The drinking of cocktails in a crummy bar in Los Angeles or a dive on West Fifty-second Street is like the renewal of life itself to these creatures of night: the rotten ones who blackmail or betray as well as the wounded angels who keep their romanticism concealed, sometimes even from themselves. And if cocktails are code for the consummation of a romance, it makes linguistic sense. "Cocktail" is a fusion of two words, "cock" and "tail," as if to signify the sought-for conjugation of the two sexes.

Chandler, justly famous for his similes and wisecracks, saw kisses in cocktails and the promise of sex in the first drink of the evening in a quiet bar. The twist is that the promise of sex always exceeds in pleasure any possible fulfillment. "Alcohol is like love," Terry Lennox says (and Marlowe agrees) in *The Long Goodbye.* "The first kiss is magic, the second is intimate, the third is routine. After that you take the girl's clothes off."

6

The Last Cigarette

Every cigarette is the last cigarette.

A cigarette is an invitation. When, in *The Lady from Shanghai* (1947), able-bodied Irish sailor Michael O'Hara (Orson Welles) meets Elsa Bannister (Rita Hayworth) in a horse-drawn carriage in Central Park, he offers her a cigarette. "But I don't smoke," she says. Still, she wraps his cigarette in a handkerchief and tucks it away for a memento. When Elsa's husband, Arthur, hires Michael to assist on a yacht trip from New York to San Francisco via the Panama Canal, the means and opportunity are at hand for an adulterous romance. Aboard the *Zaca*, Elsa smokes like an old pro, and it's as if that unsmoked pristine cigarette in Central Park prefigured the smoldering affair.

"A CIGARETTE THAT *bears a lipstick's traces" is the first line of a sexy lyric. An airline ticket takes the smoker to the romantic places where sinners gather.*

CIGARETTES WERE CURRENCY among the new immigrants. You could tip the delivery boy with a cigarette.

MY FRIEND RON *observed the paradox of cigarettes: we smoke them because of the fear of death, not in spite of it.*

I HAVE CONSIDERED writing an ironic "modest proposal" in the vein of Jonathan Swift advocating the return of cigarettes to movies, which might shorten life expectancy and thereby ease the costs of long-term health care, but friends have dissuaded me on the grounds that the irony would not be grasped.

IN 1929, WHEN cigarettes were marketed to women as "torches of freedom," well-dressed debutante types were paid to smoke while strolling down Fifth Avenue in the Easter Parade.

"DO YOU REMEMBER the last cigarette you had when you gave them up?"
    "Which time?"

"I USED TO think that all I wanted was the respect of honorable men and the ungrudging love of beautiful women," says Philip Marlow, the hospitalized mystery writer in The Singing Detective *(1986). "Now I know for sure that all I really want is a cigarette."*

AND WHAT, MR. Marlow, is it that you crave. "A smoke. A length of ash slowly building. Oh, tube of delight. Blessed nicotine."

IN THE FIRST sentence of *Too Many Cooks* (1938), Rex Stout's narrator Archie Goodwin talks of lighting a cigarette "with the feeling that after it had calmed my nerves a little, I would be prepared to submit bids for a contract to move the Pyramid of Cheops from Egypt to the top of the Empire State Building with my bare hands, in a swimming-suit." That's quite a lift to be gotten from a smoke.
    Leave aside the rush of nicotine. Forget the ritual of opening a pack of unfiltered Luckies, Camels, Chesterfields, Pall Malls, tamping them down, pulling one out, lighting it, discarding the

match, taking the first satisfying long drag. Cigarettes are the single greatest prop of all time. Not just for your glittering Hollywood actors but also for your routine civilian getting photographed for an occasion. Not just puffing, but also taking in the smoke, drawing in a deep lungful and slowly expelling it, holding the cigarette between your index and middle fingers, motioning with that hand to underscore a point.

"Cigarettes are sublime," Richard Klein asserts in a book he wrote to console himself when trying to quit smoking.[1] Sublime, maybe; sexy, for sure. "Cigarettes had to go," the poet and noir connoisseur Suzanne Lummis concedes. "But the cinema lost a language. Aside from the smoking, the lighting of the cigarette could be handled so many ways with such different effects. Richard Conte, Robert Mitchum, all those guys—in two smooth gestures they'll slide out that silver lighter and make the flame leap up, and we get the message—this is what unflappable cool looks like, virile confidence."

There is the cigarette of loneliness, the cigarette of desperation: Jean Gabin holed up in his attic room, chain-smoking his last Gauloises, as the police close in on him in *Le jour se lève* (1939). There is the cigarette of heartbreak, the chain of cigarettes that won't help you "forget her, or the way that you love her," with all the force Sinatra can put into the singular female pronoun in "Learnin' the Blues." There is the casual automatic wake-up smoke. In *The Blue Gardenia* (Fritz Lang, 1953), the first thing Crystal

---

1. Each puff, Klein writes, "baptizes the celebrant with the little flash of a renewed sensation, an instantaneous, fleeting body image of the unified Moi." Richard Klein, *Cigarettes Are Sublime* (Durham, NC: Duke University Press, 1993). Quoted in Laura Mansnerus, "Here's Puffing at You, Kid," *New York Times Book Review*, June 12, 1994.

(Ann Sothern) does when she gets out of bed is pop a cigarette into her mouth. In the same movie, when newspaperman Casey Mayo (Richard Conte) interviews Crystal's flatmate Norah (Anne Baxter), a murder suspect, they smoke cigarettes of solidarity, and you can tell they're on the same romantic page. Alas, there is also the cigarette of intense nervousness, jeopardy, and fear smoked by Faye Dunaway in *Chinatown* (1974), stunning in a black cloche and veil with black dots. When with a shaky hand she lights up, Jack Nicholson points out that she already has a cigarette going, and says, "Does my talking about your father make you nervous?"

Lighting somebody's cigarette is a powerful gesture, suggesting intimacy or the desire for same. In *The Snows of Kilimanjaro* (1952), Gregory Peck lights Ava Gardner's cigarette and his own with the same match. "If you're going to smoke you gotta learn to carry matches," Dix (Sterling Hayden) says when he lights up Doll (Jean Hagen) in *The Asphalt Jungle* (1950). Aldo Ray does the deed for Anne Bancroft at the bar in Jacques Tourneur's *Nightfall*, and Glenn Ford performs the gallantry for Gloria Grahame in Fritz Lang's *Human Desire* (1954). When Lana Turner falters trying to light her cigarette, John Garfield does the honors, foreshadowing the adultery and murder in *The Postman Always Rings Twice* (1946). The movie producer played by Kirk Douglas teaches the selfsame Lana Turner how to smoke sexily in *The Bad and the Beautiful* (1952), while Dick Powell has the flame Claire Trevor needs in *Murder, My Sweet* (1944).

Suzanne Lummis draws my attention to the moment "when Powell fires up his lighter and Trevor puts her hand on his and moves it toward the tip of her cigarette." She: "You will help me, won't you?" He: "Am I doing this for love, or will I get paid with money?" Toward the end of the movie, when "Helen, who is actually Velma, who is actually a killer . . . rises from the shadows with her cigarette, in her gown slashed with stripes of glinting sequins," the images presage danger and disaster. Soon bullets will be flying and bodies dropping.

In her discussion of smoking, Lummis also cites *In a Lonely Place* (1950). Dix Steele (Humphrey Bogart) and Laurel Gray (Gloria Grahame) sit at a piano with other couples, listening to the silky smooth rendition of the lounge singer, vocalist and pianist Hadda Brooks: *I was a lonely one, till you*. "He lights a cigarette for her, and she takes it in her mouth, such an intimate gesture. He whispers to her. They are so in love. And it will *never* be that good again. *Nothing* is going to be that good again, for either of them. If these characters had lives beyond the credits at the end, we know that each on their dying bed looked back and thought, 'that's what happiness felt like.' And because someone who unsettles their composure enters the club, that happiness didn't even last the length of the song. *That's* noir."

A haiku: *I like to watch the stars, / in cafés and bars, / smoking in films noirs.*

In *Laura*, Gene Tierney may smoke cigarettes with Vincent Price, but she chooses Dana Andrews, a much better smoker. In *Pitfall* (1948), when showroom model Lizabeth Scott (in beret, suit, and blouse with a bow) gives married insurance man (Dick Powell) a cigarette and takes one for herself, it signifies something illicit—as is plain when they clinch instead of lighting up.

Kirk Douglas lights cigarettes for Doris Day and himself in *Young Man with a Horn* (1950), which would have been a noir if Doris hadn't been there to rescue Kirk from viper Lauren Bacall. In the same movie, Hoagy Carmichael, as trumpeter Kirk's buddy, is nicknamed "Smoke" because he always has a cig in his mouth, even while his hands are busy playing the keyboard and producing "Get Happy" or "Someone to Watch Over Me."

When Rita Hayworth (Gilda) and Glenn Ford (Johnny Farrell) share a scene in *Gilda*, one of them may be smoking, but usually not both. Rita in a strapless black dress with a lit cigarette between the index and middle fingers of her right hand is reason enough to rue the day the surgeon general condemned smoking in 1964. "Got a light?" Gilda asks, and when Johnny flicks the lighter, it is belt high and she must bend over to get the flame.

A running gag in *Double Indemnity* is that Edward G. Robinson lacks a lighter. Each time he tries to light up his cigar but finds no matches in his pocket, Fred MacMurray is on hand, smirking and providing the necessary blaze. The relationship between Keyes (Robinson) and Walter Neff (MacMurray) is as intense in its way as the connection between Walter and Phyllis Dietrichson (Barbara Stanwyck). It means something that when Neff, who has been shot, is dying, it is Keyes who lights his last cigarette. The last line of the movie is on my top-ten list of great last lines: "I love you, too." Said by Neff to Keyes.

IN THE BLACK-AND-WHITE world of noir, cigarettes are everywhere. But then they are ubiquitous in all movies, as in life, in the first half of the twentieth century. Among great smokers I think of FDR with his holder tilted rakishly upward, as if to reinforce his smile, and Ike, who smoked four packs a day of unfiltered smokes before and after Operation Overlord in 1944. Gregory Peck smokes fiercely as he types up his exposé of anti-Semitism in *Gentleman's Agreement* (1947), as if to say that smoking is an aspect of the writer's job, a sine qua non, and that an ashtray full of butts is evidence that a writer has done his work. When New York replaced Paris as the world's art capital, the art critics fell into two rival camps: Pall Malls for Harold Rosenberg, Camels for Clement Greenberg. Audrey Hepburn smokes stylishly in

Charade. Marlene Dietrich smoked brilliantly, sometimes with a cigarette holder and furs. Bette Davis is in the smokers' hall of fame, and not solely because of the end of *Now, Voyager* (1942), when Paul Henreid lights two cigarettes, one for her and one for him, sealing their intimacy, and Bette has her famous line about settling for the stars if you can't have the moon. She's got a cigarette between her fingers in *All About Eve* (1950) when she says, "Fasten your seatbelts, it's going to be a bumpy night." Paul Henreid is himself a champion chain-smoker who lights a new fag from the butt he is about to extinguish in *The Hollow Triumph* (1948). Following a clinch, Henreid snags Joan Bennett's lighted cigarette out of her mouth and puts it between his own lips, as if to seal the deal.

Chesterfield ads of the 1940s and 1950s featured Claudette Colbert, Joan Crawford, and Rita Hayworth. Camels were advocated by Teresa Wright, Alan Ladd, John Wayne, Maureen O'Hara, and a neon sign in Times Square that blew out smoke. Some of the great jingles of the 1960s went to advertise mediocre cigarettes. L&M has got the filter that unlocks the flavor. You can take Salem out of the country, but. . . To a smoker it's a Kent. The most famous of all Marlboro commercials used Elmer Bernstein's music from *The Magnificent Seven*, and Yul Brynner, who played the leader of the pack, was in fact a dedicated smoker (and made a public service announcement after he learned he didn't have long to live). Nat King Cole credited the quality of his singing voice to cigarettes. Leonard Bernstein couldn't live without them.

Addictive? A hardened criminal would rat on his best friend for a cigarette, even a bad one (Lark, Parliament, Viceroy) if he needed it. Reason not the need. Hell, the guy in solitary would smoke the butts off the floor if he needed a smoke.

Was there ever a more elegant gift than a silver cigarette case or inscribed lighter, like the one that almost got Farley Granger framed for murder in *Strangers on a Train* (1951)?

In *Dead Again* (1991), Kenneth Branagh's ode to the noirs of the 1940s, the intrepid reporter played by Andy Garcia smokes and smokes, and when we see him as an old man, decades in the future, he has a tracheostomy tube in his neck. What does he ask for— what does he crave—in return for sharing information with the detective played by Branagh? A cigarette.

Read the opening chapter of Italo Svevo's *Confessions of Zeno*. It is titled "The Last Cigarette" and narrates the hero's efforts to give up cigarettes and the lengths the addict will go to in order to satisfy his or her craving.[2]

THE CIGARETTE OF combat: According to Roger Ebert, *Out of the Past* is "the greatest cigarette-smoking movie of all time." Robert Mitchum and Kirk Douglas wage war by cigarette proxy. "The trick, as demonstrated by [director] Jacques Tourneur and his cameraman, Nicholas Musuraca, is to throw a lot of light into the empty space where the characters are going to exhale. When they do, they produce great white clouds of smoke, which express their moods, their personalities and their energy levels. There were guns in *Out of the Past*, but the real hostility came when Robert Mitchum and Kirk Douglas smoked at each other."[3]

---

2. An emeritus professor at the University of Washington advances the theory that "smoking represented for Svevo the muffled resistance of the Jewish writer toward the world of work and bourgeois Catholic respectability, just as it consti-tuted for Zeno the major 'resistance' to his psychoanalytic healing and normaliza-tion." Mikkel Borch-Jacobsen, "Svevo on the Couch," *Raritan* (Summer 2020): 87.

3. Roger Ebert, "200 Cigarettes," February 26, 1999, rogerebert.com.

The cigarette as a prize: In *The Snake Pit* (1948), a so-called "problem picture" dramatizing the plight of the mentally ill, Dr. Kik (Leo Genn) wants to reward Virginia Stuart Cunningham (Olivia de Havilland) for the progress she has made. On the wall a framed photograph of a severe Sigmund Freud looks on as the doctor kindly says, "What about a cigarette now?"

The romantic cigarette, in defeat: On television in the late fifties, Sinatra in fedora and raincoat, with a cigarette in his hand, takes his seat at the bar. It's nearly three in the morning and he begins to sing "One for My Baby (and One More for the Road)" with only Bill Miller's piano accompaniment. There's a glass, an ashtray, and an open pack of smokes on the bar. The bartender, Joe by name, pours whiskey into the glass when the singer tells him to "set 'em up," and Sinatra strikes a match, keeps it lit, stares at the flame, while telling his new pal Joe that tonight he is drinking "to the end of a brief episode." Only then does he bring the flame to the cigarette and take a puff. He keeps the cigarette between fingers, or taps the ashes into the tray, and holds the glass of whiskey while singing. The song as Harold Arlen and Johnny Mercer wrote it ends with "the long, long road," but Sinatra never reaches the period at the end of the line. After "the long," he pauses, takes a drag of his cigarette, repeats "the long," and lets the music drift off like smoke.

The macho cigarette, cool under pressure: In *The Godfather* (1972), Michael Corleone is standing in front of the hospital where his wounded father lies unprotected. Enzo, the baker, has chosen this moment to visit with flowers, and Michael enlists him to help stand guard. The two men are to stand there, impersonating gunmen, in an effort to deter the hit men driving by. Enzo, understandably nervous, needs a cigarette. Hand goes to pocket, pulls out cigarette. But his hands shake, he can't work his lighter.

Michael calmly takes the Zippo and lights him up. The ruse works. Michael has displayed initiative and imagination, and the signature of that moment is his icy calm when firing up Enzo's lighter. The unfiltered Camel that Michael smokes at the end of *The Godfather, Part II* (1974) is in contrast a mark of his aloneness. The cigarette is his only friend as he sits and broods on the end of an ethic, a family, a film.

The royalty of cigarette smokers are Humphrey Bogart and Lauren Bacall. *The Big Sleep* ends with the two of them in a car. She "guesses" she's in love with him, and he "guesses" that he's in love with her. He: "What's wrong with you?" She: "Nothing you can't fix." And next to the words THE END there is an ashtray with two smoldering cigarettes in it. Ah, cigarettes. What a wonderful prop. So sexy! Too bad they cause cancer.

7

Among My Souvenirs

The ashtray with two lighted cigarettes is a fitting image for the romance of Humphrey Bogart and Lauren Bacall in *The Big Sleep*. The pair like to smoke and drink and make witty repartee in a roadhouse café, and to complete the picture, you need a pianist tickling the keys to tunes from the Great American Songbook.

In *The Big Sleep*, the flirtatious byplay between Bogart and Bacall (who married in real life after meeting two years earlier on the set of *To Have and Have Not*) is utterly charming and utterly incongruous for much of the picture. The movie needs them to be lovers, the audience expects them to clinch, and this duly happens, but at considerable violence to the logic of the plot, which puts their characters on the opposite sides of a quarrel. Though this duality may threaten the coherence of the picture, it makes the scenes between Bogart and Bacall doubly entertaining. One scene in particular has the virtue of demonstrating that black-and-white forties flicks and jazz standards were made for each other. In an elegant restaurant, the plot requires the Bacall character to pay off the detective and urge him to drop the case, and while she is doing so, the mind-reading solo pianist in the joint obligingly plays "I Guess I'll Have to Change My Plan" (music Arthur Schwartz, words Howard Dietz). Once this plot requirement is out of the way, Bacall and Bogart get down to the real cinematic purpose of their being there: to tease and flirt and advance their budding romance while the piano player plays Rodgers and Hart's "Blue Room," which idealizes the successful outcome of such wooing. Lorenz Hart's lyric pairs boy and girl and the prospect of their betrothal and a subsequent time ever after when "every day's a holiday, because you're married to me." It is a song second perhaps only to "Tea for Two" (music Vincent Youmans, words Irving Caesar) as a fantasy of marriage so beautifully innocent it almost brings tears to your eyes.

The Big Sleep needs the two songs in the background, and not simply because they are in exact counterpoint to the course of the conversation between Bogart and Bacall. The music is as necessary in black-and-white movies of the 1940s—especially hard-boiled detective movies or noir thrillers—as the drinks the characters imbibe, the suits the men wear, the chic hats worn by the women, and the nightspots they frequent, like Eddie Mars's casino in *The Big Sleep*, where beautiful costumed girls check Bogart's coat, offer to sell him cigarettes, and vie for the privilege of delivering him a message.

Nor do the songs suffer from being relegated to background music, shorn of lyrics, of voice. The solo piano renditions insinuate themselves in your consciousness. If you don't recognize the tunes, fine; if you know them, so much the better. When you listen to an instrumental version of a song whose lyrics you know and like, what you're hearing is a metonym of the song. The text is not altogether absent if you the listener can supply it. No noir would be complete without a soundtrack that either underscores or undermines what you see on-screen. The sound is the sound of the big city—swing and jazz. You can hear the music of noir in soundtracks by Bernard Herrmann (*Cape Fear, On Dangerous*

Ground, and some of Hitchcock's best, including *Psycho* and *Vertigo*). Consider, too, this extraordinary list of composers:

- Elmer Bernstein (*The Man with the Golden Arm*, with the great Saul Bass's credits that open the film, and *Sweet Smell of Success*)
- John Lewis and the Modern Jazz Quartet with Milt Jackson on vibraphone (*Odds Against Tomorrow*)
- Miles Davis's "lonely trumpet" (*Elevator to the Gallows*)
- Duke Ellington (*Anatomy of a Murder*)
- David Raksin (*Laura, The Big Combo*)
- Miklós Rózsa (*Double Indemnity, The Killers*)
- Jerry Goldsmith (*Chinatown*)
- Roy Webb (*Out of the Past*)
- Lalo Schifrin (*Bullitt*)
- Alfred Newman (*Cry of the City*)
- Franz Waxman (*Sorry, Wrong Number*)
- Max Steiner (*The Big Sleep*)
- Dmitri Tiomkin (*Shadow of a Doubt* and three other Hitchcock movies)

Instrumentals of songs by such as Cole Porter, Rodgers and Hart, the Gershwins, Harold Arlen, Arthur Schwartz, Jule Styne, Vernon Duke, Jimmy Van Heusen, and Burton Lane provide the background music in bars and cafés.

Sometimes you get lucky at a double bill and you hear "Too Marvelous for Words" sung by Jo Stafford in one movie and by Doris Day in the other. That's Doris again singing "The Very Thought of You" in *Young Man with a Horn* and Nat King Cole with "Blue Gardenia" in the 1953 movie of that name, in which Anne Baxter is the telephone operator who suffers a blackout and wakes up wondering whether she is responsible for the corpse of the cad in the room. In *Out of the Past,* you might be watching Robert Mitchum and Jane Greer in their hot, smoky, doomed romance and not even register that you're hearing "Come Out, Come Out, Wherever You Are" in the background. In each case, the music is part of the film's vocabulary.[1] *The Singing Detective*, Dennis Potter's groundbreaking TV series, with Michael Gambon as mystery writer Philip Marlow (no final *e*), makes explicit the connection between film noir and big band music. Each episode begins with the melancholy sound of a solo harmonica playing "Peg o' My Heart." The soundtrack consists primarily of songs from the 1940s, many of which are lip-synched by a character or a group of characters. Marlow is in a hospital ward, an invalid, with an acute case of psoriatic arthritis ("I've Got You Under My Skin"), trying to escape his medical condition by mental travel. On a second narrative level, that of memory, Philip is ten years old in 1945, reliving the traumas he went through that year, including the suicide of his mother. On a third level, that of fantasy, Marlow is a romantic nightclub crooner in the Sinatra manner. On a fourth level, that of invention, he is translating his experience—filtered by his own paranoia—into the plot of the novel he is writing.

The integration of the music into the various plots helps to govern transitions from one narrative to another, while the surreal lip-synching episodes are sudden and unexpected, sometimes funny, and always in ironic counterpoint to the action at hand. A decrepit old man on his deathbed opens his mouth and out comes Dick Haymes's deep baritone singing "It Might as Well Be Spring," a song of youth and wistful anticipation. A scarecrow shows up now and then, at one point breaking into Al Jolson's version of

1. The voice on the recording of "Too Marvelous for Words" in *Dark Passage* has been attributed to Jo Stafford. Doris Day sings "Too Marvelous for Words" in *Young Man with a Horn* (1950).

"After You've Gone," at another wearing the furious face of Adolf Hitler. When the song is "Paper Doll"—a perfect lyric for a guy who fears that other fellows will steal his girl—the voices are those of the Mills Brothers, but the singers are, in order, the hospitalized Marlow, the scarecrow, Marlow's sad cuckolded father back in 1945, and the soldiers on the train that took young Philip and his mother to London when she left her husband. The effect is also magical when a group of hospital "Evangelists" join the fiercely earnest Dr. Finlay to sing "Accentuate the Positive" with the voices of Bing Crosby and the Andrews Sisters—and when doctors with reflex-testing hammers in their hands, and a chorus line of nurses, perform "Dry Bones" as recorded by Fred Waring and his Pennsylvanians. The song ends with "Now hear the word of the Lord!" and the music stops, everything returns to normal in the ward, and one of the doctors asks Marlow if he'd like to see "the padre."

The whole amounts to a Freudian murder mystery in which our hero, who meets with a hospital psychotherapist, slowly overcomes his resistance and recovers the repressed memories of what, as a boy, he had witnessed (his mother's infidelity) and done to his shame (blaming his own misdeeds on a classmate). Potter advances the idea that the body's ills are manifestations of the damaged psyche. When Marlow is discharged from the hospital, leaning on the wife he has defamed in his paranoid waking dreams, we hear Vera Lynn's "We'll Meet Again," a wonderful choice, for it is either a promise (Marlow's or the author's) or a last reminiscence of 1945 and wartime England.

HERE ARE OTHER instances of the interdependence of noir movies and popular songs:

Johnny Mercer's lyric for "Tangerine" (music Victor Schertzinger) extols the charms of a vain, sultry Latin beauty. To the strains of this song, Barbara Stanwyck and Fred MacMurray have their final showdown in *Double Indemnity*. In a flashback in *Sorry, Wrong Number* (1948), the same song plays on the car radio when Stanwyck, a neurotic heiress this time, flaunts her father's wealth to betray a friend and seduce Burt Lancaster.

As David Raksin's theme for *Laura* plays in the background, the homicide detective played by Dana Andrews becomes obsessed with the murder victim, a beautiful babe (Gene Tierney), who obligingly returns to life from her weekend in a remote cabin somewhere. (The corpse in the kitchen belonged to somebody else.) The music is so memorable that Johnny Mercer was asked to produce a lyric, and the result was a ballad that every baritone in America worth his salt could sing. "But she's only a dream." In a flashback in the same movie, Gene Tierney dances with Vincent Price to the strains of "You Go to My Head," an amazingly sexy song for female vocalists ranging from Bea Wain to Marlene Dietrich.

A Buddy Rich drum solo is performed frenetically by Elisha Cook Jr. as Cliff, the jazz drummer who has eyes for Carol (Ella Raines), in Robert Siodmak's *Phantom Lady*. The critic Jeffrey Renshaw writes that the scene "is pure Freudian innuendo, [Cliff's] face frozen in a leering rictus of lust while Carol makes come-on motions and the other players blast away on their horns. Jazz as sex? It's as open a sexual metaphor as you'll see in a Forties film, with Cliff eyeing her up and down and mentally undressing her."[2]

When, in *To Have and Have Not*, sultry Lauren Bacall stands in the doorway and huskily says, "Anybody got a match?"— addressing Humphrey Bogart and meaning by "match" something

2. Jerry Renshaw, "Phantom Lady," *Austin Chronicle*, September 24, 1999.

akin to a sexual spark—the background music is Hoagy Carmichael's "Baltimore Oriole." The song is a kind of companion piece to the same composer's "Skylark," a moody love song in the form of an address to a bird. Although Paul Francis Webster wrote most of the lyrics, Hoagy, who plays the piano in the movie's nightclub scenes, wrote the best line in "Baltimore Oriole": "Forgiving is easy, / it's a woman-like now-and-then- / could-happen-to thing."

In the same movie Bacall, accompanied by Hoagy at the piano, sings "How Little We Know," a great Carmichael tune, catching Bogart's eye across the room. Jacqueline Bouvier, who became Jackie Kennedy, liked "How Little We Know" so much she translated Johnny Mercer's lyric into French for the benefit of her Francophone friends during her junior year abroad.[3]

At Rick's Café in *Casablanca* (1942), in which the proprietor feels wronged by a perfidious woman, and in *The Mask of Dimitrios* (1944), in which a jilted lover recalls her affair with Dimitrios, we hear the strains of "Perfidia." The numbers that Dooley Wilson sings in *Casablanca* include "Knock on Wood," "It Had To Be You," and the song Ilse (Ingrid Bergman) and Rick (Humphrey Bogart) consider theirs, Herman Hupfeld's "As Time Goes By."

Somebody puts a coin in the jukebox in the diner and out comes "I Can't Believe That You're in Love with Me" (music Jimmy McHugh, words Clarence Gaskill), triggering the recollected psychodrama in Edgar G. Ulmer's strange reverie of an unreliable (unbelievable) narrator in *Detour*. The other song on the soundtrack is "I'm Always Chasing Rainbows."

---

3. See Alice Kaplan, *Dreaming in French: The Paris Years of Jacqueline Bouvier Kennedy, Susan Sontag, and Angela Davis* (Chicago: University of Chicago Press, 2012), 33. On the mistaken assumption that Jacqueline Bouvier wrote a "bilingual poem," Kaplan quotes the "third strophe" and Bouvier's translation of it.

In the nightclub scene in *The Racket* (1951), the torch singer played by Lizabeth Scott, whom the mob boss will later denounce as a "cheap, clip-joint canary," sings "This Is a Lovely Way to Spend an Evening." After she repairs to her dressing room, the band picks up with a fast-paced rendition of "Come Out, Come Out, Wherever You Are."

Rita Hayworth invites the American male in the form of Glenn Ford to "Put the Blame on Mame" (music Doris Fisher, lyrics Allan Roberts) in *Gilda.* In *The Lady from Shanghai,* the same red-haired enchantress—only this time as a blonde, shorn of much of her mane—seduces Orson Welles (to whom she was married at the time) and coyly sings "Please Don't Kiss Me" (same songwriters), a phrase that says one thing and means its opposite. (In both cases Rita moves her lips, and out comes the melodious voice of Anita Ellis.) Early in the film you get to hear it on a jukebox while Rita's husband, Everett Sloane, "the world's greatest living trial lawyer," expounds on the value of having an "edge"—in the sense that the guy singing the song on the jukebox has "an edge." Though I've no proof but my ears, the uncredited voice sounds a lot like that of Welles's old drinking buddy Frank Sinatra.[4]

In *Key Largo* (1948), Claire Trevor, playing a washed-up nightclub singer and full-time lush in the entourage of gangster Johnny Rocco (Edward G. Robinson), sings "Moanin' Low" (music Ralph Rainger, lyrics Howard Dietz) a capella, her voice faltering, and when she finishes the torch song, says, "Can I have that drink now, Johnny?"

---

4. In 1944 Welles and Sinatra campaigned for Franklin Roosevelt. On election night, when the good news came in, they took part in a drunken fracas at the Waldorf Astoria.

In *I Wake Up Screaming* (1941), an instrumental of Harold Arlen's "Over the Rainbow" is Betty Grable's leitmotif, which is a little weird, but the theme you hear more prominently in the picture is Alfred Newman's sultry, bittersweet "Street Scene," so evocative of New York City, the movie's setting.

Newman's "Street Scene" is also used in other New York–based movies. All but two of the following were produced by Twentieth Century–Fox: *Street Scene* (1931); *The Dark Corner* (1946); Eliza Kazan's *Gentleman's Agreement* (1947); two Victor Mature noirs, *Kiss of Death* (1947) and *Cry of the City* (1948); and the cinematic debut of Dean Martin and Jerry Lewis, *My Friend Irma* (1949). The music gets its fullest, lushest treatment in a comedy, Jean Negulesco's *How to Marry a Millionaire* (1953), with Marilyn Monroe, Lauren Bacall, and Betty Grable. It gets its most memorable treatment in a noir, *Where the Sidewalk Ends* (1950), in which it is whistled over the opening credits of Otto Preminger's effort to renew the magic of his *Laura* costars, Dana Andrews and Gene Tierney.

A drunken Fredric March and his game wife, Myrna Loy, dance to "Among My Souvenirs" (music Horatio Nicholls, lyrics Edgar Leslie) on his first night back from the war in *The Best Years of Our Lives* (1946). Although the movie is not a noir—love conquers all, and no one dies—*The Best Years of Our Lives* is from the noir era, the black-and-white 1940s, and can be seen to represent an equal and opposite impulse, an anti-noir. In the movie are a disabled serviceman who has hooks for hands and an air force hotshot who can't hold a job—even the lowly job of being a soda jerk fixing sundaes for kids in a drugstore. If we were in a noir, handless Homer Parrish and "fallen angel of the air force" Fred Derry would team up with, perhaps, the army vet who needs a loan to buy the land for a farm but does not meet an understanding bank executive. The three plot to rob the bank, and while they plan and rehearse the crime, they pair off with dames they meet at the bar where the piano player funds the operation and plays "The Night We Called It a Day." The man with hooks for hands has qualms about shooting an armed guard, but the ex-pilot overrules him. "It's easy to have ethics when you're ahead in the game," he says. Clinging to the roughneck would-be farmer, the tipsy nightclub singer says, "Please, Len. I'm begging you. Tell me I'm a woman."

But we are not in a noir, and director William Wyler's use of "Among My Souvenirs" is too good to let go unmentioned. Edgar Leslie's 1927 lyric communicates regret at the passing of time. Trinkets and tokens diligently collected offer some consolation but do nothing to stop the flow of tears. In *The Best Years of Our Lives*, when the US Army sergeant played by March comes home, he brings souvenirs of the Pacific war as gifts for his teenage son. But like the knife in Elizabeth Bishop's poem "Crusoe in England," when it has become a souvenir on the shelf after Crusoe returns home from his island, the mementos of conflict have lost their meaning. They seem vaguely unreal, lifeless, unlike the photograph of his wife that a hung-over March looks at the next morning. A different sort of souvenir, it has all the meaning in the world for him. And "Among My Souvenirs"—played on the piano by Hoagy Carmichael, hummed in the shower by a hung-over March, and heard as background music—unifies the whole sequence and endows it with the rich pathos that makes the song so durable a jazz standard. I recommend that you watch the movie again—and that you listen to Art Tatum play "Among My Souvenirs" on the piano or, if you can find it, a recording of Sinatra and Crosby doing it as a duet on television in the early 1950s.

III

Auteurs

You don't need to subscribe to the French auteur theory to see the convenience of a single term that can embrace such diverse creative forces as Alfred Hitchcock, Dashiell Hammett, Somerset Maugham, Eric Ambler, Rex Stout, Ed McBain, David Goodis, and Ida Lupino.

8

The Great British Spymasters

I.

Espionage fiction of the great British variety falls into two general divisions. What we might call the imperial tradition is exemplified in the novels of E. Phillips Oppenheim, such as *The Great Impersonation* (1920), in which the hero may turn out to be the villain in disguise, and elegant spies mingle among the baronets and princesses in country mansions, on Mediterranean yachts, and in Monte Carlo casinos. The books are as well written and entertaining as adventure books for boys can be. The lessons in period slang are instructive. (A lawyer of the "new-fashioned school—Harrow and Cambridge, the Bath Club, and racquets and fives, rather than gold and lawn tennis," will say "Great Scott!" where his elders would have said "God bless my soul!") Nevertheless, when Eric Ambler concedes that Oppenheim's brand of "suave, stiff, stuffed-shirted intrigue still has an engaging quality about it," what you remember are the adjectives.

The imperial style reached its baroque apotheosis in Ian Fleming's James Bond novels—and the movies made of them, with agent 007 played by Sean Connery (1962–1971 and 1983), George Lazenby (1969), Roger Moore (1973–1985), Timothy Dalton (1987–1989),

Pierce Brosnan (1995–2002), and Daniel Craig (2006–2021). The Bond of the movies is devilishly handsome, strong, confident, capable, manly, clever, resourceful, and good at games. He has a license to kill and splendid combat gadgets in his briefcase or car; arrives on the scene with own musical theme; likes his martinis shaken, not stirred; looks elegant in a white dinner jacket with a red carnation, black tie, and ruffled shirt; wins high-stakes poker games in posh casinos; has a succinctly ironic comment to suit the occasion ("shocking" when a villain dies electrocuted in a bathtub); and attracts the most gloriously glamorous women, such as the brazenly named Pussy Galore in *Goldfinger*. Bond captivated the imagination of John F. Kennedy, who listed *From Russia with Love* as one of his favorite books, much as "Moon River" sung by Audrey Hepburn in *Breakfast at Tiffany's* captivated the century's most charismatic first lady.[1]

W. Somerset Maugham, that peerless storyteller, initiated the other line of spy fiction: more plausible, less flamboyant. He joined Britain's Secret Intelligence Service during World War I, thinking he would be more useful doing that than driving an ambulance. "The work appealed both to my sense of romance and my sense of the ridiculous," he wrote in *The Summing Up* (1938). He had to learn how to elude a pursuer, to conduct secret meetings in unlikely places, to convey and receive coded messages, and to smuggle documents across a contested border. Informed by his experience as an agent in Switzerland and Russia, the linked stories of *Ashenden* (1928) rank among Maugham's finest. They

---

1. Point of information: the martinis consumed by our hero in *Casino Royale*, the first of the Bond books, are really vespers, composed of gin, vodka, and Lillet, a nice and potent concoction, a tad sweeter than a regular martini or Gibson but recognizably of the same family.

have a quality of bleak realism, an atmosphere of danger, and a central figure that resembles a romantic version of the author: a talented novelist, worldly-wise and sophisticated, not a toff in a top hat. Ashenden is Maugham at one remove: imperturbable, even-tempered, a harsh but fair judge of men, destined to be portrayed by John Gielgud.[2]

When *Ashenden* was reissued as volume three in the four-volume set of Maugham's *Collected Short Stories*, the author explained that he was sent to Russia in 1917 to prevent the Bolshevik Revolution. Although his efforts, as he wryly observes, "did not meet with success," his work as an intelligence agent taught him useful lessons. He learned, for example, that "there will always be espionage and there will always be counter-espionage." In what could stand as the entire genre's raison d'être, he writes:

> Though conditions may have altered, though difficulties may be greater, when war is raging there will always be secrets which one side jealously guards and which the other will use every means to discover; there will always be men who from malice or for money will betray their kith and kin and there will always be men who, from love of adventure or a sense of duty, will risk a shameful death to secure information valuable to their country.

Ashenden's boss, whom he knows only by the initial R., tells the agent, "If you do well you'll get no thanks and if you get into trouble you'll get no help." The same statement could be made about artists of any kind, writers included, and Maugham strategically uses literary metaphors for espionage situations. "Nothing is so foolish as to ascribe profundity to what on the surface is

2. Gielgud plays Ashenden in Hitchcock's 1936 movie *Secret Agent*, which is based on two of Maugham's stories.

merely inept," Ashenden comments, adding that "many an ingenuous reviewer" has made this error. "Just as passion will make use brazenly of the hackneyed phrase," he says in another episode, "so will chance show itself insensitive to the triteness of the literary convention"—which is to say that "dullness of routine" can easily slip into melodrama, and (for instance) the motif of the beautiful, available woman at the bar, who sleeps with the spy, steals his wallet, and leaves him either dead or penniless, may be a cliché in spy books but remains an undeniable fact of life.

R. tells Ashenden that a man with the code name Gustav writes the best reports of all his agents. "His information is always very full and circumstantial," he says, instructing Ashenden "to give his reports your very best attention" and to use them as a model. A year later, however, R. suspects that "some hanky-panky" is going on, and he dispatches Ashenden to investigate. It doesn't take Ashenden very long to determine that the last report Gustav has filed from Germany is a phony; the spy was ensconced in his home in Basel at the time he dated his letter from Mannheim. Confronted, Gustav cheerfully admits to deceiving his spymasters. "Do you think I was such a fool as to risk my life for fifty pounds a month? I love my wife."

When his firm stopped sending him to Germany, Gustav continued to send dispatches to British intelligence because it was easy money. "I got a lot of amusement out of sending you reports and letters." Ashenden assures Gustav that there are no hard feelings. "Your reports will remain in our archives as models of what a report should be." He even encourages the spurious spy to report on "what the Germans are doing with a spy of theirs in Lausanne." The report comes, Ashenden can tell it's fabricated, and after holding the paper up to the light to see the watermark—confiding with self-deprecating irony that "he had no reason for doing this except the sleuths of detective novels always did it"—he sets a match to it and watches it burn.

The idea of the fake but clever spy whose reports are read at home with the greatest interest is developed by Graham Greene in *Our Man in Havana*, his send-up of the espionage genre, though Greene himself, in his retrospective *Ways of Escape*, attributes the idea for his book to his own experience in intelligence work. In West Africa during World War II he "had learned that nothing pleased the Service at home more than the addition of a card to their Intelligence files." When he submitted a review of a bogus report—the incompetent agent was illiterate, could count only up to ten, and knew only one of the four cardinal compass points—the Home Office ranked the incompetent spy's report "most valuable."

A Maugham insight that informs the work of Greene and John le Carré is the inherent contradiction in intelligence work—the awareness that unsavory and morally indefensible actions may be required in the pursuit of theoretically just aims. The sad cynicism of human nature comes to the fore in *Ashenden*, as does the fallibility of men and women, no matter how able and professional. The "bigwigs" are "ready enough to profit by the activities of obscure agents of whom they had never heard" but "shut their eyes to dirty work so that they could put their clean hands on their hearts and congratulate themselves that they had never done anything that was unbecoming to men of honour." Ashenden reports that for £5,000, a man will kill the pro-German king of a small Balkan country. R. is indignant and tells Ashenden he should have knocked the fellow down. If, however, the chap wants to manage the assassination without pay, or with pay provided by Ashenden himself, R. will have no objections.

Many readers like best the chapters dealing with the "Hairless Mexican," a sublimely self-assured assassin who is given to saying things like "Anyone can pull a trigger, but it takes a man to use a knife." One of the highlights of the book occurs when, in Naples, Ashenden deciphers a cable. The message, itself in code: "Constantine Andreadi has been detained by illness at Piraeus. He will be unable to sail. Return Geneva and await instructions." It takes Ashenden a minute before he realizes what the message means. For once he loses his self-possession. "You bloody fool," he tells the assassin. "You've killed the wrong man." End of chapter.[3]

"Giulia Lazzari" is Eric Ambler's favorite episode in *Ashenden*. The title character, arrested for espionage in England, is given a choice. She can go free if she betrays her lover, Chandra, "one of the gang of Indians that were making trouble for us in Berlin," or she will be arrested and perhaps shot. Chandra is madly in love with her, and Giulia does her best to confound British intelligence. Though she sends Chandra the letters her captors dictate, pleading with him to come to where he will be captured and killed, she tries to get word to him about what's up. In the end, it's her life or his, and she does what is asked of her, albeit bitterly. After Chandra is eliminated, Ashenden meets with Giulia Lazzari, expecting to hear

3. An echo of this memorable line was sounded in the context of what the journalist Jefferson Morley has called "the Rosetta Stone of postwar American history"—the assassination of President John F. Kennedy on November 22, 1963. According to *Mob Lawyer* by Frank Ragano (cowritten with *New York Times* reporter Selwyn Raab), the assassination was a mob hit. Ragano's client, the Florida Mafia chieftain Santo Trafficante, admitted his involvement in the plot. He spoke in Sicilian shortly before his death in 1987: "Carlos è futtutu. Non duvevamu a Giovanni. Duvevamu ammazzari a Bobby." (Carlos fucked up. We shouldn't have killed John. We should have killed Bobby.) "Carlos" was New Orleans Mafia boss Carlos Marcello; Bobby was Robert F. Kennedy, who, as his brother's attorney general, had made enemies ranging from organized crime syndicates to Jimmy Hoffa and the Teamsters Union. See Jeffrey Frank, "The J.F.K. Files and the Problem of Trust," *The New Yorker*, November 1, 2017, https://www.newyorker.com/news/daily-comment/the-jfk-files-and-the-problem-of-trust.

an outburst of ire or sentiment smacking of pathos. But she merely says, "There is one thing I should like to ask." It turns out to be "the last thing he expected." She asks for the wristwatch she had given her lover for Christmas. "It cost twelve pounds."

The realism Maugham brings to Ashenden has nothing to do with world-weariness. There are times when there is nothing for an agent to do but wait, and even an agent who doubles as a writer— and for whom all that is happening is so much "raw material"— feels like a lonely cloud wandering in the sky. In Geneva, where Ashenden is staying at a good hotel, he has the leisure to hire a boat or wander down old streets, to reread Rousseau, to dine well. Yet he can feel the onset of boredom. Ashenden, who had always prided himself on possession of the inner resources that keep boredom at bay, has "just escaped being bored," and only by virtue of his next assignment: to lure a man from neutral Switzerland into France, a British ally. He gets his instructions from R., who shows Ashenden a photograph. "That's him." What will you do with him? "R. chuckled grimly. 'Shoot him and shoot him damn quick.'"

In *The Summing Up* (1938), Maugham reviews his critical reputation by decade. "In my twenties the critics said I was brutal, in my thirties they said I was flippant, in my forties they said I was cynical. In my fifties they said I was competent, and now in my sixties they say I am superficial." Does anyone read him today?

If creative writing programs were serious about teaching the art of fiction, they would require students to read Maugham's short stories. His rules are simple to state, difficult to follow. A good story, he writes, "should have coherence and sufficient probability for the needs of the theme; it should be of a nature to display the development of character . . . and it should have completeness." In Aristotle's terms: a beginning, a middle, and an end. Maugham is an opinionated and passionate guide to great books (see *Ten Novels and Their Authors,* 1954) and an able teacher. He observed that the work of an intelligence agent is largely "monotonous." The experience is a jumble until the author makes it "coherent, dramatic, and probable." This was his achievement in *Ashenden,* which makes it one book that every survey of espionage fiction must include.

II.

Eric Ambler was the most apt of Maugham's pupils. When he read *Ashenden,* Ambler found the antidote to novels of intrigue and adventure in which the villains tend to be unbelievable and the typical hero could be "a tweedy fellow with steel-grey eyes and gun pads on both shoulders or a moneyed dandy with a taste for adventure. He could also be a xenophobic ex-officer with a nasty anti-Semitic streak. None of that really mattered. All he really needed to function as hero was abysmal stupidity combined with superhuman resourcefulness and unbreakable knuckle bones."

In the half-dozen novels he wrote in the years leading up to World War II, Ambler injected the dose of seriousness that made the spy novel a politically savvy vehicle for sustained suspense in that decade of threat and appeasement, secret pacts, the persecution and forced exile of whole sectors of the populace, and the intervention of one government into the affairs of another. He traded in real fear and palpable danger, and the effect was to enhance rather than diminish the genre's entertainment value. Nor did Ambler give in to the temptation to overwrite that critical acclaim sometimes triggers. One hallmark of his novels, from *Background to Danger* (1937) to *The Care of Time* (1981), is a cool, understated prose that efficiently serves the exposition of the author's intricate plots.

James Sandoe borrowed a locution from Raymond Chandler to salute Ambler's accomplishment: "Ambler took the spy story by the scruff of its well-washed neck, whipped the monocle out of its astonished eye and pushed it down among people, away from the world of diplomatic mummies."[4]

Here Lies Eric Ambler (1987), the title of Ambler's tight-lipped memoir, reflects the author's self-deprecating reserve. It is as though what follows is the ironic epitaph of a spy writer convinced that "only an idiot believes that he can write the truth about himself."

One episode stands out. On a vacation in Marseilles one summer, Ambler was fleeced at poker by a local barman. Out of money, he confined himself to his hotel room and "planned an assassination" to take his mind off his hunger. From his window he pointed an imaginary rifle at a spot where the barman was likely to walk. "It was quite a shock, a few weeks later, to see on the newsreels that same piece of the Canebière with the intersecting tramlines," Ambler writes. "The spot I had chosen for my sniper shot at the barman had also been chosen by the Croatian assassin of King Alexander of Yugoslavia." He took it as a sign, a foreshadowing of fictions to follow. "In the Mediterranean sunshine there were strange and violent men with whom I could identify, and with whom, in a way, I was now in touch."

An Englishman who traveled a lot and took up residence on the continent for extended intervals, Ambler set his novels in exotic but seedy locales, in cities like Istanbul and Milan, Sofia and Belgrade. The atmospherics are superb. Consider this evocation of the capital city of an unnamed Balkan dictatorship. The year is 1951,

4. James Sandoe, "Dagger of the Mind" (1946), in *The Art of the Mystery*, ed. Howard Haycraft (New York: Grosset & Dunlap, 1946), 260

the book *Judgment on Deltchev*: "The sun had not yet set, but the shadows of a church spire and the dome of a mosque stretched like a finger and thumb across the St. Mihai Square." From the sides of "a tall, narrow building with massive ferro-concrete balconies . . . rusty weather stains drooled down the walls." In the opening of one chapter in *Cause for Alarm* (1938), Ambler succinctly conveys his grasp of the European situation. The narrator remarks on the habit of designating as "black" the day of a disaster as ghastly as the stock market crash of 1929. But "almost daily acquaintance with large-scale catastrophe had deprived the custom of its point," with the result that the norm is a "drab grey" punctuated by days of "sooty blackness" in the life of an unsuspecting, law-abiding production engineer in charge of the continental office of a Midland firm, who got the job because he is fluent in Italian.

Like Hitchcock, Ambler favored variants on the wrong man theme. When the hero's quarters are ransacked in *Epitaph for a Spy* (1938), he is shocked to realize that the person responsible "is real, he is alive, he is one of those people outside." He treats himself to an unspoken reprimand: "He doesn't look like a spy, you nitwit. He hasn't got a vicious look and a revolver in his hip pocket. He's real. . . . He may be a patriot or a traitor, a crook or an honest man, or a bit of each. She may be dark or fair, intelligent or stupid, rich or poor. And, whoever it is, you incompetent fool, you're not doing the slightest good sitting here."

The Ambler hero is invariably a man who is highly competent in his professional field of endeavor but a rank amateur when it comes to the secret world of espionage. He may be an engineer on a business trip to the continent, or a detective novelist on holiday, and the first things he must learn are that spying is not "melodramatic" but prosaic; that he has stumbled blindly into an affair of international intrigue and that, therefore, assassins in black velour homburgs may be tracking his movements in Mussolini's Milan. In *Cause for Alarm*, our innocent abroad, Marlow by name, learns the essential truth of his situation when an Axis operative tries to persuade him to do his bidding. But, he protests, that would make him a spy. "My dear Mr. Marlow," the agent says, his voice thick with contempt, "you already *are* a spy."

In his prewar novels, Ambler aimed to shatter the reader's complacency. The titles of the books themselves told the story. The *Background to Danger* was everywhere in the European thirties, the *Cause for Alarm* immediate. Nations were metaphorically criminals that differed only as to type. "The French criminal is a snake, the American criminal a wolf, and the English criminal a rat," a well-informed Frenchman observes in *Epitaph for a Spy*. A different but equally memorable metaphor is proposed in *Cause for Alarm*. In the map of Europe, as Hitler and Mussolini conceived it, the Rome–Berlin Axis is said to extend from the Frisian Islands in the north to Sicily, "the toe of Italy in the south," and that toe "is waiting to kick Great Britain in the pants."

Not law but Nietzschean principles prevailed in the Europe Ambler depicted in his five great prewar novels. Herr Schimler in *Epitaph for a Spy* praises *The Birth of Tragedy*: "Fancy diagnosing Socrates as a decadent. Morality as a symptom of decadence! What a conception." Twenty years later, Herr Schindler continues, Nietzsche rejected his early allegiance to Hegel. He now felt that "contradiction is the root of all movement and vitality." Our protagonist tells us he has a hard time following the discussion, but Ambler has raised the issue. "A man is an ape in velvet," says a character in *Journey into Fear*, supporting the theory that the murderous orangutan in Poe's "Murders in the Rue Morgue" is the archetype of all subsequent culprits in detective fiction.

Of Ambler's postwar novels, *The Levanter* (1972) has a particular pertinence today. The background to danger here is the Ba'athist coup that took place in Syria in 1963, a revolution that continues to have dire effects on the population of that besieged nation. The villain of the piece is a terrorist from a splinter group that would be considered extreme even by the standards of Hamas. Michael Howell, the book's narrator and hero, is in the Middle East because he is a Levanter by parental origin and because he runs the family business, which includes an agency that operates a fleet of small cargo vessels in the eastern Mediterranean. He has learned to decipher an official news announcement in Damascus; a bombing blamed on "Israeli saboteurs" may be the work of "local Palestinian guerrillas" armed with the Maoist playbook. The strategy of the terrorist narrative depends on rhetoric and control of the means of communication. "The magic labels 'Palestine' and 'Palestinian' could transform the most brutish killer into a gallant young fighter for freedom."

The narrator of *A Coffin for Dimitrios* (1939), Ambler's best book, is Charles Latimer, a mild-mannered author of popular detective novels, and the book functions as a corrective to the sagas of omniscient sleuths. In his journey from Turkey to Paris by way of Athens, Belgrade, and Geneva, Latimer encounters "*real* murder: not neat, tidy book-murder with corpse and clues and suspects and hangman, but murder over which a chief of police shrugged his shoulders, wiped his hands and consigned the stinking victim to the coffin." The 1944 Warner Brothers movie directed by Jean Negulesco under the novel's British title, *The Mask of Dimitrios*, features Peter Lorre as the detective story writer on Dimitrios's trail, Sydney Greenstreet as his unlikely companion, and Zachary Scott as Dimitrios, elusive, cunning, totally unscrupulous, and motivated entirely by self-interest. Mobster Richard Conte's line in Joseph Lewis's 1955 movie *The Big Combo* could be his motto: "First is first, and second is nobody."

Latimer is brought back, after a thirty-year hiatus, only to be killed off in *The Intercom Conspiracy*, Ambler's 1969 thriller. It's as if, in the frigid air of the Cold War, an aging innocent like Latimer may not live to tell the tale of intrigue in which he has got himself embroiled. What's missing from the book is terror; but it makes up for the lack with its ingenious plot. Two clever NATO veterans take over a disreputable right-wing newsletter, use it to leak classified information, and blackmail rival intelligence outfits. It becomes evident that enemy intelligence outfits mirror each other. Each side knows the other's secrets but knows also that "the conventions must be observed and the pretenses maintained, that outsiders may not look in on our foolishness and that both sides have a common enemy—the small boy who saw that the emperor was naked."

The shopworn metaphor is a sign of fatigue, but we forgive the author because the parable is on point and because in resurrecting Charles Latimer, Ambler has outfitted him with a splendid pocket biography, as if he were a heteronym in the manner of the Portuguese poet Fernando Pessoa. Best known for his mystery novels, such as *A Bloody Shovel, Murder's Arms,* and *No Doornail This,* Latimer is a professional historian, the author of books "about the Hanseatic League, about the growth of banking in the seventeenth century and about the Gotha Programme in 1875"—pretty recondite stuff, and even better when you look these things up.[5] And *The Intercom Conspiracy* has this sentence of dialogue, which puts us

---

5. The Gotha Programme was the party platform of a socialist group in Germany that set out to abolish wage labor and eliminate all social and political inequality. Karl Marx hated it. See his *Critique of the Gotha Programme.*

squarely in the world of Eric Ambler: "'Monsieur Carter,' he asked softly, 'has anyone ever tried to kill you?'"

III.

The Cold War caused a revolution in espionage fiction. Ideally, the genre involves a conflict between good and evil, but "Us" and "Them" were easier to conceptualize in a hot war with the Nazis than in a frigid conflict with the Soviets, where a state of peaceful coexistence was conditioned on the threat of mutually assured destruction. The conflict was conducted not out in the open, with troop movements and supply lines, but with threats, strategies, back channels, spies in the guise of diplomats plotting a coup. The battles resembled games of chess that took place in conjecture or in theory.

In some of the most compelling spy novels of the postwar era— Graham Greene's *The Human Factor* (1978), for example, and John le Carré's *The Spy Who Came in from the Cold* (1963), his best book—the deeper drama is that of seduction and betrayal, conflicting duties of love and friendship on one side and of citizenship on the other, as if the genre were perennially working out the moral drama E. M. Forster sketched when he so famously asserted that, if presented with the conflict, he hoped he would have the guts to betray his country rather than his friend.

Le Carré adapted the thriller to a universe that was not only morally ambiguous but metaphysically treacherous as well—where the nature of reality is in doubt and paranoia seems a sane mode of apprehension. No one, including your own spymaster or boss, is reliable. It was still Us and Them, but it had become much harder to tell them apart. In a book such as *Tinker, Tailor, Soldier, Spy* (1974), the relation of the CIA or MI6 to the KGB is a little like the relation of *Time* to *Newsweek* in the heyday of those magazines: there is a certain amount of mutual mimesis between rival organizations, and plenty of distrust between putative allies. In the shadow world that the agents inhabit, individuals are of no importance. Only one thing is certain: betrayal. Only one thing heroic: the refusal to betray. In this light, it is almost a natural career move for the disgruntled employee of the CIA or MI6 to switch sides and work for the KGB, or the other way around.

In Martin Ritt's 1965 film version of *The Spy Who Came in from the Cold*, the squalid life that Richard Burton (as Alec Leamas) leads when he playacts the part of a disaffected ex–British agent in London—the little winter love that he and the librarian played by Claire Bloom find in a dark corner—is pure noir, though Bloom is an unwitting femme fatale and though Burton is not quite a chump in the sense that Robert Mitchum is in *Out of the Past*.

At the conclusion of both the book and the movie, le Carré's hero chooses to die at the Berlin Wall rather than escape, since in escaping he would feel implicated in the sacrifice of his lover. The death of Alec Leamas at the Berlin Wall—the hero whose one heroic deed is to choose to die there—is the supreme moment of Cold War espionage fiction. The book's last sentence achieves a pathos the author would find difficult to equal in his subsequent work: "As he fell, Leamas saw a small car smashed between great lorries, and the children waving cheerfully through the window."

9

The Limits of Logic

TRENT'S LAST CASE
(E. C. BENTLEY)

A key element of the detective novel is its exploration of the idea that crimes—no matter how carefully planned, how artistically executed, with false alibis at the ready, misleading clues, and blind alleys around each corner—can be solved by the application of logic. *Trent's Last Case* (1913) puts this thesis to the test. It initiated what is often called the genre's golden age. The idea was to contrive a seemingly insoluble mystery that could ultimately be solved, and not in just one but in multiple ways.

Edmund Clerihew Bentley, the book's author, wore many hats. In his student days, he was president of the Oxford Union. He was a veteran journalist, a close friend of G. K. Chesterton. He invented a light verse form, which in his honor is called the clerihew. Here's a self-explanatory example from W. H. Auden's *Academic Graffiti*, a triumph of the form: "When Karl Marx / Found the phrase 'financial sharks,' / He sang a Te Deum / In the British Museum."

To Jacques Barzun and Wendell Hertig Taylor, *Trent's Last Case* is an "undoubted classic"; Julian Symons acknowledges it as the "most famous novel" of its time, though he finds the writing "stiff and colorless." True, the prose is pedestrian; and I agree with Barzun and Taylor that the novel has one turn of the screw too many. Nevertheless, the novel is prized for its ingenuity, not its literary excellence. With the complexity of the case, the brilliance brought to bear upon it, and the incongruous clues strewn like souvenirs around the crime, *Trent's Last Case* sets the stage for the most cunning contrivances of Agatha Christie, Dorothy Sayers, John Dickson Carr, Ngaio Marsh, Margery Allingham, Ellery Queen, Michael Innes, Cyril Hare, and the rest of the gang. Sayers called it "the one detective story of the present [twentieth] century" that "will go down as a classic."

Philip Trent, Bentley's well-bred detective, establishes a type. He quotes poetry liberally. "From childhood's hour I've seen my finest hopes decay," he says, quoting the Romantic poet Thomas Moore without attribution. He paints; has old-fashioned ideas about gentlemanly behavior and honor; works as a correspondent at large for a major London newspaper. About the last, Bentley knew more than a thing or two: he was the lead editorial writer for the London *Daily Telegraph* for twenty-two years. Still, it is not *who* the detective is that interests us here but what he does; how he brings logic to bear upon a somewhat outlandish murder that on the surface seems impossible to explain.

The corpse of the unloved Sigsbee Manderson, a financial shark, whose death no one regrets, turns up outside the Manderson mansion. He has been shot. It happened a little past midnight. Witnesses attest to his having been in the house as midnight approached. No one saw him leave the house. No one heard a shot. He is fully dressed, but sloppily, and is missing his dentures, something no one who wears them would leave the house without. The coroner says that Manderson's violent end was the work of a person or persons unknown, which seems correct as far as it goes. But what about the clue of the false teeth? How could he be in his bedroom and among the hedges and gardens outside at the same time?

The means of death are obvious: the gun that was left beside the hand of the corpse.[1] The opportunity is unclear, but this is a problem that Trent can solve. It is the motive that defeats him; there are too many motives, which is what makes Manderson the prototype for the universally despised victim, a staple of the genre. Of the many others in the pattern, I would cite George in Nicholas Blake's *The Beast Must Die* (1938), not only because he is said to have been "a most unmitigated swine all around," but also because his fate illustrates another generic convention introduced in *Trent's Last Case*—the need to eliminate suicide and accident as the cause for death before the charge of murder can be leveled.

From the forensic evidence, the testimony at the inquest, the details at the scene of the crime, and the interviews with suspects and witnesses, Trent's solution to the puzzle of Manderson's violent end is flawless. Yet his hypothesis, we learn in the book's penultimate chapter, is wrong; he had based it on a safe assumption taken on faith that was subject to misinterpretation from the start. A second explanation is offered in the form of a statement—and, in its way, a confession—by the suspect wrongly accused of the deed. And even this turns out to be wrong when Trent learns at the very last that Manderson's demise was the result of neither a murder, as he supposed, nor a suicide, as the revised theory has it, but—why should I give away more than I already have done?

The "false bottom" is one more precedent established in *Trent's Last Case*. In many novels to come we will get a satisfactory

1. As Ed McBain writes in *Like Love*, "The means of murder were always fairly obvious, and [McBain's hero, Steve Carella] couldn't imagine why anyone outside of a motion-picture cop confronted with exotic and esoteric cases involving rare impossible-to-trace poisons got from pygmy tribes would be overly concerned with what killed a person; usually, you found a guy with a bullet hole in the middle of his forehead, and you figured what killed him was a gun."

solution in the penultimate chapter, only to have it exploded at the end. The knowledge that pure logic can fail, because more than one set of facts can fit the same pattern, serves Trent as a reproof and accounts for the title of the book. The chastened sleuth swears off the crime-solving habit. He declares that this shall be his "last case. His high-blown pride at length breaks under him."

10

Dashiell Hammett's Priceless Patter

The *Jeopardy* category is Opening Lines, and the literary answer is "Two Bars, Fifty-second Street." You need to ask what works begin in such venues. One comes to mind quickly enough: W. H. Auden's "September 1, 1939."

Written on the grim Friday when Nazi Germany invaded Poland and World War II began, Auden's poem finds the poet sitting at "one of the dives / On Fifty-second Street" as a "low dishonest" decade reaches its foul culmination. In its heyday, Fifty-second was "the street that never sleeps." Signs today identify it as "Swing Street" because it once boasted a plethora of jazz clubs including Jimmy Ryan's, the Three Deuces, and Kelly's Stables, where Coleman Hawkins played his tenor sax. The 21 Club was also located on Fifty-second Street, and the original Birdland, which came along in 1949, was right around the corner on Broadway. On September 1, 1939, Auden wrote his poem at the Dizzy Club, a gay bar at 62 West Fifty-second, in a space recently occupied by a Beefsteak Charlie's.

The other important literary work emanating from the spirit of Fifty-second Street in that decade is Dashiell Hammett's *The Thin Man*. Published in 1934 but written when Prohibition was still the law of the land, the novel opens with its reluctant detective hero,

Nick Charles, "leaning against the bar in a speakeasy on Fifty-second Street," waiting for his wife to finish her Christmas shopping so she can join him for cocktails and wisecracks. *The Thin Man* is the last and, in some ways, the least characteristic of Hammett's five novels, but its charm endures, and readers unfamiliar with this pioneer of the American hard-boiled tradition may well want to start here, if only because of the air of compulsive intoxication and gallows humor that pervades the writing and gives it a glow of romance not ordinarily found in the genre.

Although in tone the two works could not be more different, *The Thin Man* illustrates a prime assertion Auden makes. The decade was "low [and] dishonest" not only because, on the macro level, would-be statesmen convinced themselves that appeasement of an intransigent and ruthless foe was a wise policy, but also because Prohibition effected a structural dishonesty in urban American life. Until Prohibition was repealed on December 5, 1933, anyone having a drink was breaking the law, and people continued to drink, and to do so with gusto, to such an extent that violating the Eighteenth Amendment became a badge of honor. The excessive drinking in *The Thin Man*, a book in a genre resting on principles of justice, is thus a sign of a certain desperation and ennui as well as a winking dishonesty in law enforcement.

The Thin Man features the husband-and-wife team of Nick and Nora Charles and their schnauzer, Asta (a fox terrier in the 1934 movie in which suave William Powell is Nick and Myrna Loy is his irresistible mate). The Charleses have come to New York from San Francisco for the holidays. Nick left the detective business when his wife came into a comfortable inheritance six years earlier, and he would much rather drink another scotch and soda, wake up hung over, and pour himself a fresh one to "cut the phlegm" than engage in any shenanigans with shysters and gonifs. But when an eccentric inventor disappears and the missing man's secretary is murdered, Nick gets involved; he knows the people. And after as many cocktails as clues, Nick fingers the killer in the next-to-last chapter, in which, in classic fashion, all the suspects assemble for the final revelation and showdown around a dinner table.

The thin man of the title refers not to Nick Charles but to a character who isn't there, a character "as thin as the paper" that bears his name on checks, letters, and telegrams. When the killer is unmasked, Nick—who has only recently taken a bullet for his troubles—anticipates what will happen next. In an exquisite example of Hammett's action prose (as I think of it), he tells us: "I slammed [the killer's] chin with my left fist. The punch was all right, it landed solidly and dropped him, but I felt a burning sensation on my left side and knew I had torn the bullet-wound open. 'What do you want me to do?' I growled at Guild [the police lieutenant on the case]. 'Put him in Cellophane for you?'"

What you take away from both the book and the movie is not the sleuthing but the chemistry between Nick and Nora, the latter said to have been inspired by Lillian Hellman, with whom Hammett conducted a three-decades-long love affair. (The book is dedicated to her.) The couple guzzle copious amounts of booze, and while it may be too early for breakfast, it is never too early to get, as they used to say, "tight." In a dangerous spot, Nick slugs Nora to remove her from the line of fire, which is pretty crafty of him, but when she comes to, five minutes later, she glares at him. "You damned fool," she says, "you didn't have to knock me cold. I knew you'd take him, but I wanted to see it." One of the cops on hand all but whistles in admiration. "There's a woman with hair on her chest."

Born in Maryland in 1894, raised in Baltimore and Philadelphia, Samuel Dashiell Hammett is credited with having taken "murder out of the Venetian vase and dropped it in the alley." The words are

Raymond Chandler's, from his essay "The Simple Art of Murder" (1944), which is the closest thing to a manifesto for the American hard-boiled model. Chandler's argument is cogent and rhetorically devastating. Prior to Hammett's stories in *Black Mask*—the ones with the so-called Continental Op as their hero—the genteel detective story reigned supreme, and it was primarily a matter of artifice in the service of ingenuity. Chandler's lampooning of the genre never leaves you, even if you refuse to give up your Ngaio Marsh or Josephine Tey. Until Hammett (Chandler wrote), "it is the same careful grouping of suspects, the same utterly incomprehensible trick of how somebody stabbed Mrs. Pottington Postlethwaite III with the solid platinum poignard just as she flatted on the top note of the Bell Song from *Lakmé* in the presence of fifteen ill-assorted guests."

Hammett is Chandler's exemplar because he "gave murder back to the kind of people that commit it for reasons, not just to provide a corpse." After serving as a sergeant in the First World War, Hammett held a variety of jobs before becoming a detective for the Pinkerton Agency. During the war, he fell victim to influenza and for the rest of his life suffered from serious illnesses of the lungs. At forty-eight, he talked his way into serving as a sergeant in the Second World War. By then, he had completed or abandoned the literary career he embarked on in the 1920s, when the knowledge that he could die at any time prompted him to set up shop as a writer. The otherwise unnamed Continental Op is a short, stocky middle-aged man who works for an unglamorous detective agency in San Francisco. He is a professional and a stoic, doing his job.

Hammett doesn't waste words and doesn't editorialize, and his simple declarative sentences have a lot in common with Hemingway's. Hammett can slam a story shut as (to draw imagery from abstract expressionist painters) a Barnett Newman shuts the door after an Ad Reinhardt black-on-black turns off the lights in the room where Mark Rothko has pulled down the shades. "The Big Knockover" (1927) ends in exhilaration—"What a life!"—and "The Gutting of Couffignal" (1925) concludes with the Op's having to shoot a woman: "'You ought to have known I'd do it!' My voice sounded harsh and savage and like a stranger's in my ears. 'Didn't I steal a crutch from a cripple?'"

Another story ("The Farewell Murder," 1930) concludes with an extended conversation between the Op and the killer, who does most of the talking. The story ends as simply as such a story can: "They hanged him."

IF A STRENGTH of the classic detective story as practiced by Agatha Christie and Nicholas Blake is the cleverness of the detective in bypassing the blind alleys to arrive at the true if often outlandishly improbable solution, in Hammett quite a different pleasure awaits the reader—that of his depiction of a criminal milieu. The tone is established in the opening paragraph of his 1929 novel *Red Harvest*:

> I first heard Personville called Poisonville by a red-haired mucker named Hickey Dewey in the Big Ship in Butte. He also called his shirt a shoit. I didn't think anything of what he had done to the city's name. Later I heard men who could manage their r's give it the same pronunciation. I still didn't see anything in it but the meaningless sort of humor that used to make richardsnary the thieves' word for dictionary. A few years later I went to Personville and learned better.

Julian Symons, the distinguished British crime novelist and historian of the genre, believed *The Glass Key* (1931) to be the best of Hammett's novels. I respectfully disagree, though Hammett himself had a special fondness for this "record of a man's devotion to a friend" (Chandler's phrase). *The Dain Curse* (1929) may be the least consequential of the five novels, but it does propose an analogy between the detective (who describes himself as "a middle-aged fat man") and his novelist friend. Consider this snatch of dialogue, in which the novelist ("he") is the first speaker:

> "Are you—who make your living snooping—sneering at my curiosity about people and my attempts to satisfy it?"
> "We're different," I said. "I do mine with the object of putting people in jail, and I get paid for it, though not as much as I should."
> "That's not different," he said. "I do mine with the object of putting people in books, and I get paid for it, though not as much as I should."

I would venture the opinion, without needing to issue a spoiler alert, that *The Dain Curse* works out the exact degree of generic resemblance, and ultimate difference, between detective and novelist.

The sociologically inclined may advocate *Red Harvest* as Hammett's novel of choice, perhaps because the city, whether pronounced "Personville" or "Poisonville" in the beloved Brooklyn manner, is a vision straight out of Thomas Hobbes's *Leviathan*. It is like a fleshed-out footnote to the Hobbesian notion that man, if his impulses are left unchecked, will lead the life of anarchy, each out for himself, with chaos and bloodshed for all. Although Hammett, in 1937, may have joined the Communist Party USA (he became a leftist hero when, in the 1950s, he refused to name names and had to serve five punishing months in jail), his point of view may be said to be not Marxist but Hobbesian, as Columbia professor Steven Marcus writes in an influential essay: "It is a world of universal warfare, the war of each against all, and of all against all."

The Thin Man may take place in New York, *The Maltese Falcon* (1930) and *The Dain Curse* in San Francisco, but Poisonville is the default landscape of Hammett's imagination, a place lacking the central superego that Freud considered vital to civilization. Very few of Hammett's characters do the right thing except when it coincides with their own self-interest. Many more are as aloof from the concepts of right and wrong as from those of good and evil.

READING CHANDLER'S "THE Simple Art of Murder," you get the idea that Hammett's superiority to, say, Margery Allingham has to do with the latter's gentility and the former's true grit. Hammett's prose has a terse eloquence, and a bite. In *The Maltese Falcon*, which is Hammett at his best, each wisecrack adds its touch to the portrait of detective Sam Spade, the book's hero. Spade is a loner by instinct, though when the book begins, he is part of the firm of Spade & Archer. When his partner is killed, Spade spends no time grieving. In the aftermath of the shooting, one of the first things he does—besides fending off the advances of Miles Archer's widow—is to order his secretary to have the front door repainted with his erstwhile partner's name removed.

No sentimentalist, Spade can, as the situation requires, disarm a gunman, turn the tables on a burglar, endure a Mickey Finn, talk his way out of a sticky situation, and feign a temper tantrum to get what he wants. When a character says accusingly that Spade has a smooth explanation for everything, the latter replies: "What do you want me to do? Learn to stutter?" This is more than a witty comeback; it conveys something essential about the character of a detective in the kind of world Hammett depicts. Your confidence is half of what you bring to any case. Spade conveys his attitude in little asides throughout the book. When a cab driver remarks sympathetically that a detective's way of earning a living is "a tough racket," Spade replies, "Well, hack-drivers don't live forever."

"Maybe that's right," the cabbie says, "but, just the same, it'll always be a surprise to me if I don't." This remarkable exposition of a trait of human nature shuts Spade up for the rest of the ride.

Like Hammett's novel, John Huston's 1941 movie of *The Maltese Falcon* is a fast-paced, quick-talking excursion into a criminal milieu of heartless cold-bloodedness on the one hand and of a certain delightful eccentricity on the other. Gutman the "Fat Man" (Sydney Greenstreet); Joel Cairo, stinking of cologne (Peter Lorre); Brigid O'Shaughnessy, ruthless but skillful at putting on a helpless act (Mary Astor); and Wilmer the undersized gunsel seething in frustration (Elisha Cook Jr.): not one is easily forgotten. All are in pursuit of a priceless bauble—the "dingus," Spade calls it—with a fabulous history. It is the statue of a falcon, painted jet-black, the paint concealing the jewels that make the object worth millions.

The main characters are no more plausible than the dramatis personae of your standard mystery, in which we meet such types as the retired army colonel and his shrewish wife, the rich widow with the timid paid companion, the starlet who has a secret, the surgeon with a résumé of indiscretions, a couple of loud American tourists, and the beautiful, self-centered newlywed who has antagonized all the others, including her husband. The difference is one of style, and to some extent of nationality. In their setting, their language, and their emphasis on action rather than cogitation, Hammett's murder mysteries are American with a vengeance, not least in their ability to convey the illusion of the real in dialogue and descriptive prose that is as vigorous and unliterary as the native vernacular at its most vivid.

FOR THE SAKE of possessing the bejeweled bird, four men die during the course of *The Maltese Falcon*, all but one of them offstage. The elusive bird has most recently traveled from Hong Kong to

San Francisco on a steamship, *La Paloma*, whose captain delivers it to Spade. It is the last thing Captain Jacobi (played by the director's father, Walter Huston) gets to do.

When the cast reassembles to examine the prize, the statue turns out to be a fake. There are no jewels beneath the skin. The black bird in Spade's apartment is a mere replica. The disappointment is immediate (Cairo to Gutman: "You imbecile! You bloated idiot!") but short-lived. Gutman, the Fat Man, does the math. He has spent seventeen years looking for the Maltese falcon. If he must now go to Istanbul and spend an extra twelve months on the quest, that would add only "five and fifteen-seventeenths per cent." "I go with you!" Cairo enthusiastically chimes in.

For the sake of the falcon, Gutman is also willing to provide a fall guy to take the rap for a murder. He sacrifices his own body-guard to the cause. In another priceless piece of patter, he addresses Wilmer: "I want you to know that I couldn't be any fonder of you if you were my own son; but—well, by Gad!—if you lose a son it's possible to get another—and there's only one Maltese falcon."

CASUAL VIEWERS MAY be excused for not detecting the salient differences between Sam Spade in *The Maltese Falcon* and Philip Marlowe in *The Big Sleep*, both of them portrayed by Humphrey Bogart. Sam Spade is the more ambiguous figure. In the first paragraph of *The Maltese Falcon*, we learn that Spade "looked rather pleasantly like a blond satan," the *rather pleasantly* softening the image of a satanic hero. Sam dares the world to surprise him. At the end of the chapter, Spade's partner leaves the office to do what Brigid O'Shaughnessy, alias Miss Wonderly, has hired the firm to do. Spade: "What do you think of her?" Archer: "Sweet!" and "Maybe you saw her first, Sam, but I spoke first," in response to which Spade "grinned wolfishly, showing the edges of teeth far back in his jaw," before rolling a cigarette. "You've got brains, yes you have," he says. It is as if part of him would not be surprised if he were seeing Miles Archer alive for the last time. And sure enough, the phone call that wakes him in the middle of the night is not good news.

Unlike Marlowe, "a shop-soiled Galahad" (Chandler's phrase) who keeps his hands off his female clients unless she is played by Lauren Bacall, Sam in *The Maltese Falcon* takes up Miss Wonderly's blatant offer: "Can I buy you with my body?" He thoroughly enjoys his physical and sexual dominance. I use the phrase advisedly, because Sam's handling of Brigid can be seen most accurately, I think, within the context of domination and submission, in which sexual activity involves an exchange of power. When searching for a missing thousand-dollar bill, for example, Sam orders Brigid to strip in the bathroom, keeping the door half shut, so only he can see her naked, while the three other sinister characters—the Fat Man, Joel Cairo, and the gunsel Wilmer—sit and grumble in the living room.

In a book full of reversals and revelations, the ultimate one occurs when Sam and Brigid are alone, their former companions having fled from the apartment. Now, finally, Sam confronts Brigid with Miles Archer's murder—the one formal problem in the novel, as Chandler points out. Back in chapter two, Hammett gives us the only clue we really need when police detective Tom Polhaus shows Spade the corpse of his partner. "His gun was tucked away on his hip," Tom says. "It hadn't been fired. His overcoat was buttoned. There's a hundred and sixty-some bucks in his clothes." Spade's opinion of Archer is unflattering—"He was as dumb as any man ought to be"—and yet in pursuit of a gunman he would not have entered a dark alley with his gun holstered and his overcoat buttoned. "But he'd've gone up there with you, angel, if he was sure nobody else was up there." Brigid, appealing to her sexual bond with Sam, tries desperately to talk her way out of the accusation. In vain. "I'm going to send you over," he says. "If they hang you I'll always remember you."

SAM COOLLY SAYS to Brigid: "I'm not going to play the sap for you." The phrase resonates in both book and movie, not merely because *sap* alliterates with the detective's name but because the worst thing a sapient being can be in this moral universe is a sap. (Earlier, when Spade tries to sell police lieutenant Dundy on a cock-and-bull story he has devised, he uses the word for its rhetorical force: "Don't be a sap, Dundy.") Sam isn't a sap. No, he is "a character" (as Gutman says), "wild and unpredictable" (as Brigid says). That he is unpredictable is undeniable, and if his actions confuse, it is deliberate. Barbara Deming, in her 1969 book *Running Away from Myself: A Dream Portrait of America Drawn from the Films of the Forties*, articulates the problem:

> Why does he entangle himself with this woman to begin with? The moment they meet, he knows her for what she is; he doesn't exactly believe her story. "This is hopeless," he says—then makes the case. "Loyalty is a good word from you!" he mocks—and then walks into her embrace. This is the sequence of things. And then finally, "I won't play the sap for you," he says, "because all of me wants to," and he painfully disentangles himself from her arms. A curious sequence.

Well, yes and no. Film noir depends on the male capacity for being a sap and for generating sap, the one activity leading to the other. Spade, no sap, gets paid—not exorbitantly—in cash. ("We didn't exactly believe your story," he says. "We believed your two hundred dollars.") You may suppose he gets his rewards in romance, sex, and adventure, but it is easy to overestimate the glamour of living in jeopardy. Aside from her sexual favors, Brigid, too, can be described, in the most complimentary sense, as "a character." "I am a liar," she blurts out at one point, with the hush of melodrama that Mary Astor provides. "I have always been a liar." Why, to echo Deming's question, does Sam "entangle himself with this woman to begin with?" Because, for one thing, the private eye can't choose among clients. Because all clients are fundamentally as risky and unreliable and false, though not all are as attractive or as sexually available as Brigid. Because she does have something to offer him, something that begins but does not end with her body. And because the detective's best line of defense in this universe is to be "wild and unpredictable"—to get what you can, enjoy it, but choose wisely at the life-or-death moment.

EACH OF THE "three women" in the chapter of that title is, in her own way, in love with Sam Spade. And each is kept at bay. Brigid O'Shaughnessy is the femme fatale—to associate with her is to court death and disaster—and the main drama centers on Spade's relationship with her. But Effie Perine—Spade's gal Friday, resourceful and smart—is not to be overlooked. Spade mostly calls her "angel," but once he salutes her with "You're a damned good man, sister." The third of the three women is Iva Archer, Miles's widow, who is depicted as one half of a bad marriage. She calls on Sam, asking him whether he shot Miles and hoping the answer is yes. "That louse wants to marry you, Sam," Effie says "bitterly," which tells us all we need to know about Iva, and quite a lot about Effie. But equally telling is Effie's reaction to Spade's decision to turn in his murderous client. "She did kill Miles, angel," Sam tells Effie, snapping a finger to show just how casual a killer Brigid is. Effie recoils from Sam: "I know—I know you're right," she says. "You're right. But don't touch me now—not now." She says it "brokenly," like a child disturbed by an unhappy ending and by the renewed proof that Spade may be good at what he does but is neither a gentleman nor a saint.

What we have in Sam Spade, then, is our old friend the romantic rebel, jaded in the Byronic manner, who views human nature as something incorrigible and whose mask of defense manifests itself in his "wild and unpredictable" behavior and in his self-reliance and competence. Not an ascetic, not self-righteous, he enjoys the company of women but refuses to sentimentalize them. In the end he adheres to a code, albeit a pragmatic one. He is a detective and must identify the culprit, whether it's a he or a she, a beautiful temptress like Brigid or a dandified Levantine like Joel Cairo. As he explains to Brigid in a moment of rare earnestness: "When one of your organization gets killed it's bad business to let the killer get away with it. It's bad all around—bad for that one organization, bad for every detective everywhere."

Spade's quips and retorts are there not just for the sake of crackling dialogue but to develop the complexity of Hammett's "blond satan" and to tell us the terms on which he is determined to meet an unreasonable world. There is a reason why Sam Spade—especially when portrayed by Bogart—appeals to us as a model, a rhetorical model or a model for the wounded hero who is down on human nature, given to understatement, and nevertheless capable of making the unexpected lofty gesture, sometimes a sacrifice, sometimes a dare.

11

Paperclip (Raymond Chandler)

When you are given 250 words to review a book, a knockout quote may be your best option. This ran in the New York Times Book Review, *May 20, 2001.*

"It doesn't matter a damn what a novel is about," Raymond Chandler wrote in a letter to an editor at the *Atlantic Monthly*. "The only fiction of any moment in any age is that which does magic with words." Chandler, the premier practitioner of the American hard-boiled detective novel, elevated the wisecrack into a rhetorical figure somewhere between sarcasm and simile. For the Chandler fan, *The Raymond Chandler Papers*, edited by his biographers Tom Hiney and Frank MacShane, is a treasure trove. Chandler was an opinionated man capable of aphoristic pith: "The detective story is a tragedy with a happy ending"; "The cult of failure is embedded in all highbrow aesthetics."

Then there is Chandler's eloquent "theory" of detective fiction. What readers are looking for without realizing it, he wrote, is

> not for example that a man got killed, but that in the moment of death he was trying to pick a paper clip up off the polished surface of a desk, and it kept slipping away from him, so that there was a look of strain on his face and his mouth was half opened in a

kind of tormented grin, and the last thing in the world he thought
about was death. He didn't even hear death knock on the door.
That damn paper clip kept slipping away from his fingers and he
just wouldn't push it to the edge of the desk and catch it as it fell.

12

"Grim Grin" (Graham Greene)

*Young British novelists came up with "Grim Grin" as a nickname
for Graham Greene by approximating how a Frenchman would
pronounce the novelist's name. In "The Escape Artist," written
shortly after Greene's death in 1991, a phrase is lifted from* The
End of the Affair, *and there is a reference to Greene's experi-
ments with Russian roulette as a young man.*

1. The Human Factor

The gambler knows nothing's
more addictive than deception
with the chance that the betrayed one,
the spouse or the State, is pretending
or consenting to be deceived
for motives of vanity and greed
not different from his own,
leaving him with a choice to make
between his mistress and his self-respect—
which may be why the ideal reader
of Graham Greene's novels went
to a parochial school, was married
and divorced, has lived abroad
in Europe or Asia, plays in a weekly
small-stakes poker game, works
for a newspaper, lies to make a living.

2. The Escape Artist

A dark green room: the experiment fails,
And the leaves change color before their time.
He felt, though he had not committed a crime,
Like a gangster disguised in a top hat and tails,

Entering the lady's East Village apartment
To seduce her. If he should arrive out of breath,
It's because he knows he has a date with death,
Though that's not what the church fathers meant.

She called him a romantic fool, but she didn't mean
To make him feel bad. She just wanted to love him
In the attic, where the lights had grown dim.
Yet the darkness was green, however drab the scene,

Where danger took him by the hand, and the heroine
In his arms was someone he had met before,
In a novel about a murderer and a whore,
And didn't expect to meet again

In the seedy familiar hotel room with the bullets flying
All around them. They were busy dying,
But the imaginary spies of childhood were still spying
On them, the sinful and tormented ones,

Hungry for ordinary corrupt human love, and bound
To turn up wherever a lively crisis could be found:
A lost breed, the sort of chap who knew all about guns,
Having used them for Russian roulette, and won.

13

Rex Stout

THE EMPEROR OF
COURONNE DE CANARD

When, on the road, jazz singer Lena Horne got homesick for New York, she would turn to Nero Wolfe, she says in the preface to a paperback edition of Stout's 1958 mystery *Champagne for One*. I share her enthusiasm. We read a Nero Wolfe mystery not for the plot or puzzle but for the richness of the two leading characters and the evocation of New York City as the capital of glamour—the place we miss.

Rex Stout's singular achievement was to refresh and refashion the partnership of mastermind sleuth and good-hearted narrator. He adapted the model of Sherlock Holmes and Dr. Watson from late Victorian England to metropolitan Manhattan, circa 1935–1965. The cogitation is done by the obese, beer-drinking, orchid-loving detective with the imperial name who doesn't budge from his West Thirty-fifth Street brownstone; his right-hand man-about-town Archie Goodwin does the work on the ground and tells the tale.

Consider the duality. In *Too Many Women*, page one, Archie introduces himself as "the heart, liver, lungs, and gizzard of the private detective business of Nero Wolfe, Wolfe being merely the brains." Archie is good-natured; Wolfe, curmudgeonly. Archie likes the ladies; Wolfe can't abide them. Archie gets paid a weekly salary plus room, board, and a modest expense account; Wolfe is as wealthy and eccentric as a decadent Parisian aristocrat in 1890. Archie likes tooling around in his car; Wolfe stays put.

Archie has a lively narrative style. A client enters the brownstone, and Archie sizes him up this way: "He wasn't too old to remember what his wife had given him for his fortieth birthday, but neither was he young enough to be still looking forward to it." In the same story, Wolfe and Goodwin are having one of their quarrels about whether to take on a case. Wolfe is reluctant as usual, but after his "regulation two hours in the plant-rooms," he interrupts Archie, who has been typing up his notes. Wolfe asks, "Did you take that man's money?" Archie replies: "What do you think? If I say I took it you'll claim your attitude as you left plainly indicated that he had insulted you and you wouldn't play. If I say I refused it you'll claim I've done you out of a fee. Which do you prefer?" Archie has landed a blow. Wolfe says only: "Do your typing. I like to hear you typing. If you are typing you can't talk."[1]

Wolfe always out-duels long-suffering, cigar-smoking police inspector Cramer, whose patience is nearly always near an end. In *The Red Box* (1937), "Inspector Cramer got us [on the phone], and reported that his army was making uniform progress on all fronts: namely, none." When a fed-up Cramer tells him to "go to hell," Goodwin says, "I didn't let the elevator take me that far, but got off at the main floor." In *And Be a Villain* (1948), Archie is in the deputy commissioner's office, and Wolfe, on the phone, tells him what to say. "Mr. O'Hara is a nincompoop. Tell him I said so," Wolfe instructs. Archie looks at O'Hara and says, "He said to tell you that he says you're a nincompoop, but I think it would be more tactful

---

1. From "Instead of Evidence" in Stout's *Trouble in Triplicate* (1946).

not to mention it, so I won't." In a dramatic monologue in his office, Wolfe invariably announces the mystery's solution to a captive audience of suspects, clients, Inspector Cramer, and Goodwin.

It is tempting to imagine that Rex Stout invented the imperious heavyweight Nero Wolfe by extrapolating from his own name. Wolfe's girth and irascible temperament distinguish him from other fat detectives. In *Too Many Women* (1947), he weighs in at 340 pounds. In *The Rubber Band* (1936), Archie reveals that his boss lately acknowledged "that he weighed too much—which was about the same as if the Atlantic Ocean formed the opinion that it was too wet." In part because of his great bulk, Wolfe refuses to leave his premises and does so only when beckoned by the temptations that no gastronome can easily decline. "I am not immovable, but my flesh has a constitutional reluctance to sudden, violent or sustained displacement," he informs a client in *The Red Box*. He is nothing if not bossy, and I like to imagine Charles Laughton in the role: "'You undertake to stampede me into a frantic dash through the maelstrom of the city's traffic—in a taxicab! Sir, I would not enter a taxicab for a chance to solve the Sphinx's deepest riddle with all the Nile's cargo as my reward!' He sank his voice to an outraged murmur. 'Good God. A taxicab.'"

Wolfe solves murders not out of the goodness of his heart but because a little exercise is good for the brain and because the manner in which he is accustomed to live obliges him to take on clients. He has a live-in chef (Fritz Brenner), a live-in horticulturist (Theodore Horstmann), thousands of prize orchids on his roof, and a typical menu featuring broiled squabs for tidbits and a main course consisting of thin slices of tender lamb marinated for several hours in red wine and thyme, mace, peppercorns, and garlic. (He also relishes deviled grilled lamb kidneys with a sauce he and Fritz have concocted. On griddle cakes he prefers wild thyme honey from Greece.)

Wolfe doesn't bother to hide his nature: "If I offer anything for sale in this office that is worth buying, it certainly is not a warm heart and maudlin sympathy for the distress of spoiled obtuse children."

The state of the relationship between the two men is faithfully summarized in many of the books. Archie describes his duties in *Too Many Cooks* (1938): "I wasn't under contract as a valet—being merely secretary, bodyguard, office manager, assistant detective, and goat." Though, like every couple, they squabble a lot, Wolfe trusts Archie implicitly, and even praises him occasionally. Archie's "discretion is the twin of his valor," Wolfe says in *The Red Box*. There are, Archie tells us in *Too Many Women*, "coolnesses" between the two men ("about four a week, say, a couple of hundred a year"). Between the events described in that book and those in *If Death Ever Slept* (1957), Wolfe has lost sixty-five pounds:

> He owned the house and everything in it except the furniture in my bedroom. He was the boss and paid my salary. He weighed nearly a hundred pounds more than my 178. . . . We were both licensed private detectives, but he was a genius and I was merely an operative. He, with or without Fritz to help, could turn out a dish of *Couronne de Canard du Riz à la Normande* without batting an eye; I had to concentrate to poach an egg. He had ten thousand orchids in his plant rooms on the roof; I had one African violent on my windowsill, and it wasn't feeling well.

The culinary metaphor in *A Right to Die* (1964) is apt: "Wolfe is the cook; I only wait on table."

While Wolfe is as impossible in his behavior as some of the puzzles he solves, I cannot dislike the man who, in the opening chapter of *Gambit* (1962), tears out pages from *Webster's Third* and burns them in his fireplace. Everyone's favorite is dashing, self-deprecating Archie hoofing it to Fifth Avenue in the Eighties in *Champagne for One* or to Sullivan Street in the first book in the series, *Fer-de-Lance* (1934). He has a roguish charm and sharp intelligence you don't find in Dr. Watson, and he is a ladies' man, forever singing the praises of one pretty woman or another, managing nevertheless to remain single. "You are headstrong and I am magisterial," Wolfe tells Archie in *Champagne.* "Our tolerance of each other is a constantly recurring miracle."

Rex Stout is particularly inventive in the way he opens his Nero Wolfe novels. *And Be a Villain* begins with Archie filling out tax forms in sentence one and Wolfe reading the poems of Mark Van Doren in sentence two. *Before Midnight* (1956) opens with the partners discussing an ad campaign for a perfume called Pour Amour. The manufacturer is running a weekly contest requiring entrants to identify "a woman recorded in non-fictional history in all its forms, including biography, as having used cosmetics." The clues are in the form of rhymed quatrains. Number one is easy. "Though Caesar fought to give me power / And I had Antony in my grasp, / My bosom, in the fatal hour, / Welcomed the fatal asp." Archie nails it. But only Nero Wolfe would know whose "eldest son became a peer, / Although I couldn't write my name; / As Mr. Brown's son's fondest dear / I earned enduring fame."[2]

Of Stout's seventy-two Nero Wolfe novels, Jacques Barzun and Wendell Hertig Taylor prefer *Too Many Cooks.* I vote for *And Be a Villain.* But you can't go wrong with *Too Many Women, The Silent Speaker* (1946), or *The Second Confession* (1949) if the place you'd like to escape to is New York in the late 1940s, to my mind Stout's best period. And though, as Barzun and Taylor (in *A Catalog of Crime,* 1971) note, "the plot is transparent and the detection is

2. Number one is Cleopatra. The illiterate woman of enduring fame is Nell Gwynn, the English actress.

fairly simple" in *The Doorbell Rang* (1965), it has a special place in my heart for a quartet of reasons. One: a vital clue is a young woman's appropriation (and revision) of some lines in Keats's "Ode to a Grecian Urn." Two: I read the novel, my first experience of Nero Wolfe, in 1972, the year of Watergate, and the book's plot has much to do with illegal wiretaps and abuses of power in high places. A third reason is that I bought the book at the original Murder Ink bookstore on New York's Upper West Side; Dilys Winn, the owner, recommended it to me. A fourth reason is that one suspect's alibi is that she was attending a lecture at the New School on Twelfth Street at the time of the murder. I taught literature and writing in that same building for twenty-two years but cannot corroborate her story.

14

Ida Lupino

THE FIRST LADY OF NOIR

At a time when female directors were few, Ida Lupino directed several important taboo-busting films. *The Bigamist* (1953), which she directed and acted in, for example, is among the most unconventional of all movies that connoisseurs tag as noirs. In a typical crime drama, adulterous lovers kill the spouse who stands in their way, as in Billy Wilder's *Double Indemnity* and Henri-Georges Clouzot's *Diabolique* (1955), titles I juxtapose to illustrate how much variation there can be in the basic formula.

No one gets beaten up or shot in *The Bigamist*. No one robs a bank or steals a payroll, and the culprit's downfall is signaled by nothing more violent than a baby's sudden cry from out of the dark. Yet it qualifies as a noir, this smoky black-and-white study in human failure, thwarted desire, and quiet desperation. When you add that *The Bigamist* is implicitly critical of the conventional moral standards governing romantic triangles, you get a sense of what distinguishes Ida Lupino's films and why I have dubbed her "the First Lady of noir."

Born in London in 1918, Lupino contracted polio at age sixteen, combated it, and overcame it. A theme in her work is that self-pity sabotages the will and must be warded off—as by the blind woman she portrays in *On Dangerous Ground* (1951), who is vulnerable but brave, and able to touch and redeem Robert Ryan, a cop so consumed with rage he is like "a gangster with a badge." Lupino took over the direction (uncredited) of *On Dangerous Ground* when the movie's original director, Nicholas Ray, suffered a nervous breakdown.

In effect Lupino acted in movies to subsidize her real career aspiration: to direct them. Two of the films she directed address the subject of female independence. The protagonist in *Not Wanted* (1949) is an unwed mother. In *Never Fear* (1950), it is a ballerina afflicted with polio. A "message movie" of the kind that was popular in the late 1940s (*The Snake Pit*, *Home of the Brave*, *Gentleman's Agreement*), *Never Fear* argues that a conscious act of will is needed to surmount the affliction. Psyche must assist soma. All the therapy in the world will do little good unless the polio patient overcomes the defeatism to which all patients are prone.

Never Fear features a terrific square dance with wheelchairs. I also love the fact that when Carol (Sally Forrest) is diagnosed, the upbeat doctor offers her a cigarette in her hospital bed. She says no. He lights up. He assures her that she will walk again but first must endure physical therapy and "muscle reeducation." Before he leaves the room, the doctor gives her the pack of cigarettes. "You may want one later," he says. Later, Carol evolves from being "a cripple" ("That's what's wrong with me") to "feeling ashamed of myself for being so full of self-pity."

In *The Bigamist*, the man with two wives is far from odious. Lupino and her screenwriter wrote to understand, not to denounce. Harry (Edmond O'Brien) is simply weak though well meaning, and the sympathetic portrayal of his plight is in its way as radical as Preston Sturges's hilarious *The Miracle of Morgan's Creek* (1943), the story of Trudy, a woman who is impregnated when drunk by a soldier on his last night before reporting for duty.

She doesn't even know his name. Far from being punished, Trudy is blessed with a devoted husband and with sextuplets who make the nurses jump for joy, grab headlines, demoralize Mussolini, and cause Hitler to throw a tantrum. But *The Miracle of Morgan's Creek* is a comedy made for a wartime Christmas. There are no laughs in *The Bigamist*. There is only grim disappointment.

Neither of the wives—Eve, the ambitious blonde business-woman in San Francisco (Joan Fontaine), and Phyllis, the melancholy brunette waiting tables in a Chinese restaurant in Los Angeles (Lupino)—is the movie's protagonist. The spotlight is squarely on Harry, the traveling salesman caught between them. Technically he is a cad, but he is too nervous, and too much at cross-purposes with himself, to resemble the stereotypical two-timer. If we can trust Harry's narration, and the film expects us to do so, he loves both his wives—although the love that connects him to Eve, his first wife, is a complicated mix of pity, sympathy, debt, co-dependence, and emotional blackmail.

The ads for beer advise us to "drink responsibly." It is impossible for the bigamist to love responsibly.

Eve, the less likeable wife, has a professional career that she enjoys and is good at. Despite dropped hints, she is blissfully unaware of what her husband may be doing on his regular jaunts to Los Angeles. Is it a coincidence that she, the career woman, is unable to conceive and yet desperately wants a child?

Phyllis, of frail constitution and limited means, has a sense of humor and a quality of warmth that the ever-cheerful Eve lacks. Phyllis doesn't complain about Harry's other life. When she and he meet for the first time, it is as strangers taking a bus tour of Hollywood. After he lights her cigarette—so often the initiating gesture for a romance—she lets him pick her up, because what she sees in him are loneliness and need, not lust.

Harry accepts his fatherhood of Phyllis's baby. At the same time, when Eve suggests that she and he adopt a child, he agrees. Does he realize the jeopardy that the adoption process will put him in? Does he want to be caught?

Caught he is by the adoption agency's Mr. Jordan (Edmund Gwenn, who played Santa Claus to great applause in *Miracle on 34th Street* and whose Hollywood home is pointed out by the tour bus driver in *The Bigamist*). The jig is up when the benign but increasingly suspicious Mr. Jordan, completing his background check of the prospective parent, visits the Los Angeles house where Harry and Phyllis make their home and hears their baby crying. The movie ends in a courtroom scene. Harry is guilty as charged, the crowd disperses, and when Phyllis and Eve, left alone, look at each other, the viewer is desperate to know what each is thinking about the other.

In *cléo: a journal of film and feminism*, Elise Moore asserts that *The Bigamist* "directs its criticism at patriarchal, institutional monogamy's failure to accommodate complicated emotional, work, and financial needs and responsibilities." Is this, translated into the jargon du jour, what I'm saying? I don't know, but I definitely concur that *The Bigamist* is not just "a plea for understanding for one hapless, misguided man."[1]

It can only add to our appreciation of the picture that Collier Young, its screenwriter and producer, was, at the time of the filming, Joan Fontaine's husband and Ida Lupino's ex.

Aside from *The Bigamist*, the Lupino movie that noir-istas must see is *The Hitch-Hiker* (1953), with Edmond O'Brien as Roy, a

---

1. See Elise Moore, "Everyday Untidy Love: Ida Lupino's *The Bigamist* and Douglas Sirk's *There's Always Tomorrow*," *cléo: a journal of film and feminism* 5, no. 3, http://cleojournal.com/2017/12/19/everyday-untidy-love-ida-lupinos-bigamist/.

mechanic, and Frank Lovejoy as Gil, a draftsman, buddies of long standing who leave their families behind to go on a nostalgia-soaked fishing trip. The fellows amiably pick up a hitchhiker, but he is Emmett Myers (William Talman), the "Kansas desperado" who robs and shoots the motorists who stop for him. Myers is one scary dude, like a figure out of Poe, radiating menace, with one paralyzed eye that never closes.

It is an emphatically male picture, with no molls, no dolls, no widows, and no wives. Much of it takes place in the claustrophobic interior of an automobile, and it is not so much a movie of pursuit and capture as it is a study in sadism. Once Myers has the car he has no need of the two men. Why doesn't he ditch them in a deserted spot and speed away? There is no monetary gain; no motive other than the exercise of power. And that's the point. The psychopath enjoys torturing his captives. He is constantly comparing them, invariably to Roy's disadvantage. Frank admits to being a pretty good shot, and so, in the movie's most arresting sequence, Myers makes Frank shoot a beer can out of Roy's hand at twenty paces.

It is possible that *The Hitch-Hiker* is allegorically about the helplessness of rape victims at the hands of a bully with a gun.

15

Black Friday *(David Goodis)*

"David Goodis was a poet of the losers," Geoffrey O'Brien has written. Goodis's noir mysteries are as bitter and as chilling as the wind between two rivers of a raw Philadelphia winter. *Black Friday* (1954) begins with the Delaware's "icy flavor" mixed with the "mean gray frost" of the Schuylkill. A "skinny" hero shivers in a cheap flannel suit without an overcoat. His name is Hart, perhaps because it is that organ that keeps exposing him to danger. He "had put in a couple of years at the University of Pennsylvania" and is, or was, or wanted to be an artist. But Hart remains an enigma. It is not clear where he has come from, how he got there, or why, after spending a dime for beer, he has only eighty-three cents in his pocket.

The theft of an overcoat kicks off a plot that has the immediacy of a nightmare without any of the comforting commentaries, interpretations, and explanations that occur upon waking. Running from the clothing store, Hart eventually reaches the dark alley that exists for him to dart into it. There he hears the groans of a dying man, who gives him a wallet. In short order he is confronted by two thugs, one of whom beats him until Hart knees him in the balls. In the scuffle a gun goes off. The thug will die, and Hart will fall in with the gang of thieves, the sort of guys who reach for their weapons during the endless games of pinochle or poker with which they pass the time until their next job.

This is no ordinary mob; the gang and the house they hole up in amount to a kind of allegorical representation of a family romance gone terribly wrong. Charley, the gang boss, suffers from what was then not known as erectile dysfunction. Frieda, his fleshy mistress, wants Hart to service her, and he doesn't mind. It doesn't matter that their repartee is witty in a strictly inadvertent way. "I got plenty in here," she says, tapping her temple. "Really?" he replies. "Then let's discuss Schopenhauer." Her eyes narrow. "You getting fancy with me?" Afterwards he stares in distaste at "this chunk of sleeping animal that had no connection with him" and hopes she is not a light sleeper.

Goodis's first description of Frieda can be read as a hymn to Big Beautiful Women: "She was one-sixty if she was an ounce, more solid than soft, packed into five feet five inches and molded majestically. He guessed she didn't wear a girdle and when she turned her back to him and leaned over slightly he was certain of it." You can almost hear the author smack his lips as he brings the paragraph to an end. "Her calves were the same as the rest of her, solid round fat coming down rhythmically to slim ankles giving way to high-heeled shoes."

Just to make things more complicated, Myrna, sister of the fallen thug, has fallen hard for Hart, and he for her. The theme of fratricide will trump the fetish of the big blonde. It turns out that in the vastness of the past Hart had killed a man—and not just any man but his own brother. It was a mercy killing, and therefore he has suffered all the woes of a man on the lam wanted for homicide with the added twist that he is a guilty amateur and not a true "professional" and will therefore never fully win the trust of Charley.

For most of the novel, the characters wait impatiently. Charley depends on two trusty noir aids, booze and jazz: "Charley took the bottle and began pouring the gin into a water glass. He got the glass three-quarters full. He lifted the glass to his mouth and drank the gin as though it was water. The radio was playing more bebop. It was Dizzy Gillespie again and Dizzy's trumpet went up and up and up and way up." When the day of the heist finally arrives, Charley makes each of the gang recite his part, and—in what could serve as an epigraph for all such capers—"there were no questions because everything was clear and it was really a brilliant plan." Of course the plan goes awry. A Doberman kills one of the thieves. And Myrna, in an act of supreme self-sacrifice, flings herself in the path of the bullet Charley has intended for Hart. The simple last sentence of *Black Friday* sums up much of the noir impulse and the strange appeal it continues to exert: "He had no idea where he was going and he didn't care."

Goodis's other novels include *Street of No Return* (also from 1954), which begins on skid row and ends there after one of three bums sitting on the corner wanders off to relive his entire life in a plot move that is somewhere between a digression and a flashback. Two other Goodis novels were made into memorable movies: Truffaut's *Shoot the Piano Player* (1959), with Charles Aznavour, and *Dark Passage* (1948), with Humphrey Bogart as an ex-convict with a new face, Lauren Bacall as the art student who believes in him, and Agnes Moorehead as a nasty piece of goods.

16

Orange Noir (Charles Willeford)

You can read *The Burnt Orange Heresy* as either a murder mystery or a parable about the hoax element in modern art. Charles Willeford's 1971 novel gives satisfaction on both counts. It is an inverted detective story in the approved noir manner: the first-person narration takes us into the killer's mind. Yet not until digesting most of the book does the fallible reader guess who is to be murdered and why.

The plot centers on a painter named Jacques Debierue, avatar of "Nihilistic Surrealism," whose most famous work is *No. One.—* meaning both "number one" and "nobody." Debierue, a European transplant, lives in Willeford country: Palm Beach, Florida. James Figueras, an art critic with his eye on the main chance, obtains an interview with the great recluse. To ingratiate himself with an influential collector, he agrees to steal one of Debierue's paintings.[1]

The catch is that there are no paintings to steal. Like a version of Mallarmé as dreamed by Borges, Debierue believes his ideas are so

1. In 2019, the film adaptation of *The Burnt Orange Heresy* (directed by Giuseppe Capotondi) moved the location from south Florida to the shores of Lake Como, Italy, casting the Danish actor Claes Bang as Figueras, Donald Sutherland as the reclusive artist (renamed Jerome Debney), and Mick Jagger as the art collector.

far superior to any possible execution that in logical consequence he does not paint. Instead he has committed his life to the "unfulfilled *preparation* for painting." He puts in his four hours daily, "a slave to hope," yet always refuses in the end to violate "the virgin canvas."

Figueras has no such compunction. After breaking into Debierue's pristine studio and discovering there is nothing to pilfer, he sets fire to the place, counterfeits a painting by Debierue, forges his signature, then writes the article that offers the definitive interpretation of works that never existed. In a curious way it is as if painter and writer have colluded to invent Debierue's "American period."

Willeford, highly esteemed for his Hoke Moseley novels, weaves the aesthetic theory and the criminal mischief expertly together. *The Burnt Orange Heresy* is a rich enigma: a monument to "a qualified Nothing," suggestive of "deep despair" on the one hand and total "dedication to artistic expression" on the other. It is noir not only in the sense of Ad Reinhardt's black-on-black canvases but also in the violent romantic sense of an Otto Preminger or Fritz Lang movie.

Willeford's *Pick-Up* (1955) is a darker and even more gripping novel. Reading it you can see why this American genre held such an appeal for the French existentialists. The pick-up of the title takes place on page one. He is thirty-two, works as a counterman in a diner, "and when I'm not working, I drink." She is a year older, petite, pretty, a runaway: "I don't work at all. I drink all the time." Love is a lighted cigarette: "I lit a fresh cigarette from the end of mine, put it between her lips, and sat down on the edge of the bed." To live is to drink. Suppose we quit drinking, he wonders. No way. "Why not? We aren't getting any place the way we're going." "Who wants to get any place?" This is dangerous thinking and the narrator knows it and comes to his senses. "'Pass me the bottle,' I said."

Alcohol, sex, cigarettes; a cheap hotel in San Francisco, a suicide pact, a psychiatric ward; bandaged wrists, sudden death, a jail cell. A strong wind and a hard rain as a lonely figure climbs a deserted hill. Not until the penultimate sentence do we learn a crucial fact about the narrator and hero of the story, who describes himself earlier as "a free man" when the police let him go—but immediately doubts whether the phrase could possibly apply to him.

17

Ed McBain

THE MAN FROM ISOLA

As a graduate student at Cambridge University, I bought *Like Love* (1962), my first Ed McBain purchase, on the assumption that the title alluded to W. H. Auden's "Law Like Love," which ends with a stanza in which every line begins "Like love." The assumption was mistaken, but it turned out that the book, and most of McBain's police procedurals, do have a poetic element and are addictive.

Like Love begins with a disconsolate young woman on a high ledge who jumps to her death because of a love gone wrong. The title phrase occurs three strategic times in the course of the novel. The first is in a dialogue between detectives Carella and Hawes. Twisting Hamlet to his purposes, the former says there are more things in heaven and hell than are dreamt of in your philosophy:

"Like what?" Hawes asked.
"Like love," Carella answered.
"Exactly. And you have to admit that this thing has all the earmarks of a love pact."

This "thing" is the discovery of a dead man and woman, both semi-nude in bed, who have left a suicide note asking for forgiveness "for this terrible thing."

The second mention of the title occurs in a conversation over-heard in the "Brio Building," where musicians and songwriters and agents "filled the air with the musical jargon of Hip." A girl singer is doing the talking, as if she were a character in the pub scene in part two of *The Waste Land*: "Like I said to him why should I put out for you if I don't put out for anybody else on the band, and he said like this is different, baby. So I said how is it different? So he put his hand under my skirt and said this is like love, baby."

The final mention returns us to the supposed "love pact" that turns out to be a faked double suicide. Again the phrase is mouthed by a character, this time in a confession, with the *like* implying arti-ficiality rather than a rough similitude, a verbal tic, or a means of specification: "Then I stood in the doorway and looked into the room for a minute to see if it still looked like love, and I decided that it did, and that was when I went into the kitchen and turned on the gas."

That is getting the most out of your two-word title, a phrase that works as a simile and an alternative way of saying "for example." Beyond the snappy dialogue and authenticity of police procedure, McBain is a very careful writer.

In McBain's novels, the city of Isola—patterned after New York City—is evoked with a deep affection, as if it were the recipi-ent of four seasonal odes each year. Here are the opening sen-tences of four of his books: "The city could be nothing but a woman, and that's good because your business is women." "She came in like a lady, that April." "Nobody thinks about death on a nice spring day." "He thought of the city as a galaxy."[1] It is this sort of thing—combined with the love McBain bestows on his

1. From *The Mugger* (1956), *The Heckler* (1960), *Ten Plus One* (1963), and *Long Time No See* (1977).

87th Precinct cops—that Julian Symons has in mind when he remarks, a bit too harshly perhaps, that McBain's "characteristic flaw is his sentimentality."

What I mean by the poetic element in McBain's books is not this feeling for the city but the associative and sometimes literary logic that animates them. Many of McBain's titles announce the leitmotif that will pop up again and again, unifying the book. In *Ice* (1983), the title can be taken literally, or it can refer to jewelry or a form of ticket scalping. (Consider Marilyn Monroe's advice in "Diamonds Are a Girl's Best Friend": "get that ice, or else no dice.") It is also a verb. A dancer in a Broadway musical is "iced" by a bullet fired at her. A witty jewel thief hides stolen gems in a tray of ice cubes. The criminals use their profits to buy "snow," a narcotic also known as "flake," "sleigh ride," and "star dust." And the whole book takes place in the dead of winter.

This leitmotif approach serves McBain less well in *Lightning* (1984), mainly because the noun designated by the title is more decorative than intrinsic to the plot. Lightning shatters the sky during a rape scene in an alley; "Lightning Strikes Twice" is the tabloid headline when a former Olympic track star is arrested by the homicide squad. The murders and rapes are weirdly motivated. One series is the result of a once-famous man's desire to get his name in the newspapers; the other is the work of a pro-abortion activist, whose wife is always pregnant, and who stalks righteous Catholic women who heed the Vatican's injunction against using birth control. It's a stretch, but I have a weakness for the book if only because a sympathetic fireman is named Lehman, and this a mere year after I raved about *Ice* in *Newsweek*.

The author began his life in 1926 as Salvatore A. Lombino but changed his name to Evan Hunter after attending New York's Evander Childs High School and Hunter College. As Evan Hunter, he wrote acclaimed novels (such as *The Blackboard Jungle*) and screenplays (most famously the one for Hitchcock's *The Birds*). In 1956, as Ed McBain, he introduced the homicide squad of the 87th Precinct in Isola. Against the isolation of life on the island of Isola (which means "island" in Italian), the detectives stand as a humane community. McBain turned out fifty-five 87th Precinct novels, and while some are superior to others, not a one is dull, and there are a half-dozen or more masterpieces.

To those who are suspicious of heroic policemen, and assume that the author is a right-wing fanatic, let it be noted that the villain in McBain's *Hail to the Chief* (1982) is a stand-in for the Richard Nixon of Watergate notoriety. Robin Winks makes this point in *Modus Operandi* (1982), viewing McBain's novels not as political statements but as an advance in realism. "Seldom does detection in the normal sense of the word take place in procedural fiction," he observes. "This, too, is surely true. For if it is realism we seek, we must realize how often police work must wait, depending on the lucky break, the informer, the simultaneity of chance occurrences."

Steve Carella, McBain's central hero, is the Italian American author's projection of himself as a professional, a family man, a good guy, who moves with the casual grace of an athlete. Carella is married (and faithful) to a beautiful woman who happens to be a "deaf-mute." Also happily married is his colleague, the bald and somewhat philosophical Meyer Meyer, whose father named him that way as a Jewish joke. Sometimes Carella partners with Cotton Hawes, named after Cotton Mather, a tall, seemingly rustic fellow who has red hair with a white streak over the left temple. Bert Kling is the James Dean of the group, handsome, blond, sensitive, with vulnerable girlfriends. (In 1961's *Lady, Lady, I Did It*, his fiancée is killed in the store where she happened to be shopping when a holdup man with a gun goes berserk during a shootout; in 1981's *Heat*, a Kling girlfriend is targeted by a thug with a grudge against the cop who collared him.) Latecomers to the squad include the moody but popular Arthur Brown, a big brawny African American man, whom you want by your side if you "walk unarmed down any dark alley at two in the morning" (*Kiss*, 1992). Detective Annie Rawles, who is tough as nails but wears very sexy underwear, pairs off with Hawes. Undercover specialist Eileen Burke dates Kling. Bespectacled Sam Grossman capably runs the forensic lab. The comic tag team of Monroe and Monaghan shows up at homicides. And every precinct has to have its Andy Parker, "who could remain unfazed by police work" solely because he "abdicated it" (*Ice*) or its Fat Ollie Weeks, a bigot with the annoying habit of imitating W. C. Fields.

McBain's great achievement was to move the police procedural forward from the stodgy days of Freeman Wills Croft, whose Scotland Yard detective (introduced in 1924) is the painstaking Inspector French. "They say that genius is an infinite capacity for taking pains," Sherlock Holmes says with some scorn in *A Study in Scarlet*. "It's a very bad definition, but it does apply to detective work," and Inspector French embodies the notion. French (a very English fellow) specializes in cracking "cast-iron" alibis by doggedly checking train schedules and other minutiae. The genre as defined by Croft is aptly named "police routine." Fastidious attention to dull detail is key: the mark left by the fourth nail on the left-hand side of the suspect's shoe; the railway timetable for the local service from King's Cross to Grantham. As Henry Wade writes in *The Hanging Captain* (1933), a first-rate police procedural, "the sort of task upon which the art of criminal investigation in England is based" calls "for infinite patience and care; there was no brainwork in it, only care, thoroughness, and method."

In contrast, the "routine" in McBain's *romans policiers* doesn't overwhelm the prose. McBain's Isola has the feel of New York City in the second half of the twentieth century. A corpse turns up in a robbed liquor store with shards of broken glass on the floor. A crazed killer targets blind people exclusively. A distraught woman commits suicide and the man she loved turns sniper to avenge her death. A criminal mastermind triggers a race riot to distract the police while he and his confederates steal contraband narcotics. Muggers prey upon the defenseless, dope peddlers and pimps get what's coming to them, kidnappers snatch the wrong kid, everyone is lying, men will do foolish things "for two inches of real estate slit vertically up the middle" (*Heat*), rapists repeat themselves, cops get killed, and "a long blonde hair tangled in the sharp cutting edge of an ax shrieked more loudly than the corpse of the woman lying on a slab in the morgue" (*King's Ransom*, 1959).

The typical McBain plot is a series of three murders with the detectives having to figure out what links them—the tripartite structure of Christie's *ABC Murders*. The books are formulaic in the manner of a verse or musical form requiring three movements that represent thesis, antithesis, and synthesis.

From the McBain opus, which stretches over six decades, I like best the books he wrote in the first ten years of the series, such as *Like Love*; *Killer's Choice* (1957); *King's Ransom*, which Akira Kurosawa used as the basis of his movie *High and Low*; *Lady, Lady, I Did It*, in which four people are killed in a bookstore, one deliberately, the other three as collateral damage; and *Ten Plus One* (1963). These versions of urban nightmares are soluble as puzzles, and to that extent they are hopeful; they promote the idea that ours is a society of laws and the related fact that we are more dependent on the police than people are willing to admit. The hope endures, though at times the cops feel they are fighting a losing battle, if only because politics and crime are "maybe synonymous," juries acquit killers, and a city that survived war and depression "could not survive crack" (*Kiss*).

There are wonderful set pieces in the books: the professional cartoonist in *Ten Plus One*; the TV producer in *Eighty Million Eyes* (1966); the lesson in five-card stud poker that the brainy villain teaches his henchman in *The Heckler* (1960); the joke in *Mischief* (1993) culminating in "Not so fast, Seaman Shavorsky." And there are bizarre puzzles that only a madman with a touch of the artist can construct. In *Hark!* (2004), the squad's very own Professor Moriarty, known here as the Deaf Man, leaves at the scene of each crime a quote from Shakespeare as his signature and as a clue. In *Long Time No See* (1977), the detectives will not crack the case unless and until they can correctly interpret the dream that haunts a veteran of the Vietnam War. And this is the second way the books are hopeful: they affirm that there *is* a figure in the carpet that can be discerned by men and women of determination and skill.

18

Hitchcock's America

When you pitch an article to a magazine editor, the trick is to sell the idea in the fewest number of words. When I said "Hitchcock's America," I got the go-ahead from Richard Snow of American Heritage, *which published the piece in 2007.*

When I think of Alfred Hitchcock's America—the vision of America that you get from watching the films that he made during his prime Hollywood period—these are some of the images that come to mind:

- Heavy rain, poor visibility. The exhausted driver pulls up to a motel with a vacancy on a forlorn highway (*Psycho*).
- A low-flying crop duster takes aim at the well-dressed man running in a wide-open Midwest cornfield devoid of people or places in which to hide (*North by Northwest*).
- At Grand Central Station, the lovers (Ingrid Bergman and Gregory Peck) embrace at the gate and then go on to board the train together, and the uniformed ticket taker looks flabbergasted, because most couples who kiss at the gate go their separate ways after the buss (*Spellbound*).
- The avuncular traffic cop in the street stops an agitated teenager (Teresa Wright) from crossing against the light and says: "Just a minute, Charlie. What do you think I'm out here for?" (*Shadow of a Doubt*).

- Judy (Kim Novak) puts on the same necklace that the legendary Carlotta Valdez wears in the portrait in the museum to which Madeleine (also Kim Novak) had earlier paid rapt attention while Scottie (James Stewart) furtively watched (*Vertigo*).
- At the base of the Golden Gate Bridge, Scottie saves Madeleine from drowning in San Francisco Bay (*Vertigo*).
- At the tennis championship in Forest Hills, all heads in the crowd move back and forth, back and forth, to follow the progress of the ball—all except for one man, Bruno Anthony (Robert Walker), who keeps his eyes squarely on one of the players, Guy Haines (Farley Granger in *Strangers on a Train*).
- Glamorous model Lisa Fremont (Grace Kelly), looking like a million pre-inflation bucks, lets in a red-coated waiter from the 21 Club to serve a lobster dinner for herself and her wheelchair-bound photographer boyfriend (*Rear Window*).
- The merry-go-round at the "Magic Isle" amusement park is spinning out of control (*Strangers on a Train*).
- All that keeps a man from falling to certain death from the top of the Statue of Liberty is his jacket sleeve clutched by another man, and the sleeve is ripping apart (*Saboteur*).
- The menacing image of birds on telephone wires (*The Birds*).
- A montage: the hand of Cary Grant lifting Eva Marie Saint to safety atop Mount Rushmore and then, in the wink of a camera eye, making the same gesture to lift her to the upper berth of a train compartment, followed a frame later by a shot of the train entering a tunnel (*North by Northwest*).
- The silhouette of an arm wielding a knife, a torn shower curtain, and Marion Crane (Janet Leigh) slumps lifeless in the tub, the blood oozing out of her and flowing down the drain (*Psycho*).

I STOPPED MYSELF after a baker's dozen of such images or scenes, though I know I can easily double or triple the list. What do these cinematic moments, emblematic as they seem to be, suggest about Hitchcock's America?

The first thing I need to declare is the filmmaker's genius. In his lifetime considered the preeminent maker of thrillers, Sir Alfred Hitchcock (1899–1980) acquired a knighthood and the sobriquet the "master of suspense." He was a welcome visitor to American living rooms in his 1950s television series *Alfred Hitchcock Presents*, which used Gounod's "Funeral March of a Marionette" as a theme. Hitchcock, the host, prefaced the week's scripted mystery with macabre humor delivered deadpan. In the 1950s and 1960s, French "New Wave" film directors such as François Truffaut, who published a book comprising his conversations with Hitchcock, venerated him, and Hitchcock has long since gained general if not universal recognition as one of the major filmmakers—and thus one of the major artists—of the twentieth century. Truffaut remarked in admiration that Hitchcock's "love scenes were filmed like murder scenes, and the murder scenes like love scenes." It was as if Hitchcock's films demonstrated Freud's thesis in *Beyond the Pleasure Principle*: the idea that Eros and Thanatos, the love and death instincts, overlap and share a core identity.

An Englishman by birth and upbringing, the son of an East End greengrocer and his wife, "Hitch" was brought up in a strict Catholic household. One day his father gave the boy a letter and had him deliver it by hand to the local police station, where the officer on duty, after perusing the contents, locked young Alfred up in a cell for ten minutes, then released him. This enhanced the boy's appreciation of the police and helped to plant in him the seeds of a somewhat cruel sense of humor that expressed itself in practical jokes. The heavyset Hitchcock signed his films by making cameo appearances in them, usually at the start of the picture. In *North by Northwest* (1959), Hitch is ready to board a New York City bus when the doors slam in his face; in *Lifeboat* (1944), the director's image turns up on a scrap of newspaper among the debris in the boat—in a before-and-after advertisement for a weight reduction program.

Educated by Jesuits before enrolling at the University of London, Hitchcock made a number of superb black-and-white films in the Britain of the 1930s. *The 39 Steps* (1935) and *The Lady Vanishes* (1938) are the most celebrated of these early films. When Hitchcock and his wife, Alma, visited America in 1937 and 1938, it was not a calculated decision; he loved England and hadn't planned on leaving it, but when Hollywood producer David O. Selznick offered him a seven-year directorial contract, Hitch signed on the dotted line. In the end, the reason he abandoned London for Hollywood is simply that the latter could far more easily accommodate his aspirations than could England's more provincial film industry. And in truth Hitchcock, who became a United States citizen, made his greatest movies in his prime American period, which began with *Rebecca*, his first Hollywood venture, in 1940. Although he kept making movies through *Family Plot* in 1976, the ones I find worthiest of attention in this limited context, by virtue of their aesthetic excellence on one side and their American character on the other, are *Saboteur* (1942), *Shadow of a Doubt* (1943), *Spellbound* (1945), *Notorious* (1946), *Strangers on a Train* (1951), *Rear Window* (1954), *The Wrong Man* (1956), *Vertigo* (1958), *North by Northwest* (1959), *Psycho* (1960), *The Birds* (1963), and *Marnie* (1964).

If there is an overriding theme in Hitchcock's America, it is not that there are dangerous paranoids among us, though that is the case; it is that paranoia is sometimes a reasonable response to events in a world of menace and violence, with threats to safety and complacency close at hand, sometimes in the most intimate of places or from the most trusted of friends or relations. As the homicidal Bruno remarks to the traveler who shares his train compartment in *Strangers on a Train*, "My theory is that everybody is a potential murderer." And it follows that everybody else is potentially a victim, an accomplice, an accessory after the fact, a witness, or a sleuth. The life of man, said the English philosopher Thomas Hobbes, is "solitary, poor, nasty, brutish, and short," with each man for himself and against all others. The life of man according to Hitchcock is not quite so bleak. It is a life spent on the run, escaping from falsehood toward truth, from false accusation to triumphant vindication, and it rewards the risk-taking protagonist with excitement, intrigue, and often romance. Life is a cliffhanger.[1] There comes a moment when the hero, or his adversary, or his lover, or a bystander may have to hang from a rooftop or from the top of a lofty monument, and while there's no guarantee of survival, the reassuring thing is that someone is on hand to try to save the endangered person. That's part of the picture too.

Hitchcock's America is vast and dwarfs the individual. Man is as alone as Roger Thornhill (Cary Grant) on that wide-open cornfield in *North by Northwest*. If Man is lucky, Woman comes along, and they may learn to like each other against their own initial inclinations, as happens to Barry Kane (Robert Cummings) and Patricia Martin (Priscilla Lane) when they are handcuffed together in *Saboteur*. Robert Donat and Madeleine Carroll, the leading man and lady in *The 39 Steps*, also spend a lot of time handcuffed together, which appears to be Hitch's view of romance and marriage. (In *Saboteur*, Barry and Patricia quarrel fiercely, and a woman overhearing them says, "My, they must be terribly in love.") If our hero is extremely lucky, he looks like Cary Grant and the lady who comes along appears to be in league with the bad guys but turns out to be a friendly double agent with a feminine touch played by the magnificently attired Eva Marie Saint (*North by Northwest*).

---

1. Films with cliffhanging scenes in them include *Vertigo, Rear Window, North by Northwest, Saboteur*, and *To Catch a Thief*.

If, however, our hero is unlucky, the dame who comes along is a femme fatale in a plot so fantastic that only a detective writer could devise it. If the intricate psychological scheme at the heart of *Vertigo* isn't enough to make Scottie (James Stewart) paranoid, there must be something really wrong with him.

When I see a Hitchcock movie, as when I read a novel by Graham Greene, I know I have entered a universe in which evil exists. Murders happen for the usual reasons (greed, ambition, jealousy, the desire to be rid of a cumbersome parent or spouse) and sometimes for psychologically complex motives. But there is an undercurrent of sin and damnation in even a good-natured nightmare with a happy ending like *North by Northwest*. Just prior to the cornfield scene, Roger Thornhill in his steel-blue suit and tie looks completely out of place as he stands in the road with another gentleman waiting for the 3:30 bus. Out of the sky comes the crop duster. "That's funny," the other man says before boarding the bus. "That plane's dusting crops where there aren't crops." And as the bus departs, leaving Thornhill alone and unprotected in his natty city clothes, it becomes clear that the plane (whose pilot we never see) means to run him down, to crash into him or even decapitate him. Evil in Hitchcock's America is this inhuman and malevolent flying creature bearing down on a man who is desperately out of his element. Evil stands out in a crowd, the way Bruno's head remains fixed on Guy while everyone else's head turns to follow the tennis ball in *Strangers on a Train*. Evil is a disturbance of nature, but it can have the force of a natural phenomenon, as when flocks of birds thought friendly and harmless prove to be neither in *The Birds*. But evil is also the shadow that enters the room stealthily, taking its place noiselessly among us but turning out to be the thing that doesn't belong in the picture. In *Shadow of a Doubt*, Uncle Charlie (Joseph Cotten), with his contempt for "all-American suckers," is like a Satan who has sneaked into Eden, in this case the movie's "ordinary little town" with "average" people in Sonoma County, California, which he corrupts by his very presence, though it takes the sleuthing of his niece, young Charlie (Teresa Wright), to see through his amiable and charming façade.

The natural progress of paranoia is illustrated in the fate of Marion Crane (Janet Leigh) in *Psycho*, the bank teller who steals a wealthy depositor's $40,000, has sex outside of wedlock with her boyfriend in a hotel room, and emits the scent of guilt as she flees the city in a newly purchased used car. She has begun to act like a guilty person: fearful, jittery. When she pulls over to the side of the road, exhausted, and is approached by a highway patrol officer, she is a bundle of nerves. The officer asks, "Is anything wrong?" "Of course not," Marion says. "Am I acting as if there's something wrong?" "Frankly, yes," says the cop. He means to be kind in his gruff manner when he warns her against sleeping in her vehicle on the side of the road. "There are plenty of motels in this area. You should've . . . I mean, just to be safe," he says. The terrible irony of this statement becomes apparent only on a second viewing of the movie, for Marion would have been much safer in her car than in the motel where she does stop. The guilt and paranoia have run their therapeutic course when in the rain and gloom of night she sees the vacancy sign at the Bates Motel. What happens next is that her drama is swallowed by someone else's larger and more lethal nightmare. It is not her dream that matters, but the more lunatic dream of Norman Bates (Anthony Perkins). In *her* movie, the events are comprehensible even when things go astray: a woman gives in to temptation, takes something that isn't hers, runs away, begins to think better of it, and may even, with the benefit of a good night's sleep, decide to make a clean breast of things. In *his* movie, however, none of this matters; all that matters is that she is beautiful as sin. To the two sides of Norman Bates's split personality, Marion Crane is either (a) a sexy blonde female and therefore a natural object of desire, or (b) a sexy blonde female and therefore wicked as Jezebel. And so Marion is dispatched in the shower scene, stabbed by Norman's "mother," before the movie is half over. The greatest danger is the nearest, and one reason the shower scene in *Psycho* is the scariest and most threatening in all of Hitchcock is that it violates the defenseless heroine in the most private and intimate of places. It is rumored that Janet Leigh never again took showers, preferring to bathe, after playing the part of Marion Crane.

In the mythic landscape that is Hitchcock's America, the murderous or perilous coexists with the homely and domestic. People aren't who they claim to be. A son can impersonate his dead mother (*Psycho*). A salesgirl in a San Francisco department store can impersonate an industrialist's wife (*Vertigo*). Murder is the result, premeditated in one case, spontaneous and unplanned in the other. But if murderers and their accomplices reinvent themselves, the hero, too, must be nimble enough to employ a fictive identity. In *Saboteur*, Barry Kane's very name suggests that he starts with a strike against him. When his friend Ken Mason perishes in the fire at the airplane factory where they work, and the fire is determined to be the result of industrial sabotage, Kane is the chief suspect because he was seen handing Mason a fire extinguisher that the saboteur had filled with gasoline. (Unfortunately, no one saw the villain, Frank Fry, hand the extinguisher to Kane.) Though he is innocent, good-hearted and good-natured, there is a sense in which Kane has repeated Cain's crime in Genesis: he has not been his brother's keeper. And he must suffer the fate of Cain, who was sentenced to wander the earth. Barry Kane must cross America in his quest to absolve himself by fingering the real saboteur. The episodic film begins in Los Angeles and ends in New York harbor. When on the run Barry claims that his name is Barry Mason, conflating his own first name with the last name of his slain buddy, we know he's on the right path, for the progress of a Hitchcock hero is often a parable of identity, and names are sometimes changed along the way.

There's a wonderful variety of bad guys in Hitchcock's America. There are psychotics and con men out there, also kleptomaniacs and traitors and thieves, and sometimes just an ordinary husband who has had enough of his wife's nagging and turns murderous. From the back window of his apartment, L. B. Jefferies (James Stewart), the laid-up photographer in *Rear Window*, monitors the lives of the people who live in the apartments around their common courtyard in Greenwich Village during a hot summer. He has given nicknames to some of the neighbors, and in each case we can extrapolate an entire movie from the little we learn—as if each window he observes were a movie screen, and the voyeur in the wheelchair with the camera were a stand-in for the film director himself. There are the newlyweds, who live mostly behind shut curtains. There is the songwriter, who plays "Mona Lisa" as if in unconscious homage to Lisa Fremont, the Grace Kelly character in the movie. Rebuffed at romance, Miss Lonelyhearts is in despair and on the verge of suicide, but then she begins a hopeful new friendship with the songwriter. Miss Torso, the sexy dancer with the acrobatic body, fends off handsome suitor after suitor, reserving her warm embrace for the least prepossessing fellow, who turns up at the end, a short man with a receding hairline in a US Army uniform. It is a little community in a back alley, but behind one window lives one whose existence threatens all, for Lars Thorwald (Raymond Burr) has killed his wife and chopped her into pieces that fit in valises. There's a wail in the middle of the movie when one of the neighbors discovers that her pet dog has been strangled. Behind that wail is an accusation—*one of you did this*—that is also a challenge to the community. So it turns out to be fortunate, after all, that the film director is a snoop: Jefferies proves that "we've become a race of peeping toms," but his paranoia is justified; his peeping leads to the apprehension of the guilty one, who must be expelled for the community to go forward. This is in miniature the logic of the generic detective story, with the twist that the *Rear Window* of the title is unmistakably a movie screen in metaphor, and we the spectators are implicated in Jefferies's voyeurism.

When a criminal design is put into effect, it takes on a velocity of its own, like the out-of-control merry-go-round in the amusement park where the villain meets his end in *Strangers on a Train*. It was in the park's tunnel of love that the out-of-control Bruno Anthony had earlier approached Miriam, Guy Haines's unfaithful wife, and strangled her to death. An amusement park is a made-to-order Hitchcock setting, a place dedicated to wholesome fun, with songs like "Ain't She Sweet," "And the Band Played On," and "Oh, You Beautiful Doll" playing in the background when the violence occurs. In Hitchcock's America, men and women are surprisingly vulnerable—to lunatics of various stripes, criminals ingenious and banal, and even flocks of birds that, for no apparent reason, attack people with murderous fury.

Yet for all that, Hitchcock's America is also the America of the grateful immigrant, émigré, or refugee: a haven of freedom, a light in the storm of World War II. There is something benevolent in American institutions symbolized by public monuments or by people in uniform. The cop in the street stops young Charlie Newton (Teresa Wright) from crossing against traffic in *Shadow of a Doubt* because this is Santa Rosa, California, small-town America, where the librarians help to educate you and the police keep you out of mischief. (Thornton Wilder, author of *Our Town*, wrote the screenplay.) America is the cheerful determination of Doris Day singing "Que Sera, Sera," in *The Man Who Knew Too Much* (1956). And though Hitchcock has a sense of humor that has been characterized as sadistic,[2] the counterweight to his dark view of humanity is also in his movies. It takes the form of an unrelenting insistence on justice, and sometimes poetic justice, and a reiteration of basic American values. Young Charlie in *Shadow of a Doubt* has a special bond with the uncle whose name she shares. She has always adored him. When she has reason to suspect him of being the Merry Widow murderer, seducer and betrayer of wealthy widows, it nearly breaks her heart. But not only does she prove her mettle as a sleuth; she also opposes her uncle's evil with a commensurate force of goodness, and that is why she prevails. On the basis of one purloined page clipped from a newspaper and one critical clue—the ring her uncle has given her bears the same initials as one of the murdered widows—she confronts him and gets him to confess. But he doesn't have to tell her that he has strangled three women. She knows. What persuades her is not so much the evidence as the contemptuous way the killer talks about the "ordinary" people in the "ordinary little town" of Santa Rosa. When Uncle Charlie says, "The world's a foul sty. If you rip off the fronts of houses, you'd find swine," it's as good as an admission of guilt.

Young Charlie in *Shadow of a Doubt* embodies America in the same way that brash Barry Kane does in *Saboteur*. They radiate the optimism and innocence of an ordinary person to whom

2. "He took a gleeful delight in devising indignities for Madeleine Carroll to undergo [in *The 39 Steps*], getting her drenched and dragged about and generally off her super-*soignée* high Hollywood horse." John Russell Taylor, *Hitch: The Life and Times of Alfred Hitchcock* (New York: Berkley, 1980), 120.

nothing truly bad has yet happened, and then one day it does, and it troubles her, and she is no longer innocent in the sense of being unaware, but she is able to resist her cynical uncle mentally and physically, and it is he who falls out of the train to his death when they struggle. Santa Rosa is where Hitchcock and his family lived, and the benevolence and kind-heartedness of small-town America may be most apparent in *Shadow of a Doubt*. But you can sense the director's affection for American ideals in *Strangers on a Train* when the US senator played by Hitchcock stalwart Leo G. Carroll says, "Let me remind you that even the most unworthy of us has the right to life and the pursuit of happiness." You hear the patriotic strain loudly in *Saboteur* when a blind man, our heroine's uncle, fearlessly welcomes the fugitive Barry Kane to his rustic cabin in a rainstorm though he can tell the man is in handcuffs. "It's my duty as an American citizen to believe a man innocent until proved guilty," Uncle Philip tells his skeptical niece Patricia.

American monuments turn up in Hitchcock's movies too often to lack significance. Take the United Nations, site of a key scene in *North by Northwest*. The knife that kills the United Nations diplomat in the movie was intended for someone else, which in the abstract sounds like a cutting comment on the institutional successor to the League of Nations. But while Hitchcock's intentions may never lack irony, they do not consist solely of irony, and to an important degree the monuments in his films—Mount Rushmore in *North by Northwest* or the Lincoln Memorial in *Strangers on a Train*—are invoked for the ideals they stand for.

The Statue of Liberty at the conclusion of *Saboteur* takes its place as the nation's favorite monument, evoking our preferred idea of ourselves. On the observation deck, waiting for Barry Kane and the police to arrive, the blonde heroine finds herself alone with the traitorous Frank Fry. Patricia Martin flirts with him to detain him,

and when he grows suspicious, she stands her ground and defiantly recites the great peroration from Emma Lazarus's "The New
Colossus": "Give me your tired, your poor, / Your huddled masses
yearning to breathe free, / The wretched refuse of your teeming
shore. / Send these, the homeless, tempest-tost to me."[3] The final
confrontation takes place on the outside of the statue—between
the thumb and forefinger of the hand holding the torch. The villain Fry will fall to his death, after promising "I'll clear you" to
Barry Kane, who tries to rescue Fry, holding onto his jacket sleeve
until it rips apart. The placement of Lady Liberty here is as ringing
an endorsement of American values—and, in particular, the open
door to immigrants that Lazarus's poem commends—as the playing of "The Marseillaise" at the end of *Casablanca* is an endorsement of the French Resistance.

A favorite Hitchcock plot motif is that of the wrong man—the
innocent man falsely accused of a crime, usually murder. Often he
must elude his pursuers and track down the true culprit. *Saboteur*
is a straightforward version of this design; *Spellbound* a baroque
one (in which the suspect on the run is an amnesiac whose dreams
are choreographed by Salvador Dalí); *The Wrong Man* a grim one
made in a semi-documentary style; *Frenzy* (1972) a British version;
and *North by Northwest* a comic apotheosis of the theme. Both
Spellbound and *North by Northwest* are cases of mistaken identity
and can be interpreted as existential parables: the hero needs to

3. Lazarus wrote "The New Colossus" in 1883 to help raise funds to pay for
the statue's pedestal. The sonnet enjoyed little celebrity in its author's lifetime
and was not recited when the Statue of Liberty was dedicated in 1886. In 1903 a
plaque with the poem on it was placed on an interior wall of the statue's pedestal,
where it remained virtually ignored for another generation. Not until the 1930s,
when Europeans in droves began seeking asylum from fascist persecution, was
the poem rediscovered, and expressed the monument's true meaning.

discover who he is, or must adopt a made-up identity to become his true, adult self. The quest for the villain, and the need to subdue him and foil his plot, amounts to the hero's rite of passage.

The tension between aesthetic and moral impulses adds an edge to Hitchcock's movies. The better the villain, the better the movie, was a Hitchcock maxim, in which *better* has a strictly aesthetic meaning. Often enough it is the villains who steal the show. Certainly this is true in *Strangers on a Train*, where Robert Walker playing Bruno gives a considerably more interesting, threatening, and complex performance than the tennis pro played by Farley Granger. Claude Rains in *Notorious* (1946), James Mason in *North by Northwest*, Joseph Cotten in *Shadow of a Doubt* are, for all their villainy, attractive, charming, urbane, even sympathetic. The male lead in some Hitchcock films—Robert Cummings in *Saboteur*, Farley Granger in *Strangers on a Train*, Rod Taylor in *The Birds*—comes close to being a generic figure: the nice guy framed for something he didn't do, or implicated in a crime he didn't commit, or beset by natural forces gone hysterically out of control. None of the other male characters in *Psycho*, and there are quite a few, including those played by John Gavin and Martin Balsam, can hold a candle to the schizophrenic culprit as a figure of interest.

The male lead in a Hitchcock movie has heroic qualities but is decidedly a regular guy with flaws or wounds, and even when he is played by an Englishman, he seems a type of the American. Roger Thornhill, the successful Madison Avenue advertising executive in *North by Northwest*, is a commitment-averse mama's boy who drinks too much. As the film begins he leaves his New York office building accompanied by his secretary, dictates an insincere apology to a miffed girlfriend, and, in the time-tested New York manner, swoops in and takes a taxi someone else had hailed. Cary Grant, who plays Thornhill, is the perfect Hitchcock actor.[4] But James Stewart, the unpretentious average guy, who played the protagonist in Frank Capra's *It's a Wonderful Life*, is a close second. Either Hitchcock found something dark that was previously untapped in Stewart or he liked capitalizing on the discrepancy between the actor's amiable image and his character in the film at hand. As Jefferies, the invalid photographer in *Rear Window*, Stewart has less interest in his girlfriend than in spying on his neighbors. In *Vertigo* he plays the plainclothes police detective John "Scottie" Ferguson, who is hampered by a psychological weakness that the film's criminal mastermind exploits to the hilt: Scottie has acrophobia, gets dizzy in high places, and this in San Francisco, city of steep hills and towers. When the film begins, a uniformed cop dangling from the edge of a rooftop clings for his life to Scottie's hand. But Scottie, beset with vertigo, lets go and the cop tumbles to his death.[5]

Scottie is not the only Hitchcock character to suffer from a guilt complex. Gregory Peck in *Spellbound* arrives at the asylum as its new director, Dr. Anthony Edwardes, but is soon revealed to be an impostor, an amnesiac, and a suspect in the murder case of the real Dr. Edwardes. (In a flashback resembling a psychoanalytic breakthrough, he recovers the repressed boyhood memory of sliding down a New York banister in the snow and accidentally pushing his younger brother to his death.) For much of the movie, Gregory Peck doesn't even know who he is, proving thereby that in the asylum the doctors and the patients are hard to tell apart. The Peck

4. Besides *North by Northwest*, Cary Grant gives winning performances in *Notorious*, *To Catch a Thief*, and *Suspicion*. At least two of the four—*North by Northwest* and *Notorious*—are masterpieces.

5. It can be said that Scottie fails the cliffhanger test that Cary Grant passes at the end of *North by Northwest* when he saves Eva Marie Saint from falling off a presidential nose atop Mount Rushmore.

character learns that his real initials are J. B., and when he checks into a hotel as "John Brown," this represents considerable progress, for the entire film is metaphorically a case study in psychoanalysis in which the patient reveals his dreams, talks about his repressed memories, and discovers at long last that his name is John Ballantyne, and that though he was the immediate cause of his brother's death, it is now past time to shed the burden of guilt.

Some of the wounded men in Hitchcock's movies have their chance at regeneration and redemption. Gregory Peck gets well through the love and ministrations of sympathetic psychoanalyst Dr. Constance Petersen (Ingrid Bergman), Hollywood's greatest homage to Freudian psychology. Cary Grant in *North by Northwest* shows himself so adept at eluding pursuers and escaping from hot spots—by, for example, hilarious antics improvised at an elegant auction house—that by the end of the movie he has proved himself worthy of Eve Kendall (Eva Marie Saint). As in *Saboteur* and other Hitchcock movies, a change of name spells a change in fortune in *North by Northwest*. Cary Grant thinks he is ad man Roger Thornhill until he is abducted and people start calling him George Kaplan. There is even a hotel room in the Plaza in Kaplan's name, with a suit of clothes in the closet. From the moment he answers to the name Kaplan for the first time—thereby embodying the purely notional spy that the CIA has concocted to lead the bad guys astray—the hero begins his journey through terror toward redemption. In this case, redemption is epitomized by his union with Eve Kendall in that railway compartment as the train enters the tunnel and "The End" appears on the screen.

Guy Haines in *Strangers on a Train*, who plays a mean game of tennis and is earnest and decent but weak and irresolute, enjoys a fate perhaps better than he deserves, as befits a character adapted from a novel by Patricia Highsmith, who exalts criminal creativity.

Guy hasn't quite agreed to Bruno Anthony's proposal that each kill the other's nemesis—Guy's wife, Bruno's father—but he has entertained the notion and that's all the encouragement Bruno needs. The elimination of the tennis professional's wife is something he had wished for—it removes the major obstacle to a new marriage—and so there is a sense in which Guy gets away with murder as no one else I can think of does in a Hitchcock film, with the exception of Gavin Elster (Tom Helmore), mastermind of the perfect murder in *Vertigo*. Gavin Elster is one of several characters who disappear in the middle of this movie, Hitchcock's most enigmatic, in the same way that the Fool disappears in *King Lear*.

Hitchcock's female lead is almost always a blonde beauty: Ingrid Bergman, Grace Kelly, Doris Day, Kim Novak, Eva Marie Saint, Janet Leigh, Vera Miles, Tippi Hedren, Laraine Day. In the era of the universal hausfrau she can be surprisingly accomplished. She is sometimes a professional and sometimes a pink-collar working girl. The psychiatrist in *Spellbound* faces down a killer with a gun pointed at her and calmly walks out the door to safety while he turns the gun on himself. The model in *Rear Window* has the daring of a burglar and willingly puts herself in danger to help bring a guilty man to justice. Patricia Martin, Priscilla Lane's character in *Saboteur*, is likewise a model with pluck. The very sound of Doris Day's rich singing voice works wonders in *The Man Who Knew Too Much*. Eve Kendall in *North by Northwest* is about as suave as an intelligence agent can be. Though still a teenager, young Charlie (Teresa Wright) in *Shadow of a Doubt* is the only person in her family clever enough to see beneath her homicidal uncle's veneer and courageous enough to confront him.

It is possible that no Hitchcock heroine undergoes an ordeal as perilous as Ingrid Bergman's in *Notorious*. Bergman plays Alicia Huberman, the daughter of a Nazi spy. The news of his conviction

is a terrible burden for her to have to bear. It is, the opening sub-
title tells us, April 20, 1946. The war has officially ended, but there
are committed Nazis who will not say die. Alicia, who lives in Florida, is a patriotic American, but her life's a mess; she drinks too
much and is said to be promiscuous. She also has connections that
Allied intelligence would like to exploit, and Devlin (Cary Grant),
an American agent, recruits her for an espionage mission in Brazil.
Devlin and Alicia begin to fall in love, but there will be a fog of
mutual distrust between them because of what the spy agency is
asking her to do. Her mission is to seduce and, if one thing leads to
another, to wed Alex Sebastian (Claude Rains), one of the leaders
of a Nazi spy ring in Rio.

The honey-pot plot is not nearly as difficult to arrange as one
might suppose, because Sebastian has met Alicia and was, we're
given to believe, very taken with her. In the opposition between
the dashing, mistrustful and somewhat callous Devlin (a name
that includes an anagram of "devil") and the urbane if insecure
Sebastian, there is more than a little ambiguity. Let Roger Ebert
state the case: "By the time all of the pieces are in place, we actually
feel more sympathy for Sebastian than for Devlin. He may be a
spy but he loves Alicia sincerely, while Devlin may be an American agent but has used Alicia's love to force her into the arms of
another man." In effect Devlin has acted as a pimp. He has put
Alicia into extreme danger. How can he be sure that Alicia loves
him and not Alex? He can't. And she is even less able to know how
he feels about her.

Alex and Alicia have been Mr. and Mrs. Sebastian for some time
before the deceived man catches on that he is the target of a coun-
terespionage operation. Devlin's visits to the Sebastian mansion
arouse Alex's suspicions, and the clue of a missing key confirms
the bitter truth. "Both men love her but the wrong man trusts

her," Ebert observes, and Alex's barely suppressed fury of self-loathing and shame is painful to watch. After the duped husband, like a chastened schoolboy, confesses to his fearsome domineering mother (Leopoldine Konstantin) that he is "married to an American agent," she puts Alicia on a strict regimen of arsenic and coffee served in elegant chinaware. Even if, in the end, Devlin arrives to rescue her, Alicia has been cruelly used and abused. As she and Devlin descend the stairs to freedom, the hapless Sebastian can do nothing but climb back up the same stairs in obedience to the voice of a ruthless Nazi bigwig: "Alex, will you come in, please? I wish to talk to you." The movie ends with this death sentence, and we can only hope that Alicia will recover at the hospital and marry the spy who loves her.[6]

Not that all the leading ladies are heroic. The title character in *Marnie* (Tippi Hedren) is a kleptomaniac. Luckily, Mark Rutland (Sean Connery) is devoted to her and there is a Freudian solution to her habit, resist it though she will. "You, Freud. Me, Jane?" she snaps at him. She gets off this great line: "Oh, men! You say 'no thanks' to one of them, and BINGO! You're a candidate for the funny farm." Marnie is a nihilist, because of a traumatic incident when she was a tot. "I don't believe in luck," she tells Mark. "What do you believe in?" he responds. "Nothing," she says.

Marnie is saved, but others are punished severely for their crimes or sins. In *Vertigo*, Judy Barton (Kim Novak) gets the role of a lifetime, and plays it perfectly, but she is an accomplice to murder and she will die not once but twice. The feat is owed to the director's sleight of hand, the director in this case being the fellow who planned the crime, auditioned the leading lady, and

6. Roger Ebert, August 17, 1997, https://www.rogerebert.com/reviews/great-movie-notorious-1946.

cast James Stewart as either a fall guy or an unwitting accomplice, or both.

In some ways a Hitchcock film functions as a morality play. In *The Lady Vanishes*, the cast of characters stranded on a stalled train act out the appeasement-versus-confrontation debate in Britain in the face of German aggression in the late 1930s. The underrated *Saboteur* is a series of episodic lessons in democracy. When Barry and Patricia throw themselves upon the mercy of circus performers, the troupe—in a flamboyant scene written by Dorothy Parker—debate whether to offer refuge to the fleeing pair. And then they vote. The quarreling Siamese twins cancel each other out. The fat lady declares herself neutral. The leader of the troupe votes for the couple, the malignant midget against. And so Esmeralda, the bearded lady with her hair in curlers, casts the decisive vote, and it is in favor of the fugitives. *Lifeboat*, about the survivors of a shipwreck marooned in a small lifeboat, is allegorically not only a parable of survival but also a contest between American democracy and German totalitarian efficiency. *The Birds* sounds a prophetic call for an ecology movement that had not yet got off the ground in 1963. In the absence of an explanation of the birds' warlike behavior, the viewer imagines that it must be payback for man's spoiling of the environment—a version of birds "coming home to roost."

The Harvard philosopher Stanley Cavell has argued that *North by Northwest*, whose title echoes one of Hamlet's famous declarations ("I am but mad north-north-west. When the wind is southerly I know a hawk from a hand-saw"; *Hamlet*, 2.2.367–68), is in fact a symbolic reworking of *Hamlet*, and you don't have to agree with this unusual thesis to find the argument fascinating. *Rear Window* is allegorically about moviemaking and voyeurism. *Vertigo* and *Psycho* are allegories of the interior life of the wounded psyche.

Vertigo, based on the French novel *D'entre les morts* by Pierre Boileau and Thomas Narcejac, has the most uncanny plot in Hitchcock, though it's what the director does with the plot that is most audacious. For one thing, he gives away the solution to the mystery long before the movie's climax, indicating thereby that the psychological drama of Scottie Ferguson's obsession with Madeleine Elster rather than Gavin Elster's murderous scheme is the essence of the matter. A plot summary is in order. Elster hires Scottie, a retired police detective with a debilitating fear of heights, to follow his allegedly suicidal wife, Madeleine. Elster tells Scottie that Madeleine has premonitions of a violent death by her own hand in a repetition of the fate of her tragic ancestress Carlotta Valdes. The secret is that it is not Madeleine that he follows but the equivalent of a body double: a working girl named Judy Barton, who looks broadly like Gavin Elster's reclusive wife and is made up to resemble her closely. Scottie saves "Madeleine" from drowning, takes her for a drive to Muir Woods in Marin County, wines and dines her at Ernie's, falls in love with her. On an outing to the Spanish mission of San Juan Bautista, about one hundred miles south of San Francisco, she abruptly climbs to the top of the bell tower, and Scottie is unable to follow. His vertigo has rendered him a helpless onlooker when she leaps to her death. In fact, Elster has already murdered his wife, and it is her body that Scottie and we see falling (and Judy's scream that we hear). But because the false Madeleine has established a history of suicide attempts, to which both Elster and Scottie can testify, her death is ruled a suicide. Elster is in the clear and presumably out of the country, living on his wife's money, while Scottie, rebuked for "his weakness" by the coroner at the inquest, suffers a nervous breakdown that leaves him in a catatonic state in an asylum.

In a witty essay that provides some of the intellectual founda-
tion for the detective story as a genre, Thomas De Quincey argued
that a murder can resemble a work of art. Gavin Elster's scheme,
making up in ingenuity for what it lacks in practicality, is artistic
in this sense. Yet it is surpassed in aesthetic interest by Hitchcock's
cinematic plot, for what happens in the second half of the movie is
an uncanny repetition of the events in the first half. Released from
the asylum, Scottie is more, not less, obsessed with Madeleine. One
day in the street he sees a young woman who resembles her. He
introduces himself, learns her name is Judy Barton ("from Salina,
Kansas"), woos her, and proceeds to make her over in clothing,
hairdo, and makeup so that she is a double for the fallen Madeleine. What he doesn't yet realize, and what lifts the story out of
the realm of the plausible and into that of the parable, is that she
is the fallen Madeleine. Only when she puts on the necklace that
Madeleine wore do the scales fall from Scottie's eyes. Only when
the simulation is complete and Judy has merged with Madeleine
down to the last detail can he tell that he has been deceived. His joy
in the re-creation has lasted only for the length of a kiss captured
in a 360-degree pan.

Now he drives her back to the scene of the crime. He doesn't
say where they're heading but it looks like the long drive south
to San Juan Bautista and you can see the panic on her face. Leading her by the hand to the top of the mission tower, he speaks
angrily. "Did he [Elster] tell you exactly what to do, what to say?
You were a very apt pupil too, weren't you? You were a very apt
pupil! Well, why did you pick on me? Why me?" But then suddenly it is no longer Judy standing there, and his tone changes.
"I loved you so, Madeleine." As the film moves inexorably to its
conclusion, he calls her by both names. He still can't tell the real
from the imitation, and that is inevitable, because the real has

been an imitation all along. He drags her to the top of the tower, hoping to cure himself of vertigo, and he does, but he loses her in the doing—loses her for a second time. Surprised by the sudden appearance of a nun, she slips and falls to her death. There is no telling what will happen to Scottie now. "God, have mercy," says the nun, and the movie ends.

Look at some of the things the movie has done. It has dramatized what Freud calls the compulsion to repeat. Both Scottie and Judy succumb to the lure of that elusive thing, the second chance: the chance to undo a past error or make the same mistake twice. The false Madeleine is conceived as the second coming of Carlotta Valdes; Judy is a repetition of Madeleine; Scottie twice falls in love with a specter and twice sees the object of his desire fall from the top of a tower, as if to embody and reinforce the precise phobia he suffers from.

Always inventive in his use of familiar public spaces as backdrops of action or meditation, Hitchcock makes inspired use of San Francisco in *Vertigo*. Madeleine fakes her suicide attempt near the Golden Gate Bridge, a historically appropriate spot. (It was, for example, on a ramp to the bridge that the poet Weldon Kees's car was found in July 1955; he was presumed to have drowned.) In a moment of surpassing strangeness, Madeleine addresses a gigantic sequoia in Muir Woods as if the centuries were inscribed on it: "Here I was born, and there I died. It was only a moment for you; you took no notice." There is one sequence in which Scottie is in his car tailing Madeleine in hers, and she seems to be driving aimlessly, tentatively, up and down the steep city streets. He is puzzled: What is she up to? It turns out that she is looking for his house in order to thank him for his gallantry in saving her from drowning. She says she searched for and finally recognized his street from its alignment with Coit Tower in the distance. "First time I've been grateful for Coit Tower," Scottie says, most aptly given the part that a tower will play in the drama.

The sequence does more than show off the hilly streets of a beautiful American city. The irony is that Scottie follows all her winding peregrinations just to end up at his own place, which he need never have left. What draws them together is an urge that flies in the face of all common sense and can coexist with pretense and deception. Neither Scottie nor Judy can resist the other, though each knows on some level that their love is doomed and may prove catastrophic. The movie is at once a study in Scottie's wounded psyche, a variation on the Pygmalion myth ("He made you over just like I made you over," Scottie says), and an allegory of the Hollywood starlet who, for her part in the movie, is entirely made over and given a new name, as "Judy" in *Vertigo* becomes "Madeleine," with the unexpected result that, as in Henry James's story "The Real Thing," the counterfeit image is more compelling than the genuine article. *Vertigo* is allegorically the story of the making of such a starlet, the transformation of Norma Jean Baker into Marilyn Monroe or Margarita Carmen Cansino into Rita Hayworth.

Vertigo and *The Birds* are two major movies that end without the usual resolution that we expect in a murder mystery. In other Hitchcock films as well, the element of threat is what endures beyond the solution of the puzzle at hand and the restoration of order. In a Hitchcock movie, an object can vibrate with meaning and serve as a metonym for danger: Guy's cigarette lighter with crossed tennis racquets on it, which Bruno wants to plant at the scene of the amusement park murder in *Strangers on a Train*; the victim's smashed eyeglasses in the same picture (does any other image convey vulnerability so well?); the crack of light beneath the asylum director's door in *Spellbound*; the key to the wine cellar in *Notorious*; the glass of milk Cary Grant carries up the stairs to Joan

Fontaine in her bed in *Suspicion* (1941); the necklace Kim Novak puts on in *Vertigo*. Hitchcock's poetry of objects, as I think of it, could stand as a lesson for modern poets weaned on Ezra Pound and William Carlos Williams.

There is this in Hitchcock, and there is some of the most glorious music ever written for the movies by Bernard Herrmann, Dimitri Tiomkin, Franz Waxman, Erich Korngold, Miklós Rózsa, and others.[7] There is also glamour in Hitchcock, as when Grace Kelly flirts with Cary Grant in *To Catch a Thief* (1955) or wheels in an elegant repast for James Stewart and her to consume in his bohemian pad in *Rear Window*. And there is the good old-fashioned Hollywood buss that ends the spectacle, as when Ingrid Bergman and Gregory Peck clinch at the gate in Grand Central Station at the end of *Spellbound*. But I would save the last word for Hitchcock's humor and the marvelous way it coexists with the macabre. In *Shadow of a Doubt*, there is a running conversation between young Charlie's father, Joseph Newton (Henry Travers), and his neighbor and friend Herbie Hawkins (Hume Cronyn) in comic counterpoint to the plot of the Merry Widow murderer. Both gentlemen are addicted to detective stories and make a competitive parlor game out of planning the perfect murder as a strictly theoretical pastime. When we first meet Joe, he is carrying a magazine titled *Unsolved Crimes*. The best way to commit a murder, he tells Herb, is with a blunt instrument. In a later scene, Herb jokes that he could have poisoned Joe's coffee unseen. Both men are oblivious to the drama unfolding in the very house in which they drink their coffee and discuss methods of murder.

7. See Jack Sullivan, *Hitchcock's Music* (New Haven, CT: Yale University Press, 2006), and "Hitchcock, Thrilling the Ears as Well as the Eyes," by Edward Rothstein, *New York Times*, January 8, 2007.

When Emma Newton (Patricia Collinge) describes her husband and Herb as "literary critics," she is more accurate than she can know, for the pair have the same fuzzy relation to the crimes in the movie—murder by strangulation rather than poison or a lead pipe—that many literary critics have to literary art. This comic subplot, which might seem to underscore the theme of our general vulnerability, is a variant on the archetypal story of the scholar who, with his eyes fixed on the stars, falls into a ditch. Most of us are looking elsewhere and do not see the peril immediately before us. This may make us easy prey. But the comedy is benevolent, because the "ordinary people" in *Shadow of a Doubt* are decent, warmhearted, and generous, the backbone of Hitchcock's America.

IV

DREAMS THAT MONEY CAN BUY

*T*his section, comprising essays on individual films and actors, takes its title from Hans Richter's 1947 film about an indigent poet who discovers that people will buy the dreams he can produce. In Dreams That Money Can Buy, *the contents of clients' minds are reassembled into more or less surrealistic sequences directed by Richter, Max Ernst, Man Ray, Marcel Duchamp, Alexander Calder, and Fernand Léger. The same idea, minus the surrealism, animates films noirs.*

19

Straight Down the Line

BILLY WILDER'S
DOUBLE INDEMNITY (1944)

Double Indemnity (1944) is the *ne plus ultra* of noir movies, and if we were to give out noir awards on the model of the Oscars, I believe it would win the Falcon for best picture, best screenplay (written by Raymond Chandler in collaboration with director Billy Wilder), best femme fatale (Barbara Stanwyck), and best supporting actor (Edward G. Robinson). Excellent as a villain and a dupe, Fred MacMurray would get a nomination for best actor in a lead role but would lose to Robert Mitchum (*Out of the Past*).

The plot is that old reliable, homicidal adultery. Man falls for woman, but woman's husband stands in the way. To consummate the illicit affair, the couple collaborate to eliminate the obstacle. As in *The Postman Always Rings Twice*, also based on a book by James M. Cain, murder presents itself as a feasible solution. In both, the woman's husband is almost incidental to the plot—though next to the stiff to whom Stanwyck is married, the Greek diner owner who likes getting drunk and singing "She's Funny That Way" in *Postman* is a live wire. There are various triangles in *Double Indemnity*—including ones involving Stanwyck's stepdaughter Lola and her boyfriend—but in all of them the figure of the husband is almost an afterthought, like the corpse in chapter one of a classic detective novel. It is Stanwyck who dominates the picture, and the triangle in which Stanwyck and Robinson stand at opposite poles in MacMurray's consciousness is the most vital one of all.

Our narrator is the wounded Walter Neff (MacMurray), a bachelor in his thirties with a healthy libidinal appetite, dictating his confession into a recording device: "How could I have known that murder can sometimes smell like honeysuckle?" It's his point of view we're getting, the chump, who works for an insurance company and knows that, because of the so-called "double indemnity" clause, the firm pays double for accidental deaths incurred while the policyholder is traveling. The idea is to amend the husband's policy before bumping him off. Then Neff will impersonate the husband and fall off a moving train, though one that is not going very fast. He and Phyllis Dietrichson (Stanwyck) will plant the corpse on the tracks. Plausible on paper, but it smells bad to an experienced insurance investigator; and then, to paraphrase Dana Andrews in *Laura*, the dame pulls a switch on you. It turns out that her co-conspirator has been doing Phyllis's bidding all along. She's in it not for love but for her husband's dough. She loves somebody else—to the extent that she loves anyone other than herself. By the time Neff gets cold feet, it's too late. "The machinery had started to move and nothing could stop it."

Some favorite moments:

1. Stanwyck as traffic cop, MacMurray as speeding motorist, when he first calls on her, hoping to get her husband to renew his life insurance. Mr. Dietrichson is not at home. Mrs. Dietrichson is scantily clad at the top of a staircase. She descends. Sparks begin to

fly. Walter has come on a bit strong, and the dialogue is a wonderful fencing match:

> *Phyllis:* There's a speed limit in this state, Mr. Neff. Forty-five miles
> an hour.
>
> *Neff:* How fast was I going, officer?
>
> *Phyllis:* I'd say about ninety.
>
> *Neff:* Suppose you get down off your motorcycle and give me a
> ticket.
>
> *Phyllis:* Suppose I let you off with a warning this time.
>
> *Neff:* Suppose it doesn't take.
>
> *Phyllis:* Suppose I have to whack you over the knuckles.
>
> *Neff:* Suppose I bust out crying and put my head on your shoulder.
>
> *Phyllis:* Suppose you try putting it on my husband's shoulder.
>
> *Neff:* That tears it.

When Stanwyck scolds her partner in love and crime, she proves
to be the tougher of the two. "Nobody's pulling out," she says. "We
went into this together and we're coming out at the end together.
It's straight down the line for both of us. Remember?" It is not an
accident that the last name of Phyllis Dietrichson, this paragon of
the femme fatale, includes "Dietrich."

2. The speech made by Edward G. Robinson as Barton Keyes,
claims manager (and MacMurray's boss) at Pacific All-Risk Insurance, refuting the theory that Phyllis's husband killed himself.
Death by suicide would let the insurance company off the hook,
so naturally it is the theory favored by Mr. Norton, the head of the
firm. But Keyes will have none of it:

> Why, they've got ten volumes on suicide alone. Suicide by race, by
> color, by occupation, by sex, by seasons of the year, by time of day.

Suicide, how committed: by poison, by firearms, by drowning, by leaps. Suicide by poison, subdivided by types of poison, such as corrosive, irritant, systemic, gaseous, narcotic, alkaloid, protein, and so forth; suicide by leaps, subdivided by leaps from high places, under the wheels of trains, under the wheels of trucks, under the feet of horses, from steamboats. But, Mr. Norton, of all the cases on record, there's not one single case of suicide by leap from the rear end of a moving train. And you know how fast that train was going at the point where the body was found? Fifteen miles an hour. Now how can anybody jump off a slow-moving train like that with any kind of expectation that he would kill himself? No. No soap, Mr. Norton. We're sunk, and we'll have to pay through the nose, and you know it.

Keyes has a soft spot for Neff but wises up in time. "I thought you were a shade less dumb that the rest of the outfit," he says. "Guess I was wrong. You're not smarter, Walter. You're just a little taller." Robinson stood five foot seven, MacMurray six foot three.

There are lovely subtleties and secret puns in the screenplay. When Walter first visits the Dietrichson house and is waiting for Phyllis to descend the staircase wearing her alluring anklet, the maid tells him the liquor cabinet is locked, and he replies that he brought his own keys.

3. The movie's last line ("I love you too") as MacMurray dies in Robinson's arms in what Suzanne Lummis characterizes as "the pietà that closes *Double Indemnity*, where instead of mother and crucified son it's Boss kneeling by his fallen Star Employee, insurance salesman Walter Neff, blood seeping from his bullet wound. Turns out it was a love story after all—the kind the Greeks called philia."

WHEN *DOUBLE INDEMNITY* was released in 1944, the critical reaction was mixed, with Bosley Crowther of the *New York Times* complaining that the lead actor and actress lacked "attractiveness" and that, though "diverting," the movie had a "monotonous" pace and was too long.[1] In *The Nation*, James Agee characterized it as "essentially cheap." Hollywood gossip queen Louella Parsons was much closer to the mark when she called the film "the finest picture of its kind ever made." Alfred Hitchcock told the director that since the release of *Double Indemnity*, "Billy" and "Wilder" had become "the two most important words in motion pictures."

1. Crowther's limitations as a critic (and writer) may be inferred from his reaction to the original *Ocean's 11* (1960). He felt that the movie's defects were that (a) "there is no built-in implication that the boys have done something wrong," and (b) "a wholesale holdup of Las Vegas would not be so easy as it is made to look." Bosley Crowther, "Sinatra Heads Flippant Team of Crime," *New York Times*, August 11, 1960.

20

Strangers and Mirrors

ORSON WELLES'S *THE STRANGER* (1946)
AND *THE LADY FROM SHANGHAI* (1947)

O rson Welles directed and starred in two late-forties noirs. He is the hapless hero in one; in the other, the dastardly villain. In *The Lady from Shanghai* (1947), Welles cast himself as the itinerant Irish sailor Michael O'Hara, who narrates the film and is the fall guy in an intricate homicidal plot. In *The Stranger* (1946), Welles plays an unrepentant Nazi. In both, the acting up and down the cast is superb, and the direction a marvel.

The Stranger has the more straightforward plot and is the more righteous of the two films. It includes newsreel footage informing an incredulous public of the atrocities committed by Nazi Germany. It is also the only movie Welles made that showed a profit when it was first released. *Variety* called it "a socko melodrama."

Franz Kindler (Welles), a bigwig in the Third Reich, who is said to have "conceived the theory of genocide," has reinvented himself as Charles Rankin, an instructor at the exclusive Harper School for Boys ("established 1827") in an idyllic Connecticut village. An imprisoned Nazi fanatic (Konstantin Shayne) is released in the hope that he will lead the authorities—in the person of pipe-smoking Mr. Wilson, agent of the war crimes commission (Edward G. Robinson)—to Kindler.

Rankin has married Mary (Loretta Young), the daughter of a Supreme Court justice. "And the girl is even good to look at," Welles tells Shayne, with the roguish twinkle that would serve him well in *The Third Man*. As the evidence against her husband mounts, Mary is understandably reluctant to accept that the dynamic prep school teacher she married is a villain capable of strangling a man to death with his bare hands.

A suspension of disbelief is the price of admission. Incredibly, Kindler hasn't a trace of a German accent. Yet, as if to confirm the hypothesis that the film in its larger-than-life fashion postulates, history has given us a procession of forgetful ex-Nazis in high places.

Mr. Wilson is present at the dinner where Rankin tries to deflect suspicion by heaping scorn on the German national character. But Rankin, polished though he is, makes a slip when Karl Marx is mentioned. "Marx wasn't a German, he was a Jew," Rankin blurts out, and Wilson wakes up in the middle of the night and knows his man, because only a Nazi would have made this distinction. At the film's denouement, atop the village church's clock tower, Edward G. Robinson gets to say, "You're finished, Herr Franz Kindler."

Whereas *The Stranger* takes place in a picture-perfect New England village dominated by its clock tower and monitored by the checkers-playing proprietor of the drugstore ("All your needs are on our shelves"), *The Lady from Shanghai* is in constant motion. The movie begins in New York's Central Park after dark, where Michael O'Hara (Welles), on foot, meets Elsa Bannister (Rita Hayworth) in a horse-drawn carriage. After Michael proves his mettle by rescuing Elsa from a trio of muggers, he is recruited to join her, her husband, Arthur (Everett Sloane), and their entourage on the *Zaca*, a yacht sailing to San Francisco via the Panama Canal and Acapulco.

The Lady from Shanghai generates sexual heat of the kind that is absent from more licentious works. Rita Hayworth is a magnificent femme fatale, less of a *chingona* than Barbara Stanwyck but just as dangerous and more beautiful. When the movie was made, Hayworth was married to Welles. At the director's command, she was shorn of her long red locks in favor of short blonde hair. Apparently Welles felt that no one would believe Hayworth was a calculating killer unless he refashioned her looks. Maybe he got her wrong. "Men go to bed with Gilda and wake up disappointed that it's me," Hayworth once said. The studio (Columbia) hated what he did to her hair, and the film flopped. All the same, Rita remains a knockout in *The Lady from Shanghai*, and though (or because) the marriage ended soon after the film was released, the love scenes are intense.

There is a *meshuga* scheme involving a life insurance policy. Grisby, Arthur's creepy partner (Glenn Anders), pays Michael to sign a confession to a murder that has not been committed. When Grisby is shot, Michael is charged with the crime. Arthur Bannister, who has never lost a case but is not eager to win this one, defends him at the trial. Elsa's cuckolded husband, who needs crutches to move, can be pompous, can be nasty, but does have undeniable courtroom skills and showmanship. Called as a witness, he gets to cross-examine himself and makes the most of the moment. Two excited Chinese girls in the gallery comment in their native language until one turns to the American vernacular: "You ain't kiddin'."

Two scenes and a phrase linger with me. When Elsa and Michael have an assignation in the San Francisco aquarium, we see their silhouettes kissing in the foreground while fish dart by in tanks behind them. The effect is eerie, magical: pure noir. The other scene, in the "Magic Mirror Maze" of a Playland fun house, is where we find out who killed whom for what reason. That information is forgettable, unlike the shattering of the images in the multiple self-reflecting mirrors as Mr. and Mrs. Bannister face off with pistols, and two thirds of a romantic triangle are wiped out.

And the phrase? "Target practice," as Grisby pronounces it. It will never sound the same.

21

An Exchange of Bullets in Belfast

CAROL REED'S *ODD MAN OUT* (1947)

British director Carol Reed turned out three masterpieces in the late 1940s. With an exemplary performance from Ralph Richardson, *The Fallen Idol* (1948) does justice to Graham Greene's story "The Basement Room." *The Third Man* (1949), the most celebrated of the three, has its unforgettable zither theme, its evocation of postwar Vienna, and its extraordinary script, including the speech Orson Welles improvised at the Prater amusement park. Fierce competition, but my vote for Reed's best goes to *Odd Man Out* (1947), a modern passion play about a doomed man in the shadows and alleys of his last hours alive.

Odd Man Out foregrounds political and religious themes and differs thereby from most films noirs. Yet I wouldn't hesitate to claim it for the category. The setting is Belfast, Northern Ireland, where the people take their Catholicism seriously, and the robbery that triggers the plot is committed not by your typical thieves but by an unnamed underground movement, presumably the IRA. Thanks to the inspired cinematography—the hero's haunted profile, the desolate cityscape, the long narrow alleys—the Belfast we see is a dark and bleak war zone.

You may argue that the revolutionary cause is undermined in *Odd Man Out*, which establishes that the men who rob a mill for a cause are no nobler than those who rob banks for money. Nevertheless, the viewer's sympathy is with rebel leader Johnny McQueen (James Mason), whom the children in the street emulate in their pretend games of cops and robbers. "It's probably the best thing that Mason has ever done, and certainly the best film he's ever been in," Richard Burton observed.

Johnny, who escaped from prison six months earlier, has spent the time hiding at the house where Kathleen Sullivan (Kathleen Ryan) and her grandmother reside. Kathleen would be Johnny's natural mate if he were not wedded to "the organization." Far from a femme fatale, she is closer to a martyr or saint, embodying the Christian virtue of *caritas*. Love is the moral absolute that sustains her. There is no evidence that she and Johnny have so much as kissed. Yet she is willing to die for him or with him.

The narrative takes place all in one day. When McQueen and chums go over last-minute details of the mill heist, Kathleen implores him not to go: "You're not fit for it." Another man offers to go in his place: "Your heart's not in this job, Johnny." Johnny is rusty; his six months in hiding followed eight months behind bars. But though he is not as steady on his feet as he should be, Johnny is "the chief" and feels he must lead the four-man team.

Naturally something goes wrong. Alarms sound. Johnny has renounced violence, but now he finds himself in a struggle with an armed cashier, and when the guns go off, the cashier lies dead and Johnny has taken a bullet in his left shoulder. No one was supposed to get killed. And Johnny wasn't supposed to fall out of the getaway car—or be abandoned by his none-too-bright chums fleeing for their lives.

Dazed and bleeding badly, McQueen manages to get to his feet and stumble into a deserted air raid shelter. There is a precious moment of relief when, upon waking, he imagines that he is still in prison—and that the little girl who has entered to recover her lost ball is reassuringly a prison guard to whom he can describe the strange dream from which he has woken. Only when his hand reaches inside his jacket and feels his blood-soaked shirt does the wounded man realize that what he dreamed did happen. He is no longer safely, almost contentedly, in a prison cell. Susceptible to hallucination, hunted by the authorities, he staggers out of the shelter and into the mercy of chance encounters.

Johnny's progress is like that of a pilgrim on his way through hell to get to purgatory. As gray skies give way to heavy rain, he is seldom fully conscious but constantly on the move. Some citizens take brief pity on him—tending to his wounds, giving him liquor, sheltering him in a pub—before returning him to the streets. Sometimes luck lends a hand, as when Johnny is deposited in the back of a hansom cab, which the police do not inspect on the assumption that the passenger, out cold, is an ordinary drunkard.

The secondary characters are extraordinary. As Penn State media professor Kevin Hagopian puts it in his film notes for the New York State Writers Institute, *Odd Man Out* is "festooned with gargoyles." The crazed painter Lukey (Robert Newton) sees in Johnny's suffering face the perfect model for a masterpiece of portraiture. With the bearing of a genteel bordello mistress, treacherous Theresa O'Brien (Maureen Delaney) lets two of the bandits drink her whiskey in one room, while in another she informs the police of their whereabouts. Dimwitted Shell (F. J. McCormick), who collects birds and speaks in avian metaphors, discovers Johnny in a rubbish heap and relishes the reward he will get for turning in this bird with the wounded left wing. But Father Tom (W. G. Fay) persuades Shell that there is a greater reward than money and it is called Faith. When Shell wonders what Faith is, his roommate, a medical student, says, "It's life."

Odd Man Out is rife with dualities. Father Tom stands for mercy. A police inspector, who represents justice, distinguishes between the sphere of guilt and innocence, which is his concern, and that of good and evil, which isn't. The med student ministers to Johnny's body; the painter labors to capture his soul. As for the politics, most of the people are like the cabman who tells Johnny he's neither for him nor against him but can't afford to get mixed up in his troubles.

Movies that make intelligent use of poetry or scripture hold a charm for me, and when he is being painted, Johnny breaks from his delirium into lucid speech, quoting from 1 Corinthians 13: "When I was a child, I spake as a child, I thought as a child, I understood as a child: but when I became a man, I put away childish things." With a visionary gleam in his eyes, Johnny stands up and raises his right arm: "Though I have all faith, so that I could remove mountains, and have not charity, I am nothing."

The heavy rain has turned to snow by the time Kathleen locates her man. Johnny: "Is it far?" Kathleen: "It's a long way, Johnny, but I'm coming with you." Shots ring out. And then the clock strikes midnight.

22

Blind Accidents

JOHN HUSTON'S
THE ASPHALT JUNGLE (1950)

"If you want fresh air, don't look for it in this town," Louis the "box man" Ciavelli (Anthony Caruso) tells Doc Riedenschneider (Sam Jaffe), the mastermind of a million-dollar jewel heist, in John Huston's noir *The Asphalt Jungle* (1950). Surprise: the robbery doesn't go off as brilliantly planned. Doc, also known as "the professor" and "Herr Doktor," will end in prison along with Gus (James Whitmore), the hunchbacked counterman who is a top-notch getaway driver; Cobby, a bookie (Marc Lawrence); and Lieutenant Ditrich, a crooked cop (Barry Kelley). Louis will leave a widow and a small, sickly child, after a watchman is punched and falls to the ground, misfiring his gun, and a slug finds its home in Louis's belly. Oh, yes, "box man" means safecracker.

Based on the novel by W. R. Burnett, *The Asphalt Jungle* is the ur-example for the whole caper subgenre. The booty could be the gems in a shop on Paris's ritzy rue de Rivoli (*Rififi*), the proceeds at the track on the day of a big race (*The Killing*), or, in a comic register, the take of five Las Vegas casinos at midnight on New Year's Eve (*Ocean's Eleven*). Whatever the setting, the result is failure not because of the ratiocinative powers of the police but because of the inevitability of betrayal, miscalculation, and violent death. Nearly all of noir is founded on this assumption made somehow romantic and even almost glamorous.

In the course of *The Asphalt Jungle*, we see ex-con Dix Handley (Sterling Hayden), a tall man, walking alone, dwarfed by arched columns beside train tracks; a long crooked alley that veers to the right at a forty-five-degree angle; a narrow dark entryway to a bookie joint that makes you feel as if the walls are closing in on you; the innards of a building, exposed pipes, brick walls; and a security gate resembling the bars in a prison cell. The visuals are noir signifiers, and so is Miklós Rózsa's soundtrack. The city itself seems to wail. Says Maria, Louis's wife, the police sirens sound "like a soul in hell."

For a heist to succeed, you need to do more than remove the valuables from a safe or vault. If you're lucky enough to get away without firing a gun or incurring an injury, you need to find a reliable fence, who will take half of your ill-gotten gains. But the fellow with the smooth front may be pulling a fast one, especially if, like the well-heeled, tuxedo-clad Alonzo Emmerich (Louis Calhern) in *The Asphalt Jungle*, he has an unhappy wife at home, a glamorous babe in his beach house, and neither the dough he promised nor the guts to pull off his facile plan to fleece the robbers.

The entire cast is superb, these five especially:

• Hayden as Dix, the "hooligan" and "big hick," brawny and trustworthy, an honest crook. No genius, but his instincts serve him well. He hopes someday to buy back the farm where he grew up in Boone County, Kentucky. "We lost our corn crop," he remembers, and Corn Cracker, the tall black colt he loved, broke his leg and had to be shot. "That was a rotten year." Once he makes "a real killing" he is determined to return, and the first thing he will do is find a country creek where he can wash off "the city's dirt."

- Jaffe as Doc, a little man in a homburg and dark overcoat, who smokes cigars, speaks with an immigrant's thick German accent, and never carries a gun. In jail he was popular among the police guards, who made him an assistant librarian, a job that enabled him to hone his trade. "That square-head . . . has got plenty of guts," Dix says.
- Calhern as Emmerich, the very essence of suave, who, as Dix says, "even double-crossed himself." When Doc and Dix bring the stolen jewels to Emmerich, he greets them not with cash but with Bob Brannom (Brad Dexter), a hired gun, who shoots Dix in the side but is paid back with a terminal "hole in his pump."
- Jean Hagen as Doll, an out-of-work showgirl now that the Club Regal has been raided. Doll is sweet, sincere, and smitten with Dix. "I never had a proper home," she laments. Hagen is a remarkably versatile actress. Compare her work here to that in *Singin' in the Rain*.
- Scene-stealing Marilyn Monroe in a strapless black dress as Angela, Emmerich's trophy girl, who calls him Uncle Lon and is willing to give him an alibi. "Yipe," she exclaims about a bathing suit she has her eye on, and when a cop knocks on her door, she tells him off: "Haven't you bothered me enough, you big banana-head?"

Spoiler alert: of the three men on this short list, one will shoot himself; one will die of his wounds, but not before getting into a jalopy with his lady and driving to the horse farm of his youth; and one will be arrested, with a fortune in jewels on his person because he gives a teenage girl a roll of nickels to feed a jukebox, feasts his eyes, and is apprehended by cops he would have eluded if he hadn't stayed to watch the girl and her friends dance the lindy.

On a recent viewing, I noted that "soup" was slang for explosive and that, in the postwar era, to "bone" someone was to insult him or her in a humiliating way. (An angry Dix to Cobby, the bookie: "You boned me in front of a stranger.") As in so many noirs, the crooks wear neckties and suit jackets with peaked lapels, the getaway car looks great, and the caper and its deadly aftermath illustrate two essential precepts. Emmerich: "Crime is only a left-handed form of human endeavor." Doc: "Put in hours and hours of planning. Figure everything down to the last detail. Then what? Burglar alarms start going off all over the place for no sensible reason. A gun fires of its own accord and a man is shot. And a broken-down old cop, no good for anything but chasing kids, has to trip over us. Blind accident. What can you do against blind accidents?"

23

Epitaph for a Genre

STANLEY KUBRICK'S
THE KILLING (1956)

Adapted by Stanley Kubrick and Jim Thompson from the pulp novel by Lionel White, *The Killing* is classic noir. The plot is about an expertly planned racetrack heist that goes spectacularly wrong because the weak link in the chain of confederates is married to a two-timing frail. A cast of noir stalwarts under Kubrick's direction brings the story to life. Later Kubrick movies such as *2001* and *A Clockwork Orange* are more ambitious undertakings, but many of us with noir in our bones have a special affection for *The Killing*, a taut black-and-white depiction of futility and failure.

Just out of prison, Johnny Clay is tall, tough, taciturn, and as decent a guy as you could want in a thief and ex-con—a role Sterling Hayden was born to play. "Johnny, you were never very bright," his friend Maurice says, "but I love you anyway," which is pretty much how the viewer sees him. (The muscular Maurice, a local chess master with the strength of Samson, had observed that "the gangster and the artist are the same in the eyes of the masses," who nevertheless want to see them brought down "at the height of their glory." Johnny responded, "Like the man said, life is like a glass of tea.")

For all his mental shortcomings, Johnny has planned the robbery with a chess player's precision. An inside job, it requires the contributions of a pay window cashier named George (Elisha Cook Jr.) and a track bartender. Johnny has also recruited Randy (Ted de Corsia), a crooked cop, who drives solo in his prowl car; Nikki, a sharpshooter (played with great nastiness by Timothy Carey); and Maurice, a muscle man (Kola Kwariani, a Georgian wrestler with whom Kubrick played chess).

Nikki must shoot Black Lightning, the favorite in the high-stakes race of the day, when the colt reaches the far turn of the track just before the head of the backstretch. At the same time, Maurice will pick a fight at the bar. You need ten men in uniform to hold Maurice down, and so, amid the chaos, no one notices the cashier when he unlocks the door marked "NO ADMITTANCE" behind which men count and stash the day's take. The diversions give Johnny time enough to walk in, don a mask, brandish a submachine gun, and collect the dough in a duffel bag, which he then tosses out the window . . . for Randy to pick up and drive away. A perfect crime.

Kubrick starts and restarts the story, shifting points of view, reverting each time to the track announcer's call of the $100,000-added Lansdowne Stakes ("the horses are approaching the starting gate"). The marksman's story features a chilling scene between Nikki and a Black racetrack employee played by James Edwards. The narrative throughout is advanced by voice-over, a matter-of-fact male voice of authority and doom, accentuating the suspense.

Elisha Cook Jr., so memorable as the humiliated gunsel in *The Maltese Falcon* and as brave, lovesick Harry Jones in *The Big Sleep*, is outstanding as George the cashier, a man who, in Lionel White's novel, is said to be "crazy about his wife" but "not completely blind to her character." He knows, too, that he has "failed as a husband and failed as a man."

In short, he is the archetypal noir loser, married to Sherry (Marie Windsor), who is discontented, fickle, frustrated, and doomed.

When George confides that in the next few days he will have a lot of money, she says, with practiced cruelty, "Did you put the right address on the envelope when you sent it to the North Pole?" Sherry gets George to reveal the gang's plans.

Everything goes right until the guys gather to split the proceeds. Sherry has spilled the beans to her handsome boyfriend Val (Vince Edwards). Val and a henchman barge in to steal the dough, and in the ensuing shootout all are killed except George, who is badly wounded but has enough vitality left to stumble home and shoot Sherry before he expires. "It isn't fair," she says, making the cinematic most of the moment. "I never had anyone but you, not a real husband, not even a man."

Having transferred the loot to the biggest suitcase he could buy, Johnny Clay arrives at the scene fifteen minutes too late for the gunfight. Seeing George tumble down the front stairs, Johnny puts two and two together and drives away with the sound of sirens in his ears. He and girlfriend Fay (Coleen Gray) hightail it to the airport.

Johnny Clay does not survive in Lionel White's novel. On the last page, two bullets from George's gun make a "peculiar, plopping sound" as they enter Johnny's stomach. Under his elbow is a folded newspaper, headlined "Race Track Bandit / Makes Clean Break / With Two Million." (The novel's original title was *Clean Break*.)

The movie's ending is even better, culminating with the greatest money shot in the movies, its nearest competition being the shower of love bestowed on James Stewart on Christmas Eve at the end of *It's a Wonderful Life*. Johnny and Fay are at the airport, about to board a flight to Boston and freedom. He doesn't want to let go of the suitcase, but it is too big for the overhead compartment, so he reluctantly yields it to the airport clerk. He and Fay watch the suitcase totter atop the checked luggage in the cart conveying it from terminal to plane. When a bystander's dog runs into the cart's path, the driver swerves, and the suitcase falls off. It pops opens, and the money flies around like snow in a swirling wind. The bandit has not only lost the money but also unmasked himself as the culprit. Dazed, helpless, Johnny and Fay retreat, vainly try to hail a taxi, and are standing by the airport's front doors as two armed plain-clothed cops walk menacingly toward them. The look on Sterling Hayden's face is unforgettable.

Fay: "Johnny, you've got to run."
Johnny: "Ah ... what's the difference?"

This exchange, which ends the movie, could stand as an epitaph for all of noir.

24

Shadow of Evil

ROBERT MITCHUM
CAPE FEAR (1962)

Horror is what we feel witnessing the aftermath of a fatal car wreck. Terror is what we feel in anticipation of something terrible that has not yet happened.

What *Cape Fear* (1962) offers is a pure example of a third kind of sensation, one that attracts even as it repels: menace. Menace is Robert Mitchum as Max Cady, newly released from an eight-year prison sentence, a cigar in his mouth and a Panama hat on his head, into the heat of summer in a small southern town. Cady embodies evil and Mitchum embodies Cady, a character who is as cunning as he is vicious.

Although he plays an unreformed sex offender who beats up women and has no business gaining control of the viewer's attention, *Cape Fear* is Mitchum's picture from the moment he appears on the scene, confronting the attorney who put him behind bars. "Hello, counselor. Remember me?" Cady is back with a vengeance.

Every time Mitchum's character addresses Sam Bowden (Gregory Peck) as "counselor," his derision is palpable. And the Bowden family is vulnerable. Bowden's wife, Peggy (Polly Bergen), is right to be nervous—she will be attacked. But it is Nancy (Lori Martin), their teenage daughter, who is the primary target of Cady's lust and rage.

Cape Fear resembles the great 1949 James Cagney gangster movie *White Heat*, inasmuch as the protagonist in both cases is the bad guy. But I'm also reminded of *High Noon* (1952), in which the protagonist is the good guy (stoic, tall Gary Cooper, a figure of rectitude and resolve). Both *High Noon* and *Cape Fear* exemplify the maxim that hell hath no fury like the wrath of an ex-con set on revenge. With Cady, the maxim gets another twist: hell hath no scorn like that of a furious man intent on pushing his adversary to the brink.

Cape Fear argues that there is such a thing as evil, a darkness that cannot be rehabilitated. While *High Noon* asserts that nothing less than violence will do to eliminate evil, *Cape Fear* hedges its bets. At the film's end, Bowden points a gun at Cady but refrains from pulling the trigger, leaving his fate to the justice system.

If Peck seems uncomfortable playing the upright attorney, a role that would ordinarily serve him well, it's because from his point of view, the film is a study in frustration. Evil is powerful and corrosive. The effect Cady has on Bowden is striking: he brings out the worst in the man. As the movie progresses, Bowden's tactics to defeat Cady steadily escalate. First he prevails on the police chief (Martin Balsam) to chase Cady out of town. Because he has committed no crime, the chief refuses. Next Bowden hires a detective (Telly Savalas), hoping to charge Cady with lewd vagrancy, or worse. But the terrified prostitute whom Cady beats up refuses to file charges.

When Bowden sees Cady staring insolently and lustfully at his daughter Nancy, the lawyer punches the ex-con. But that merely augments Cady's case that he is being systematically harassed. Bowden then offers Cady $20,000 if he agrees to leave town, but Cady rejects the offer as inadequate. He makes his point persuasively by dividing the amount by eight, the number of years he spent in prison. At this point, Bowden takes up an option he rejected earlier in the film: he hires three thugs to beat up Cady, who survives the attack, tough guy that he is.

Having struck out three times, Bowden hires an accomplice, puts his family on a houseboat in Cape Fear, and makes plans to entrap Cady by catching him in a criminal act and shooting him in self-defense. This is the movie's apotheosis: the character who has undergone the most change is Bowden.

Upright is uptight in *Cape Fear*. All the sexual energy in the movie comes from Mitchum, whom we see shirtless more than once, unlike Bowden and the police chief in their suits. Cady can be characterized as the unrestrained id—with the added menace that his cunning intelligence brings to bear. Two characters call him an animal; a third calls him a beast. True enough . . . but he's played by Mitchum.

Perhaps the chief reason why *Cape Fear* is a classic is Mitchum's sensual, almost bestial appeal, which is advanced even as we are told repeatedly that he is a barbarian. In the film's most riveting sequence, Cady picks up a prostitute, Diane Taylor (Barrie Chase), at a bar. A "drifter," to use the movie's euphemism, she has just arrived in town and is full of self-loathing. "Max Cady, what I like about you is . . . you're rock bottom," she says in the car on the way to a hotel room. With bitter sarcasm, she adds, "It's a great comfort for a girl to know she could not possibly sink any lower."

When we next see the two, Taylor is asleep on the bed in a black slip. Cady stands shirtless, sizing her up. When she wakes, without either of them saying a word, Taylor immediately tries to get away, as if she has an instinctive awareness of the beating she is about to undergo. By the time the police arrive, Cady has escaped out the back, and Taylor lies on the floor with a split lip and a black eye.

As a religious question, the problem of evil has to do with how we can reconcile the concept of a benevolent, omnipotent God with an atrocity on earth. As a secular question, it asks whether there is such a thing as evil—an evil that is not simply a function of external factors and that cannot be remedied by enlightened attempts at rehabilitation. Max Cady profits from his years in the clink by acquiring not a sense of morality but legal know-how that he uses to further his criminal ends.

In 1991, *Cape Fear* was remade by Martin Scorsese, with Robert De Niro as Cady and Nick Nolte as Bowden. It is definitely worth seeing—De Niro gives a strong performance—but the original is unparalleled.

25

A Reluctant Spy's Conversion

WILLIAM HOLDEN IN
THE COUNTERFEIT TRAITOR (1962)

*T*he Counterfeit Traitor (1962), directed by George Seaton, is an underrated espionage classic in the same league as an early Eric Ambler novel or a Warner Brothers forties flick, albeit one that is set on location and in color. My best guess for why it is underrated is that the hero (William Holden) and heroine (Lilli Palmer) do not conform to accepted norms. They are played not by an all-American boy and golden girl but by two attractive and capable if decidedly middle-aged adults. Holden, who plays protagonist Eric "Red" Erickson, was forty-four in 1962. Palmer, cast with her *Mitteleuropa* beauty and charm as Frau Marianne Möllendorf, Erickson's clandestine confederate in Berlin, was forty-eight.

Like the proprietor of Rick's Café Américain in *Casablanca*, the hero of *The Counterfeit Traitor* does not begin the Second World War as the champion of a cause. He must be converted, and Frau Möllendorf is his catalyst, converting the American-born, Cornell-educated Swedish industrialist from reluctant spy to committed freedom fighter.

Erickson, an oil exporter who has continued to trade with Germany after hostilities began in September 1939, has aimed for a stance of political neutrality. But he has been denounced as a Nazi collaborator, and now, Allied intelligence, led by the sardonic

British agent Collins (Hugh Griffith), wants him to play the role with a vengeance. Repeating ugly shibboleths and breaking off relations with his best friend, a Jew, Erickson gains credibility among Nazi higher-ups, enabling him to gather vital information on German oil production facilities.

Not for the first time in his Hollywood career does Holden portray a resourceful skeptic whom the Allies need to recruit despite his reluctance to join the fray. As in *The Bridge on the River Kwai* (1957), he needs to have his arm twisted hard. You might call Erickson disillusioned, but he doesn't appear to have illusions in the first place. Virtually coerced into the role of counterfeit traitor, he sums up his situation thus: "So you want me to risk my life to get off a blacklist I didn't deserve to be on in the first place?"

Erickson and Frau Mölendorff, the wife of a German officer off womanizing in occupied France, are supposedly having an affair. This is their cover. Given the sparks between Holden and Palmer, whose elegance at high social functions conceals her idealism, the liaison turns romantic for real. Both are eligible. Eric has lost all his friends, and his wife, by acting the part of a quisling in Stockholm. Möllendorf is married in name only; but she is serious in her Catholicism and therefore doesn't sue for divorce.

When they meet, Erickson is working for the Allies because he has no choice. Möllendorf, by contrast, acts out of deep moral conviction, a revulsion with Hitler and his movement. She predicts that someday Eric "will see a stranger, a complete stranger, being bullied, beaten; and suddenly, in an agonizing moment, he will become your brother." So it happens when, as Erickson cannot help witnessing, a Nazi officer defeats a strike of famished Polish "volunteers" by picking out one of them at random and hanging him in front of the others.

Möllendorf's moral dilemma comes as an unexpected twist. Fearing that she is implicated, however indirectly, in a bombing raid that killed innocent schoolchildren, she wants to cease passing information to her Allied contacts. She feels an intense need to confess, and she enters a church, not knowing that a Gestapo agent rather than a priest is seated in the confessional box.

The movie reaches its emotional climax when Erickson is made to watch Möllendorf receive brutal Nazi justice. The Gestapo needs to decide whether his involvement with Frau Möllendorf was strictly an affair of the heart. He passes the test, but his days on German soil are numbered.

Once the movie's moral dilemmas have solved themselves, the film becomes a great escape thriller. The hero must elude the Gestapo en route to Hamburg, where his Allied contact turns out to be a sex worker in the red-light district. In the woods he must outrun German border patrol hounds to cross into Denmark. In Copenhagen he is given a cyanide tablet "in case you get caught." Arrested on a busy boulevard, he escapes the clutches of an old Gestapo antagonist thanks to an intrepid truck driver and the Danish bicyclists' form of nonviolent resistance, bringing car traffic to a standstill. A harrowing adventure on a fishing boat to Stockholm precedes a nostalgic coda.

Based on the 1958 nonfiction book of the same title by Alexander Klein, *The Counterfeit Traitor* is true in its broad contours if not in all details. The hoax Erickson and his superiors had concocted to justify his visiting oil refineries in Germany took him to meetings with top Gestapo officials, including Himmler. On June 3, 1945, the *New York Times* ran the headline "Swedish 'Pro-Nazi' Duped for 3 Years: Blacklisted by US, He Sent Allies Secret Data on Synthetic Gasoline Plants."

One reason Germany lost the war was the fuel deficit that doomed the Nazis' western offensive during the bitter winter of 1944–45. Albert Speer's industrial machine was building synthetic gasoline plants as fast as it could, but Allied bombing raids would just as swiftly cripple them. The raids could not have happened without the information Erickson and his confederates provided.

Erickson had a prodigious memory for detail, and the only documents that figure in his story are the letters he agreed to write for German businessmen who cooperated with Allied intelligence. In the event of a German defeat, these letters would protect the men and their families from partisan reprisals. If, however, the Nazis were to discover such a letter, it would fatally compromise Erickson's mission—and sentence the bearer as well as the Swedish spy to certain death. The fate of one such letter proves pivotal in the movie.

I FIRST GRASPED the importance of a pocket square with three wings in a man's breast pocket when I saw William Holden wear one at a cocktail party in *The Counterfeit Traitor*. And it was watching the movie as a fourteen-year-old that I realized for the first time that the hopelessness of a love affair accentuates its romantic and sexual intensity.

26

Gangsters in Love

SERGIO LEONE'S *ONCE UPON A TIME IN AMERICA* (1984)

Nearly four hours long, *Once Upon a Time in America* was drastically cut when released in 1984. Viewers were puzzled and reviewers panned the butchered 144-minute version that they saw. The movie makes a lot more sense at its proper length. When the eighty-five minutes of deleted footage were restored, some of the same folks who derided *Once Upon a Time in America* hailed it as Sergio Leone's melancholy masterpiece, a gangster epic that doubles as an exploration of friendship and betrayal, male competition masked as sexual desire, greed, violence, and the American dream.

The gangsters here are first-generation Jews, the locale is New York City's Lower East Side, and there are three distinct time periods. Though the story begins in the early 1920s, the movie opens in 1933, in the aftermath of a disastrous caper that only one of the gang members survives. The survivor is David Aaronson, known to all as "Noodles" (Robert De Niro).

When we first see Noodles, he is smoking a pipe in a Chinese opium den. His partners have been killed, and he feels responsible for their deaths. Hit men are out to get him. Noodles makes his way to the bus terminal where he and his buddies stashed a suitcase full of cash in a locker. But the suitcase has old newspapers in it, not money, and Noodles, a beaten man, buys a one-way ticket to Buffalo, where he will spend the next thirty-five years "going to bed early."

What really happened to Noodles in 1933? The story hinges on that question.

Most of the film is told in memories and dreams, languorous flashbacks and an abrupt flash-forward to 1968, the transition to which is managed by the appearance of a tossed Frisbee and the sound of a Muzak version of the Beatles' "Yesterday." Racked with guilt because he feels responsible for the violent deaths of his boyhood chums, Noodles is mysteriously summoned back to New York City in letters that imply that his cover ("Robert Williams") has been blown.

The scenes set in the early 1920s are perhaps the most affecting. The leading characters are played by child actors, of whom the most notable is the twelve-year-old Jennifer Connelly as Deborah. Noodles is desperately in love with her, has always been, and she loves being his object of affection but will always reject him: "He'll always be a two-bit punk, so he'll never be my beloved. What a shame!"

For his delectation, the young Deborah recites passages from the biblical Song of Songs and dances to the strains of "Amapola," played as a clarinet solo. The song, which recurs as the background music for the couple's ill-fated romance, is particularly apt, because *amapola* in Spanish means "poppy," and the grown-up Noodles smokes opium to forget his troubles.

As kids, the fellows form a gang that has fun at the expense of a dirty cop. Noodles and Maxie, his closest friend, are the gang's leaders. They get beaten up viciously by a rival gang, but get some measure of revenge when Noodles knifes Bugsy, the leader of the opposition.

When Noodles is released from prison, he is Robert De Niro and it is 1932. Maxie (James Woods) drives a hearse to pick him up. The naked young woman in the coffin "died of an overdose," Maxie says, and the girl springs to life saying, "I'm ready for another!" Intense sexual competition is a crucial element of Maxie's friendship with Noodles, and Maxie's gift is also a test. "Don't worry," the girl says when the hearse pulls up to the speakeasy the gang operates. "A pansy he ain't."

The guys form an alliance with union boss Jimmy Conway O'Donnell (Treat Williams), who will someday, like another Jimmy, become chief of the teamsters. The gangster epic allows for comic scenes, and to get what they want for the union, the gang plays a practical joke on the city's head cop (Danny Aiello). Aiello, who has fathered daughters, is over the moon because his wife has given birth to a son. The cops have been cracking down on striking workers, but they lay off after the fellows sneak into the maternity ward and, to the strains of Rossini's *Thieving Magpie* overture, switch babies from one crib to another. A blend of astonishment and fury, Aiello's reaction when he removes his baby's diaper is priceless.

To woo the ever elusive Deborah (Elizabeth McGovern), a budding actress, Noodles rents an entire restaurant by the shore. The orchestra plays for them alone. Deborah: "You dancing?" Noodles: "You asking?" Deborah: "I'm asking." Noodles: "I'm dancing." It is a most marvelous evening that comes to a horrific end when, in the hired limousine, out of pent-up frustration or pure brutishness (or both), Noodles rapes Deborah in the back seat. The violation of his beloved is the second source of his lifelong guilt.

John O'Hara wrote that Prohibition made "liars of a hundred million men and cheats of their children." And its repeal works as a wonderful plot hinge in *Once Upon a Time in America*, because the bootlegging business will have to undergo a major change in 1933. But the movie's darker truths have to do with the mimetic desire that links the male leads. There are three women who have sex with both Maxie and Noodles. The three episodes are in three different registers: comedy; gangster gothic; and high opera, with swoons and tears.

The film could have been even longer. As things stand, it is not clear what happens to Secretary of Commerce Bailey at the end of the movie, which is an ambiguity Leone intended, and we are curious about Maxie's metamorphosis. What is the meaning of the smile on Noodles's face that ends the picture? Is he on an opium high reliving his life and dreaming what might have happened in 1933?

Taking into account the brilliance of Ennio Morricone's soundtrack, the excellence of the acting, and the complexity of the movie's structure, you may find it hard to disagree with Sergio Leone's own assessment: "*Once Upon a Time in America* is my best film, bar none."

27
Rogues' Gallery

There's a special onus on the villains in crime dramas. They have to be wicked, but they also have to make that wickedness interesting. Whether by being singular in some way, or by virtue of fine acting, or because what they do is so despicable, they offend even those of us who might ordinarily root for the scoundrel. Then again, some of them simply impress us with their roguish charm or sharp-toothed wit.

Who are the greatest rogues, then? Many can be found in Hitchcock's thrillers, in which the culprit can be two people, himself and his murderous mother (Anthony Perkins in *Psycho*). Or there is madness in the man's method, and he steals every scene he's in (Robert Walker in *Strangers on a Train*). Or the villains are forces of nature wreaking havoc on humanity, which has mistreated them along with the rest of the planet (the birds in *The Birds*). But let's omit Hitchcock's bad guys, sadistic prison wardens like Hume Cronyn in *Brute Force*, as well as the homicidal freaks in movies starring Clint Eastwood and Charles Bronson, who might otherwise dominate the list.

Here are a few of my favorite miscreants.

Gregory Anton, Gaslight *(1944)*

In an effort to bury the evidence of a murder he has committed, Charles Boyer in *Gaslight* (directed by George Cukor, 1944) compounds one sin with another by mounting a campaign to persuade Ingrid Bergman that she is insane. His strategy has made "gaslight" a verb signifying the sort of mental manipulation that sadistic spouses and bosses have been known to inflict.

Waldo Lydecker, Laura *(1944)*

In *Laura*, the critic and radio personality with the unforgettable moniker Waldo Lydecker (Clifton Webb) says he writes "with a goose quill dipped in venom." Lydecker represents the movies' idea of what a critic is: vain, effete, scornful, condescending, and conceited.

Phyllis Dietrichson and Walter Neff, Double Indemnity *(1944)*

In director Billy Wilder's *Double Indemnity*, adulterous wife (Barbara Stanwyck) and insurance executive boyfriend (Fred MacMurray) eliminate the inconvenient husband, then prepare to betray each other. Says she: "We're both rotten." He: "Only you're a little more rotten."

Veda, Mildred Pierce *(1945)*

Ann Blyth plays Veda, Joan Crawford's daughter in *Mildred Pierce*, directed by Michael Curtiz. Veda is an ingrate, a liar, a blackmailer, a murderer, and worst of all, a spoiled brat.

Tommy Udo, Kiss of Death *(1947)*

In Henry Hathaway's *Kiss of Death*, Richard Widmark plays the giggling psychopath who uses an electric cord to strap a disabled woman in her wheelchair and roll her down a fatal flight of tenement stairs.

Kathie Moffat, Out of the Past *(1947)*

For a terminally treacherous femme fatale who may look innocent but kills without compunction, you can't beat Jane Greer as Kathie Moffat in Jacques Tourneur's *Out of the Past*.

Madge, Dark Passage *(1948)*

Happy only when others suffer, Agnes Moorehead in director Delmer Daves's *Dark Passage* embodies the spirit of spite. She also kills people.

Harry Lime, The Third Man *(1949)*

In director Carol Reed's *The Third Man*, Harry Lime (Orson Welles) sells tainted penicillin in postwar Vienna, and, from the top of the Riesenrad in the Prater amusement park, looks down disdainfully at the people below as if they have the significance of ants. Welles doesn't show up until the movie is half over and gets very little airtime, but he does speak—and apparently improvise—the movie's most memorable lines: "In Italy, for thirty years under the Borgias, they had warfare, terror, murder, bloodshed, but they produced Michelangelo, Leonardo da Vinci, and the Renaissance. In Switzerland, they had brotherly love. They had five hundred years of democracy and peace, and what did that produce? The cuckoo clock."

Cody Jarrett, White Heat *(1949)*

James Cagney as Cody Jarrett in *White Heat,* directed by Raoul Walsh, is an eighteen-karat psychopath. On receiving news of his adored mother's death, he freaks out so violently in the prison cafeteria that hardened criminals can only watch in awe. Jarrett dies at the height of his glory, atop a tower on fire and about to collapse. "Made it, Ma!" he yells. "Top of the world!"

Vince Stone, The Big Heat *(1953)*

Lee Marvin flings a pot of boiling coffee at girlfriend Gloria Grahame's face, disfiguring it, in *The Big Heat,* directed by Fritz Lang. There are murders and a car bomb in the picture too, but nothing equals the violence of that flung pot of coffee.

Bud Corliss, A Kiss Before Dying *(1956)*

In *A Kiss Before Dying,* Gerd Oswald's film based on Ira Levin's book of the same title, Robert Wagner plays the calculating cad who invites his pregnant girlfriend (Joanne Woodward), an heiress, to meet him at the town's municipal building, ostensibly to obtain a marriage license. Timing the meeting to coincide with the bureau's lunch break, he lures the would-be bride to the roof and hurls her to her screaming death. She has a sister, and guess who's next on his list to woo? In the 1991 remake, Matt Dillon plays the murderous monster, Sean Young plays both sisters, and the scene of the crime is Philadelphia's City Hall.

Mark Lewis, Peeping Tom *(1960)*

Mark Lewis (Carl Boehm) is the "Peeping Tom" of Michael Powell's movie. An aspiring filmmaker, Lewis slays a woman, records her death throes with a portable camera, and watches the film in his den. The movie allegorizes the cinematic experience and implicates the audience in the killer's voyeurism.

Max Cady, Cape Fear *(1962)*

The example of Max Cady as portrayed by Robert Mitchum in *Cape Fear*, directed by J. Lee Thompson, goes a long way toward refuting the notion that evil is a function of environment. Hellbent on revenge, indifferent to moral restraints, and possessed of great cunning, he embodies, in Milton's phrase, "darkness visible."

Senator John Yerkes Iselin and Mrs. Eleanor Iselin, The Manchurian Candidate *(1962)*

In John Frankenheimer's *The Manchurian Candidate*, Angela Lansbury is the brains of the assassination plot and James Gregory is her stooge of a husband, a stand-in for Joe McCarthy. The plot calls for the recurrence of a certain playing card, which triggers a hypnotic trance in which brainwashed war hero Laurence Harvey will do what he is told, including assassinating designated individuals. In Lansbury's honor, the award for best villain might be dubbed the Queen of Diamonds.

Alain Charnier, The French Connection *(1971)*

With his hat, walking stick, and enjoyment of fine French food in a tony midtown Manhattan restaurant on a cold December day, while the cop on his tail freezes his ass off holding a paper cup of coffee, Fernando Rey in *The French Connection*, directed by William Friedkin, is as debonair as he is clever. Disappearing at film's end, he escapes penalty as few criminal masterminds do.

Verbal Kint, The Usual Suspects *(1995)*

In 1864, Charles Baudelaire crafted the rogues' motto when he observed that one of Satan's "artifices" is "to induce men to believe that he does not exist." In Bryan Singer's *The Usual Suspects*, Verbal, played by Kevin Spacey offers this paraphrase, "The greatest trick the Devil ever pulled was convincing the world he didn't exist." Verbal demonstrates the validity of the statement by enduring hours of police grilling, using his powers of narrative invention to confuse the authorities, who realize only after releasing him that he is responsible for all the mayhem and murder in the film.

Julian Wilde, Lured *(1947)*

Speaking of Baudelaire and his relevance to noir, Sir Cedric Hardwicke merits dishonorable mention as the creepy "poet killer" who sends poems to the police in imitation of Baudelaire to announce his murders in Douglas Sirk's *Lured*. The film is worth seeing also for Lucille Ball as the damsel in distress and for George Sanders who, for a happy change, is cast as the misunderstood good guy.

28

Why Not New York?

In *Out of the Past*, Robert Mitchum says he used to live in New York and Rhonda Fleming says she's never been to New York and Mitchum says that if she visits the city, she'll know one reason why he's not there but in San Francisco.

San Francisco, because of its natural beauty, its hills and bridges and bay, may be the most popular location for films noirs and crime dramas. Think of *The Lady from Shanghai, Dark Passage, Impact, Woman on the Run, Vertigo, Bullitt, Dirty Harry, Jagged Edge.* These movies feature some of the distinctive landmarks of the city—Chinatown's Mandarin Theatre, the Steinhart Aquarium, and Playland at the Beach in *The Lady from Shanghai*; the Golden Gate Bridge in *Dark Passage*; Fisherman's Wharf and the Embarcadero in *Woman on the Run*; Fisherman's Wharf, Chinatown, and a cable car in *Impact*; the Presidio, Coit Tower, and Muir Woods in *Vertigo*; the Dodgers' Don Drysdale on the mound at Candlestick Park in *Experiment in Terror*; Kezar Stadium in *Dirty Harry*; Coit Tower and the Golden Gate Bridge in a cloud of fog in *Jagged Edge.*

"People who complain that Los Angeles is sprawling and without roots and has no character are uninformed," the screenwriter Daniel Fuchs writes in one of his Hollywood stories. "It just means they haven't been here long enough." Los Angeles is the locale for its share of crime dramas. *Double Indemnity*; *The Big Sleep*; *Murder, My Sweet*; *Black Angel*; *He Walked By Night*; *In a Lonely Place*; *Chinatown*; *Farewell, My Lovely*; and *L.A. Confidential* come to mind. So do *The Man Who Cheated Himself*, *The Onion Field*, and *Mulholland Drive*. Los Angeles is also where Columbo smokes his cigars and where Perry Mason, Della Street, and Paul Drake defend the wrongly accused on the television show with the fabulous entrance and exit music by Fred Steiner. Billy Wilder's great *Sunset Boulevard*, not your typical noir, is narrated by William Holden in voice-over, a screenwriter whose dead body floats face downward in a swimming pool at a Hollywood mansion, as if the film were an allegory of the writer's typical fate in the dream merchants' universe.

There are other great capitals of crime: Chicago, Miami, Boston, London, Paris. Still, as a New York native who has mastered what Auden called the art of crossing the street against the light, I must put in a plea for the "helluva town" celebrated by the three sailors on shore leave in *On the Town*. The city hosts such popular TV crime dramas as the *Law & Order* franchise, *Blue Bloods*, *NYPD Blue* in the nineties and *Kojak* in the seventies. Jules Dassin's *Naked City* (1948) is the inspired result of producer Mark Hellinger's pioneering effort to shoot the film entirely on the streets and sidewalks of New York. In Don Siegel's *Coogan's Bluff* (1968), Clint Eastwood is a deputy sheriff from Arizona who flies into the big city to nab an escaped killer in Fort Tryon Park and leave for the airport from the heliport on top of the old Pan Am Building. The viewer of *No Way to Treat a Lady* (1967) visits Lincoln Center, admires the Chagall murals at the Metropolitan Opera House, and stops for a bite at Joe Allen and Sardi's in the theater district. The situation is *echt* New York: George Segal, the cop on the case, has an overbearing mother and a beautiful blonde girlfriend, Lee Remick, who wonders, "Is a Jewish cop so wrong for me?"

"I love this dirty town," J. J. Hunsecker, the Winchell-like columnist played by Burt Lancaster, says in *Sweet Smell of Success* (1957), and while the dirt in the movie sticks to your sole like something bad you stepped into, the affection is there too, in the form of 21, Toots Shor's, the Flatiron Building, the Broadway lights, and the wisecracking of the press agent played by Tony Curtis: "Dallas, your mouth is as big as a basket and twice as empty!" "If you're funny, Walter, I'm a pretzel! Drop dead!"

Four notable New York noirs feature Dana Andrews: Fritz Lang's *While the City Sleeps* and *Beyond a Reasonable Doubt* (both 1956), Otto Preminger's *Laura* (1944) and *Where the Sidewalk Ends* (1950). In *Laura* and one other of these movies, Andrews succeeds in solving a crime and winning a woman's hand. The newspaperman hero of Fritz Lang's *While the City Sleeps* outwits the "lipstick killer," a twenty-year-old "mama's boy," who bears an odd resemblance to Bono, the lead singer of U-2, as photographed by Herb Ritts in Vienna in 1992. (Is the implication that yesterday's punks may be today's heroes, if only in style?) In *Where the Sidewalk Ends*, however, Andrews epitomizes the morally equivocal noir hero, a hardnosed cop who hates criminals because his father was one. Often enough accused of police brutality, Andrews has a hair-trigger temper, gets into a fistfight and accidentally kills the other guy, then alters the evidence at the scene of a crime. This is as subversive a view of police behavior as you can get away with in 1950, with handsome Andrews and Gene Tierney reassuringly on hand to remind you of their joint cinematic history as the hero and heroine of *Laura*: actors who look so good together, you can imagine them as a couple in real life. *Beyond a Reasonable Doubt*, in which Andrews as a journalist agrees to frame himself for murder in order to prove a point, is even bleaker, ending with a double twist that dooms him to a prison cell.

Attracted to landmarks for thematic reasons, Hitchcock concludes one film with the Statue of Liberty and another at the gate
in Grand Central Station. Henry Hathaway's *Kiss of Death* (1947)
begins with a jewel heist in the Art Deco lobby of the Chrysler
Building. Fritz Lang's *Scarlet Street* (1945) treats us to Greenwich
Village art galleries and a desolate Central Park bench at dawn—
albeit as reconstructed in a Hollywood studio. In Sergio Leone's
Once Upon a Time in America (1984), a kosher deli on New York
City's Lower East Side evolves into a Prohibition-era speakeasy in
the opening decades of the twentieth century. John Farrow's *The
Big Clock* (1948) places us in a magazine empire's midtown sky-
scraper. Robert Siodmak's *Phantom Lady* (1944) invites us into
a swinging jazz bar. In *Where the Sidewalk Ends*, the Manhattan
Bridge in the background is a constant reminder of where we are.

Not only the subway (the IND line going downtown) but also
Broadway, Penn Station, and two of the city's bridges figure in
Stanley Kubrick's second feature, *Killer's Kiss* (1955). A runaway
subway train (the number 6, heading south) is the apotheosis of
terror in *The Taking of Pelham One Two Three* (1974). In Samuel
Fuller's *Pickup on South Street* (1953), Richard Widmark plays an
experienced pickpocket who lifts a woman's wallet in the subway and the wallet happens to have strips of microfilm that the
Communists crave, and Widmark lives on a houseboat-like shack
beneath the Brooklyn Bridge, and Thelma Ritter gets offed, and
Jean Peters gets beaten up like you wouldn't believe.

Among neo-noirs and Technicolor crime films, New York is
home for most of *The Manchurian Candidate* (1962), which features Sinatra's favorite bar, Jilly's, and the Central Park lake. In *The
French Connection* (1971), critical scenes take place in the subway
and in a fancy midtown French restaurant, and there's a fantastic car chase on a long Brooklyn avenue under an elevated BMT

train. In *The Godfather* (1972), Michael and Kay go to Radio City Music Hall on Christmas Eve to see Ingrid Bergman play a nun in *The Bells of St. Mary's*. On that night they learn of the attack on Michael's father, and as events unfold, it is Michael who volunteers to kill "the Turk" and his police protector, Captain McCluskey. To elude a possible tail, the driver of the car taking Michael and his two antagonists to the Italian restaurant with the best veal in the city begins to cross the George Washington Bridge to New Jersey, then makes an illegal U-turn to deliver the group to the Bronx, where a gun is hidden in the restaurant's men's room for Michael's use.

Of the movies Martin Scorsese set in New York, I have a particular fondness for *Goodfellas* because of the long tracking shot that ushers us into the Copacabana, gangland heaven. Two "hired gun" movies by another quintessential New York City filmmaker, Spike Lee, deserve mention: the adaptation of Richard Price's *Clockers* and the bank heist-and-hostage movie *Inside Man*, set in the financial district and celebrating the city's seen-it-all attitude and its diversity as well as the daily annoyances and occasional outrages.

Die Hard with a Vengeance is a virtual tour of the town with stops in Harlem, Wall Street, the FDR Drive, Central Park, and Yankee Stadium. Both Hillary Clinton and Donald Trump are laugh lines in this 1995 movie that does its bit to combat racial prejudice by pairing Bruce Willis and Samuel L. Jackson as unlikely teammates. And you get to hear the odious villain chuckle in wonder saying, "I love this country"—his words belying his scorn for Americans, such suckers, so trusting. Mind you, this is a movie you're not supposed to like; you're allowed to call it a triumph—of "blitzkrieg action," perhaps—but only after first denouncing it as "bombastic mush."

V

THE IMP OF THE PERVERSE

*E*dgar Allan Poe introduced "The Imp of the Perverse" in the story of that title, and Charles Baudelaire ran with the concept in some of his greatest prose poems—such as "Let's Beat Up Some Beggars!" or "The Bad Glazier"—in which characters commit acts of violence either to test a hypothesis or out of a lonely impulse of delight. If there are motiveless crimes, it may be because a capricious individual is drawn to doing something wicked—as if wickedness were as instantly gratifying as a drink or a drug—and the identity of the victim is an accident or an afterthought.

Together with the idea that elements of spoof can coexist with the pursuit of truth, the imp of the perverse impels me from time to time to undertake a flight of fancy. For the Best American Poetry blog, I have experimented with the astrological profile as a genre or form on the nervy assumption that the horoscope—like the "haruspicate or scry," "sortilege, or tea leaves," playing cards, pentagrams, handwriting analysis, palm reading, and the "preconscious terrors" of the dreaming mind in T. S. Eliot's "The Dry Salvages"— may be a bust at prediction but may provide the means of poetic exploration.

Astrology, with its many mythic elements, gives the writer an assist in the form of what the metaphysical poets of the seventeenth century *called "conceits." If you leave aside the hokum, entertaining though it be, the profiles work only when they are undergirded with fact as well as psychological insight. The aim is not to lampoon a type of discourse but to steal it as a high-minded medium.*

29

Three Astrological Profiles

Barbara Stanwyck (July 16)

Born in Brooklyn Heights on July 16, 1907, Ruby Catherine Stevens was an atypical Cancer, with both her moon and her rising sign in Virgo. Gemini, the sign of the twins, ruled her mid-heaven. The last time the girl saw her parents was when she was four years old. Brought up by an older sister, she started smoking at the age of nine. She worked as a typist and at assorted other jobs before she broke in as a Ziegfeld dancer. When Ruby landed the part of a chorus girl in a play that became a hit after her part was enlarged, she changed her name to Barbara Stanwyck.

A superb actress (Mercury in Leo), Stanwyck was able to project a wide variety of women—a confidence artist, a vixen, an unflappable witness to a murder, a spurned lover, a scheming sophisticate, a bitter woman two men fight over, a scheming wife smarter than her husband, an invalid wife who anticipates her own murder—in modes melodramatic or comic. She was funny enough for Frank Capra and Preston Sturges, and played the definitive femme fatale in *Double Indemnity*.

According to Isaac Babylon in *The Charts of the Stars*, his study of Hollywood starlets from the 1940s, Stanwyck's Virgoesque self-restraint modified the gush of watery emotion that comes from having not only her sun but also her Venus, Jupiter, and Neptune in Cancer. She was a good businesswoman (Mars in Capricorn) but prone to morbidity (Saturn in Pisces). A Fire Goat in Chinese astrology, an Elm Tree in Celtic tree horoscopy, she had the same Neptune sextile ascendant as Beyoncé, Grace Kelly, Kurt Cobain, and Kate Winslet. The moon was a waxing crescent on the morning of her birth.

Stanwyck is among the actresses of the 1940s who belie the notion that women born before the age of female enlightenment lacked strong models who could keep their families together despite the stresses of war, as Claudette Colbert does in *Since You Went Away*. Why, Greer Garson could single-handedly fight off a German soldier in *Mrs. Miniver*. And doesn't young Teresa Wright solve the murder in *Shadow of a Doubt*? Katharine Hepburn may get the better of Spencer Tracy whether she is a journalist (*Woman of the Year*) or an attorney (*Adam's Rib*), just as card sharp Stanwyck gets the better of innocent rich boy Henry Fonda (*The Lady Eve*). Sure, there are plenty of molls, dancers, torch singers, and femmes fatales who don't have an actual occupation, but you'll also find a psychiatrist (Ingrid Bergman in *Spellbound*), a fast-talking reporter (Rosalind Russell in *His Girl Friday*), a taxi driver and a bookstore owner (Joy Barlow and Dorothy Malone, respectively, in *The Big Sleep*), a kooky painter (Elsa Lanchester in *The Big Clock*), an amateur sociologist (Lana Turner in *Johnny Eager*), and a pair of twin sisters, one of whom will take her deceased sibling's place (Bette Davis in *Dead Ringer* and *A Stolen Life*). The lady can plan a murder, go crazy, run a restaurant, slap a spoiled daughter, speak Chinese, commit adultery, double-cross her partner, be smarter than her husband, or risk her life as an American agent in South America during or after World War II.

There is a rumor that Barbara Stanwyck never graduated from Erasmus Hall High School in Brooklyn, and a fat lot of harm it did her. In 1944 she was the nation's highest-paid woman, earning $400,000. Thanks to shrewd investments, she grew richer. It figures that she never won an Oscar though she was nominated four times. She helped William Holden get the title part in *Golden Boy* and became Holden's lucky star. He was crazy about her, as photos taken on the set of *Executive Suite* attest. In 1939 she married Robert Taylor. They smoked beautifully together. Whisperers said it was a sham designed to get gullible people to believe the two stars were heterosexual. Taylor was four years younger than Stanny. "The boy's got a lot to learn and I've got a lot to teach," she said. She kept the ranch and horses when they divorced in 1951. For a time, she and Glenn Ford were an item. Robert Wagner said he had a four-year affair with her. Could be.

When they gave her a lifetime achievement award, she held the statue aloft and dedicated the Oscar to her "golden boy," the recently deceased William Holden. It was a touching moment. Stanwyck (whose nicknames included "Missy" and "the Queen") had a sharp tongue. She defined "egotism" as "usually just a case of mistaken nonentity." She had a proud notion of her true worth. "Put me in the last fifteen minutes of a picture and I don't care what happened before. I don't even care if I was *in* the rest of the damned thing. I'll take it in those fifteen minutes." Her repartee with Fred MacMurray in *Double Indemnity* is as good as it gets. Walter (MacMurray): "You'll be here too?" Phyllis (Stanwyck): "I guess so, I usually am." Walter: "Same chair, same perfume, same anklet?" Phyllis: "I wonder if I know what you mean." Walter: "I wonder if you wonder."

On assignment for the short-lived German magazine *Rätsel*, I got to interview Stanwyck on the day she read the script for a proposed TV series that came to nothing. The working title was "Deck Chairs on the Titanic." Stanwyck, a self-described "tough old broad from Brooklyn," took one look at the pages and started laughing. What's the matter? "Be a good lad and re-fill my glass. Scotch, rocks, no water. You know what my biggest problem is? My biggest problem is trying to figure out how to play my fortieth fallen female different from my thirty-ninth."

Graham Greene (October 2)

Graham Greene was born in Berkhamsted, England, on October 2, 1904. I was reading his novel *The End of the Affair* on the day he died in April 1991. Two thirds of the way through, the score was God 5, Adultery 2.

Greene's chart is that of an author who loves language as a fickle lover with money to burn loves the French Riviera.

In Greeneland, an antithesis is like a mathematic equation: "He was conceited with failure, and she puzzled him with the humility of success" (*England Made Me*, 1935). The mind in "the moment of fear" can be vacant: "Then my head came over the earth floor and nobody shot at me and fear seeped away" (*The Quiet American*, 1955). But the moment invites speculation: "I have wondered sometimes whether eternity might not after all exist as the endless prolongation of the moment of death" (*The End of the Affair*, 1951).

When Greene writes about spies, substitute adulterous lovers and betrayed spouses for undercover agents in your mind—and replace back-channel diplomatic negotiations with assignations behind closed curtains.

The astrological configuration at the time of Greene's birth indicates an abundance of narrative talent. Melodramatic sentences

came easily. *"With an almost superhuman effort he battled back."*
A Libra with a difference, Greene balanced himself between rival
impulses that led to the same bedroom. Scorpio was his rising sign;
his moon lurked in Cancer. *"The knife fell from his assailant's hand."*
Such a man has a respect for the occult and a gambling problem.
Greene played Russian roulette as a boy and as an older man tried
to develop a system for winning at roulette in the casinos of Monte
Carlo. He felt that adultery was a sort of aphrodisiac, always more
intense than conjugal love, especially on the Côte d'Azur.

Consider these sentences, which I wrote when trying to inhabit
Greene's mind:

> With an almost superhuman effort, he fought off the stranger.
> Dawn crept up on them. He turned around. When the stranger
> bolted into the woods, he could have cried with relief. "Don't stop."
> He looked behind him. The candle had blown out. "You can stand
> up," he told himself. Had someone followed them? There were
> three other candles. "But—" he cried. A surge of pity entered his
> heart. It was like a disease you could palliate but never cure.

The fact that Greene's Jupiter is in Aries (fifth house) may account
for his zest for life, travel, gambling, and sex with good-looking,
intelligent women of various nationalities. The fact that Pluto was
messing with his moon (and Neptune) in the eighth house suggests the morbidity of the confirmed Catholic, who faithfully sins
and repents, sincerely, and then repeats the cycle, like the hero of
a spy novel. "I hate You, God. I hate You as though You actually
exist," the narrator says in *The End of the Affair*, making sure to
capitalize the pronoun, just in case. To which the counterargu-
ment is given in *The Power and the Glory* (1940), "Hate is a lack
of imagination," and almost mystically in *Brighton Rock* (1938),
in which the morality of good and evil is deemed greater than the

ethics of right and wrong because of "the appalling strangeness of the mercy of God."

A world-besotted traveler, Greene said that he went to as many places as he did—Liberia, Mexico, Sierra Leone, Vietnam, Cuba, Haiti, Panama—not "to seek material for novels but to regain the sense of insecurity" to which the London blitzes had addicted him. His wanderlust is consistent with a tarot reading held as a lark at Balliol College, Oxford, in 1922. Among his major arcana were the Wheel of Fortune and the Chariot; he also drew the Three of Cups and the Ten of Coins. Is it any wonder he felt, as he puts it in his *Ways of Escape* (1980), that "one must try every drink once"? This philosophy extended to writing in different formats—plays, stories, novels, screenplays, film reviews. As a young man, Greene quit a secure job at the London *Times* to write novels, the first two of which flunked the publisher's test. But he persevered. *Stamboul Train* (1932) and the books he deprecated as "entertainments"—*A Gun for Sale* (1936), *The Confidential Agent* (1939), and *The Ministry of Fear* (1943)—have held up well. The setting of a Greene novel might be Mexico, Africa, Vietnam, or the Caribbean. It was as if a sixth sense told him where the action would be. In Vietnam, the locale of *The Quiet American*, Greene discovered opium, which, together with alcohol, eased the pain to which he, a five-star manic-depressive, was prone. Written before Lyndon Johnson sent half a million US troops to Saigon, *The Quiet American* is nasty to the title character, reflecting the author's dislike of America. But if the best and brightest had read *The Quiet American*, they might have thought twice about sending half a million troops to fight a land war in Southeast Asia.

Greene always gives you the impression of leaving something unrevealed. He was a man who chose the confessional box rather than the psychoanalyst's couch and transmuted his anguish into engrossing narratives. It could be argued that Greene's novels, the so-called entertainments no less than the Catholic ones, flesh out an observation T. S. Eliot made in his essay on Baudelaire: that man's glory is the capacity not just for eternal salvation but also for eternal damnation. "Good old Graham, always the saham," quipped Philip Larkin. Greene loved his morning espresso and wrote exactly five hundred words a day, not a word less or more, before downing his first martini.

Several of his best stories—"The Basement Room," "May We Borrow Your Husband?"—would test the tolerance of the thought police. He wrote at a time when a sympathetic character could be designated as "the Jew" until he comes more into focus and gets a name and an identity riding on the Orient Express. The best of Greene's stories are "Under the Garden," "A Walk in the Woods," and "Cheap in August." The first two of these are uncanny tales that Greene published in a volume brilliantly titled *A Sense of Reality* (1963).

Greene disdained symbol-hunting scholars who analyzed the names of his characters in *The Third Man* (1949). Such an individual connected Harry Lime with *The Golden Bough* and Holly Martins with Christian paganism. No way. Greene chose Lime because of quicklime, in which "murderers were said to be buried," and Holly Martins would have been Rollo Martins except that Joseph Cotton (who played the part in the movie, which preceded the novel) didn't like "Rollo." Greene went out of his way to choose Smith, Jones, and Brown as the names of the three leading characters in *The Comedians* (1966).

The phrase "trigger warning" in its ordinary usage may be meretricious, but as a metaphor for the atmosphere in some of Greene's novels it can't be beat. There are few last sentences as devastating as the one that concludes *Brighton Rock*.

Marlene Dietrich (December 27)

Marlene Dietrich musically summarizes her mystique in a couplet from a song she sings in one of her movies: "Be careful when you meet a sweet blonde stranger; / you may not know it, but you are greeting danger." With the looks of a goddess—she is the eponymous *Blonde Venus* (1932)—Dietrich gives off the scent of sex as a kind of combat, involving struggle, conquest, surrender, and perhaps turnabout. Among men whose lust overcomes all restraint, she does more than hold her own. She is the enchantress who can consume her mate in the very act of love. Born Marie Magdalene Dietrich in Berlin on December 27, 1901, Marlene was electric from the time she stepped forth in her first major film, *Der blaue Engel* (*The Blue Angel*, directed by Josef von Sternberg, 1930), as the cabaret singer feeding the fruit of the tree of knowledge to a frumpy schoolteacher (Emil Jannings), whose loss of innocence costs him everything. In Hollywood she worked with von Sternberg, Hitchcock, Ernst Lubitsch, Fritz Lang, Billy Wilder, Orson Welles. She spoke English in an accent all her own, with traces of German, schoolgirl British, and a sexy lisp. She took pride in having slept with three Kennedy men (Joe Sr., Joe Jr., and JFK), and there's a lot more gossip where that came from. A natural blonde, she measured 35–24–33 in 1930.

For nearly two decades, Greta Garbo and Dietrich were one-two in virtually all international blonde bombshell competitions. The Swedish Garbo ("I want to be alone," she says in *Grand Hotel*) was a recluse. Dietrich was not. Garbo—the code name of the Allies' most celebrated secret agent in World War II—radiated melancholy and mystery. Dietrich embodied insolence. Garbo played the lead in *Anna Karenina*, a role that wouldn't have suited Dietrich, the cabaret singer who in *Blonde Venus* lands on her feet in Paris after her beloved child is taken from her. In "You're the Top," Cole Porter rhymed "you're the National Gallery" with "you're Garbo's salary" as a superlative. In "The Most Beautiful Girl in the World," Lorenz Hart said that the lady in question "isn't Garbo, isn't Dietrich, / but a sweet trick."

Marlene's natal chart reveals a lusty Capricorn with Virgo rising. Behind the scenes swift Mercury and blonde Venus play like the frolicking gods of Olympus. Marlene's cards (the Chariot, the Moon, the Knave of Swords, the Nine of Wands) reinforce the impression of a woman of sophistication, beauty, and Old World charm mixed with a spectacular capacity for audaciousness. Her eyes say she's seen it all and a lot of it was lousy. A palm reading indicates a fluency in languages, an appetite for sex, and a pair of shapely legs. The yin in her chart outweighs the yang by a healthy margin. But there is enough cosmic ambiguity to make her the object of desire of males across the sexual spectrum. She is a role model for dominant women and an object of veneration among the submissive. Dressed in a man's suit, tie, and shirt with French cuffs, she holds an unlighted cigarette between forefinger and thumb, waiting for you to light it with your Lucifer. And you will. In a nightclub in *Morocco*, she sports a top hat and tails when she sidles over to an elegant woman and kisses her on the mouth.

The greatness achieved in the career of Marlene Dietrich implies what Frankfurt School astrologers call a "fifth house dominant personality." I do not know what this means, but it sounds authoritative and is consistent with her ability to toss off aphorisms between puffs of a cigarette in a holder held at a rakish angle: "There's a gigantic difference between earning a great deal of money and being rich." "Most women set out to change a man, and when they have changed him they do not like him." "A country without bordellos is like a house without bathrooms."

"In America, sex is an obsession; everywhere else, it's a fact." She also said, "I am at heart a gentleman." *Marlene* (1984), Maximilian Schell's documentary consisting largely of the director's conversations with Dietrich, is must viewing, in part, oddly enough, because she refused to be photographed for it. What we hear is the distillation of hours of unrehearsed dialogue, which veers from fencing match to tender reminiscence; what we see are film clips and stills. The effect is remarkable.

Dietrich sang in three languages with a distinctively husky voice that made up in sheer sexual horsepower what it lacked in vocal range and strength. "Ich bin von Kopf bis Fuss auf Liebe eingestellt," from *The Blue Angel*, is even better in German than in the English version that begins "Falling in love again, / Never wanted to." She made that song seem autobiographical, the story of an oversexed lady who can't help herself, it's her nature. The song belongs to her as "Over the Rainbow" belongs to Judy Garland—anyone else singing it is competing with a ghost—though I like the way Billie Holiday bends the notes of "never wanted to."

If Dietrich "had nothing more than her voice, she could break your heart with it," Ernest Hemingway said, and to understand her allure you need to hear her sing. A playlist should include "The Laziest Gal in Town," "You Go to My Head," "La vie en rose," "When the World Was Young," "Ich bin die fesche Lola," and Charles Trenet's "Que reste-t-il de nos amours?"[1] In *Destry Rides Again* (1939), in which her romantic partner is James Stewart, Marlene brings down the house when, playing the part of the saloon singer

---

1. "What Remains of Our Love" would be a literal translation of the Trenet song. An English version, which Dietrich sang on the London stage in 1972, is called "I Wish You Love." The English version of "Ich bin die fesche Lola" begins "They call me naughty Lola, / the wisest girl on earth, / at home my pianola / is played for all its worth."

in a cowboy town, she instructs us to see what the boys in the back room will have, "and tell them I sighed, and tell them I cried, / And tell them I died for the same." Frank Loesser, best known for *Guys and Dolls*, wrote the wonderful lyrics.

Dietrich is Circe, mixed with Carmen, confident, arrogant. The man who does things to her heart is the man "who takes things into his hands—and gets what he demands." The strong, silent type, "by moonlight, under a big palm tree." In other words, as she sings in *The Blue Angel*, "Ein Mann, ein richtiger Mann!" That raspy, intimate, seductive, threatening voice challenged or dared the manliness of any man: to impress her, you'd pretty much have to be John Wayne, whom she played opposite three times, or Gary Cooper, her co-star in *Morocco* and *Desire* (1936). In *Witness for the Prosecution* (1957), she affects a "ducky" English accent to give Tyrone Power an alibi. The ingrate thought he could double-cross her. He thought wrong. From the time the Nazis rose to power, Dietrich staunchly opposed them. Like baseball player Moe Berg, chef Julia Child, and Supreme Court justice Arthur Goldberg, she was one of the unlikely recruits assembled by Bill Donovan for the OSS, the World War II predecessor of the CIA. For the agency's morale division, she recorded an English version of the immensely popular German song "Lili Marlene," as if to take it away from the enemy. While the song appealed to soldiers on both sides, it was the translated version that the tireless star sang to entertain half a million Allied troops on her heroic tours of war stations in Europe and Africa.

At seventy Dietrich gave a triumphant one-woman stage show in London reviving her signature songs. She lived to a grand old age and died in Paris on May 6, 1992, spoiling the birthdays of astrological cousins Tony Blair, George Clooney, Willie Mays, Robespierre, Freud, the aforementioned Welles, and Professor Martha

Nussbaum. Robespierre and Freud, in an overheard exchange, expressed the hope that Nussbaum would choose between them as between "a ring of the Inferno and an intellectual Eden" (Freud's phrasing) or between "a cleansing bloodbath and a reign of error" (Robespierre's) on a campus like that of Princeton but with no politics or faculty meetings allowed.

In her movies, Dietrich had the power to witness destruction without blinking. In *Touch of Evil* (1958), she read Orson Welles's palm and knew his future was a blank card. And she kept a straight face while telling him.

She added something vital to every film she was in, from *Stage Fright* (1950), a second-tier Hitchcock effort, to *Judgment at Nuremberg* (1961), where, as the widow of a German general executed by the Allies, she spends quality time with Spencer Tracy, a judge at the trial of accused Nazi war criminals. "We hated Hitler," she tells him. In my own allegorical understanding of that film, her character, who claims that the populace didn't know about the death camps, stands for nothing less than Germany herself.

Author's Note

The Perfect Murder: A Study in Detection, my first nonfiction book, was published in 1989. A paperback edition, with a new afterword, followed eleven years later and is still in print. The book was the culmination of years of study. At Cambridge University, I wrote a thesis on the literature of crime and detection. In the 1980s, I reviewed many mystery novels and wrote a *Newsweek* cover story on the subject.

While there are times when the publication of a book exhausts your interest in the matter at hand, my love of the genre, broadly defined, keeps growing, and I've wanted for a long time to write about some pleasures treated briefly if at all in *The Perfect Murder*. These include the multiple dimensions of "noir," Hitchcock's movies and Ida Lupino's, *Odd Man Out, The Killing, The Asphalt Jungle, The Lady from Shanghai*, Somerset Maugham's spy stories, Rex Stout's refiguring of the Holmes and Watson partnership, Ed McBain's police procedurals, the importance of *Trent's Last Case*, and such stylistic props of film noir as drinks, smokes, cracks, bad romances, the swing music in the background, the fedora, the seam stockings, and the gun.

Mahinder Kingra, editor in chief of Cornell University Press, encouraged me to write this book and followed through with brilliant edits. It was my marvelous luck to work with him. It gives me pleasure, too, to thank the talented editors with whom I've worked at *The American Scholar*: Robert Wilson, Sudip Bose, Bruce Falconer, Katie Daniels, and Jayne Ross. The section of this book titled "Dreams That Money Can Buy" reflects the "Talking Pictures" column I have been writing for *The American Scholar* since December 2019.

Thanks, too, go to the editors at *American Heritage, AWP Chronicle, Boston Review, Boulevard*, the *New York Times Book Review*, and *Tin House*, who commissioned and not infrequently made me improve other pieces that I have incorporated in, or cannibalized for, *The Mysterious Romance of Murder*.

On the *Best American Poetry* blog in 2019, Suzanne Lummis and I engaged in weekly exchanges about film noir, and I owe many insights to her. Eddie Muller's *Noir Alley* on Turner Classic Movies was and is a reliable source of inspiration, as is Joe Lehman, who keeps introducing me to excellent movies. Criterion proved why a subscription to its streaming service is a must for any noir fan. There are novels I may not have read had Michael Dirda not recommended them.

I was lucky enough to have Paul Auster as an advance reader and am grateful for his suggestions. Special thanks go to my agents Glen Hartley and Lynn Chu and my wife, Stacey Lehman, always my first reader.

Authors and Books Index

Film and Television Index